DISCRETION

OTHER TITLES BY KARINA HALLE

Contemporary Romances

Romantic Suspense Novels

Sins and Needles (The Artists Trilogy #1)
On Every Street (An Artists Trilogy Novella #0.5)
Shooting Scars (The Artists Trilogy #2)
Bold Tricks (The Artists Trilogy #3)
Dirty Angels (Dirty Angels #1)
Dirty Deeds (Dirty Angels #2)
Dirty Promises (Dirty Angels #3)
Black Hearts (Sins Duet #1)
Dirty Souls (Sins Duet #2)

Horror Romances

Darkhouse (EIT #1)
Red Fox (EIT #2)
The Benson (EIT #2.5)
Dead Sky Morning (EIT #3)
Lying Season (EIT #4)
On Demon Wings (EIT #5)
Old Blood (EIT #5.5)
The Dex-Files (EIT #5.7)
Into the Hollow (EIT #6)
And With Madness Comes the Light (EIT #6.5)
Come Alive (EIT #7)
Ashes to Ashes (EIT #8)
Dust to Dust (EIT #9)
The Devil's Duology
Donners of the Dead
Veiled

DISCRETION

KARINA HALLE

Montlake
Romance

Text copyright © 2019 by Karina Halle
All rights reserved.

Published by Montlake Romance, Seattle

www.apub.com

Amazon, the Amazon logo, and Montlake Romance are trademarks of Amazon.com, Inc., or its affiliates.

ISBN-13: 9781542008532
ISBN-10: 1542008530

Cover design by Hang Le

Cover photography © 2018 by Wong Sim

Cover model: Mitchell Wick

Printed in the United States of America

For Scott (even though you didn't believe me when I said I was looking at handbags for research purposes)

PROLOGUE

OLIVIER

Ten years ago
Grasse, France

I can still taste her on my lips.

Soft, sweet musk. Nectar from a fallen angel.

I close my eyes, breathing in deep, trying to hold on while everything fades. I can feel the memory of her growing smaller, the taste turning into something bitter, like coins under the tongue.

It's over now. Everything.

Everything I've ever had, everything I've ever known.

I'm only twenty years old, and my life is about to change forever.

Across from me is the man who holds all that power in his hands, those cruel fingers that never worked a real day in their life.

My uncle.

He's just sitting there and watching me, legs crossed with ease, slowly tapping those fingers along the velvet arm of the chair.

Marine is long gone. So far gone that I fear I may never see her again. It's probably for the best, but it still does something to my heart, like an anchor has been lodged in there, slowly dragging it out.

I try not to think about her.

I try not to think about what my uncle is going to do next.

Because he is going to do something.

He always does.

My uncle's pride is as fragile as ice in springtime. Solid to the naked eye but cracking easily under pressure.

"How long has this been going on?" he finally asks me. I can't tell if seconds or minutes have passed in this dark room. It feels like an eternity. Outside, the moon is hanging low over the lavender fields, and I swear it wasn't there a moment ago.

I stare down at my hands, knowing I can't lie. I'm a damn good liar, but Uncle Gautier is better.

"Six months," I tell him.

He sucks in a sharp breath. "I see."

I could try to justify things; I could protest, tell him he has it all wrong. But again, he'd know. In fact, he's already made up his mind about what he's going to do with me.

It won't be painless.

"Olivier," he says, his voice growing quiet. He's most menacing when he's quiet, a shark hunting in silence. "What you've done violates the most sacred trust there is. Do you know what trust that is?"

I say nothing. I can't.

"The trust of family," he goes on, his fingers continuing to rap methodically against the chair. "You've poisoned the bonds between us all. Your blood, my blood, your father's blood. We're all one and the same. All Dumont. What you do touches everyone. If you bleed, we bleed. You know this. Oh, how I've been there for you all these years, Olivier, stepping in when your father was too busy to spare his time. And this is how you repay me."

Of course he would make this about him and not about Pascal.

I swallow, trying to find the remorse, to at least fake it. The problem is, there is none. I hate Pascal, which is why I didn't hesitate to begin with.

Gautier leans forward on his elbows, his watch catching the dim light from the kitchen. That watch costs $200,000, something he'll tell you more than once. He'll also tell you that hard work will get the same results. But with him, he's coasted on my father's coattails all this time. The Dumont name, the Dumont fortune, none of it would matter today if it weren't for my father.

Gautier knows this too.

It's why he's become my father's opposite. His foil. He's never had to earn any of it. He's only learned to take advantage.

My father is too trusting to see it.

But I do.

Of course, now I'm in a great deal of shit, so none of it matters anymore. I've let my own father down by giving Gautier the upper hand.

Fuck.

"You do regret it, don't you?" he asks, and when I glance up, his eyes are trained on my hands. I've been wringing them together. Out of anger, not regret, but I let him see what he wants to.

I nod. "I'm sorry."

"I was wondering when you'd say that," he says, slowly easing to his feet. He's tall, just like my father, just like all my siblings and cousins, but he wears it with menace. Pascal does too. They're so much the same.

I wonder what would have happened if it were Pascal I was talking to. He's so much more unpredictable and volatile. Gautier at least knows he can't touch me, that he can't hurt me physically. I'd be able to take him anyway.

But Pascal is a vicious, elegant beast who plays dirty. The worst kind.

My uncle slowly walks toward me until he's hovering over me, shadows falling over his face. "I could ruin you. You know that, don't you?"

Always with the questions.

I nod again.

"I could tell your father what you did. I could tell Pascal. I could tell the world. And I would make sure that you would never work again. That you would amount to nothing. Because a man who breaks the bonds of his family should amount to nothing." He pauses, tilting his head as if considering me. Perhaps considering if he should just murder me on the spot. I'm sure with his lies and manipulation, he could make it look like an accident. I know I said I can take him physically, but who knows how many people he has in his phone he could just place a call to. People who know how to get rid of people properly.

For the first time since Gautier came barging into the house, I'm afraid for my life.

The seconds stretch into minutes again, my heartbeat growing louder in my head.

Finally, he lets out a long sigh. "You're young, Olivier. You made a mistake. I see that. I remember what it's like to be twenty years old, filthy rich, the world at your feet. You don't care for anything but sex and money and power, and you'll do anything to get them. I know— don't think I don't. But youth doesn't excuse you from punishment. It doesn't unwrite your sins." He pauses. "I have a bargain for you, Olivier. The only way out of this. Would you like to hear it?"

I blink at him, my eyes trying to focus on the shadows of his face, but everything keeps shape-shifting.

A bargain with my uncle is a deal with the devil.

But what other choice do I have?

"What is it?" I ask, licking my dry lips as I talk, my words coming out in a murmur.

"It will ensure that neither Pascal nor your father will hear of your indiscretion. No one will know at all, and you'll be able to go on living the reckless, selfish, stupid life that you've been living. Fucking every-thing that walks, spending your money on pointless, vapid things. You'll continue to be Olivier Dumont, one of the many heirs to the Dumont empire, the most eligible bachelor in France."

I clear my throat. "And so what do I have to do?"

Though his face darkens, I can see the smile spread across it, the white of his veneers standing out as sharp as the Cheshire cat's.

"Sign a document, that's all."

But that wouldn't be all.

Nothing is ever that simple with the Dumonts.

"Okay," I say quietly, knowing I'll have to agree to whatever it says. I'll be signing it in blood.

CHAPTER ONE

SADIE

Nice, France
Present day

Train ticket?

Check.

Phone?

Check.

Ridiculous travel wallet that wraps around my leg?

Umm.

Well, shit.

I rummage through the compartments in my backpack, riffle through my cross-body purse, and look around the empty dorm room, frantically trying to remember where I put the damn thing. It's not like it contains my money, credit cards, *and* passport.

I'd spent the morning going for a jog along the promenade and had only taken some euros along with me for my postworkout coffee; then I spent the rest of the day hanging around the common room and munching on last night's leftovers from the hostel's BBQ. On those days when I don't have to spend my money on food, I take advantage. I'm like a jackal, but with lipstick.

Only right now I won't be able to afford another lipstick unless I find my money belt.

Then I remember stumbling to my bed last night after too many drinks at the bar and becoming suddenly suspicious of everyone in the room.

I reach over and lift the edge of the mattress.

Ta-da. My money belt.

With a sigh, I grab it and clutch it to my chest.

After two months backpacking through Europe, you'd think I'd have a better idea where I put things, but hey, at least I was being vigilant after a bottle of wine. I've heard enough horror stories from the people I've met so far to know that the worst-case scenario is always around the corner.

And currently my worst-case scenario is losing either my passport or my wallet, hence the ugly and uncomfortable money belt I wear strapped around my calf. Depending on the sketchiness of the hostel I'm staying at, that money belt sometimes stays on me as I sleep. Last night I apparently thought hiding it under my mattress was somewhat of a happy medium.

I pull up the leg of my wide linen pants, which are wrinkled beyond belief, and strap the belt on, then take one last look around the dirty, threadbare room with sagging bunks and the unshowered stink of a couple of Swiss guys who arrived yesterday. They're probably out at the clubs right now, but their sour aroma is here to stay.

Good riddance to this shithole.

When I first came to Europe, I never dreamed of staying in a run-down backpacker hostel like this one, but then again, when I first came to Europe, I was with my ex, Tom, and I had nothing but love and adventure in front of me, not to mention security for the first time in my life.

Though I'd saved up as much money as I could from working at the university bookstore after classes, it was Tom who really planned ahead for both of us. Traveling as a couple, it was rare that we stayed at a hostel, and when we did, it was always in a private room. Most of the time we were in a hotel. Nothing fancy, but nothing that smelled like alcohol-infused farts either.

Then, a month into our travels, I'd gotten an email from my friend Chantal back home, the email that changed my life. Chantal told me Tom had been sleeping with our mutual friend Jen throughout the two years we'd been together and, suffice to say, an epic breakup to end all breakups occurred, right in the middle of the train station in Vienna.

So now Tom's gone back to Seattle, and I've been staggering around Europe with a broken heart and a dwindling bank account, trying to figure out what to do with myself. I've got three weeks before I have to fly back home, and I have no idea what I'll do if I find out Tom is in most of my classes in September.

Shit, I don't even know what I'll do with myself period. Though the breakup occurred almost four weeks ago, I'm nowhere near being over him. With every new place I end up in, I can't help but wish I had someone by my side to share it with.

I sigh and pick up my increasingly heavy backpack, throwing it on with a grunt. We had started our trip in London, where I spent way too much money buying clothes and knickknacks, and I've been lugging around too much shit for just one person. I probably should start leaving things behind or sending shit home, but I'm far too sentimental for the first option and way too broke for the second.

I head out into the hall and nod at the front-desk guy, Ryan from New Zealand.

"Sadie," he says to me, pouting slightly, "you're off?"

"I've got a train to catch, remember?" I tell him, adjusting the pack on my shoulders. He's been hitting on me for the whole week I've been in Nice, and I've deftly avoided every one of his clumsy advances.

"But you're going so late," he says with a sloppy smile. "Why not stay the night and go to Barcelona in the morning?"

"No can do," I tell him. "If I catch the eleven o'clock train, I sleep overnight and I don't have to pay for another bed. Thank you for letting me keep my stuff in the dorm room, by the way."

"No problem. You sure you don't want to stay?"

"It's all booked and nonrefundable." I glance at the clock over his shoulder. "And I've got fifteen minutes to make it to the station."

I give him a quick wave and then hustle out of there before he can try to convince me some more. I loved using Nice as a base to explore towns like Menton and Cannes and even Monaco, but I'm over the French Riviera. When you don't have any money in a place like this, you really feel out of your element. I'm hoping Barcelona will be more in line with my spirit, that Spain will become the country to heal me before I return home. At the very least, it's supposed to be easier on the wallet.

The night is warm and humid, and the sea breeze coming off the Mediterranean doesn't seem to reach this far into the city. The hostel is somewhat near the train station, maybe a ten-minute walk, but it's in a sketchy section of town.

If you were with Tom, maybe you'd be staying in one of the fancy hotels on the Promenade des Anglais, I can't help but think.

But thoughts like that are futile.

I take out my phone from my purse and get walking directions through the maze of streets, but as the blocks get dirtier and more derelict—the stores boarded up, people shuffling out of alleys—I decide that flashing around my iPhone might not be the best idea.

I commit the map to memory.

Turn right on this street.

Turn left on that street.

Go straight until—

A low cough from behind me causes my heart to jump.

I look over my shoulder to see a large man walking a few meters behind me. I can't make out his face—he's looking down at the ground rather than at me, which I guess is a relief.

Still, I'm on edge. I'm walking through a strange neighborhood in Nice at night with a large backpack that's making my pace considerably slower.

Don't panic, I tell myself. *Just a bit farther.*

And yet as I take my first right onto Rue d'Alger, the man follows me.

Oh, fuck.

My mouth immediately goes dry from fear.

I swallow thickly and pick up the pace, trying to tell myself that it's a coincidence and he's not following me. I can't be suspicious of everyone.

And yet everything seems more empty and darker somehow, and I'm starting to panic, hearing his heavy, lumbering footfalls behind me.

I have to be sure.

I take another right this time, so I'm basically heading back the way I came, toward the hostel, to try to throw him off guard.

He follows.

He's fucking following me!

Fuck, fuck, fuck.

Now what do I do?

I can almost feel him at my back, getting closer and closer, the dread around my heart tightening like a vice.

What do I do, what do I do?

I grip the straps around my shoulders, my head held high with false confidence, my eyes darting from side to side, trying to see a way out of this situation. But there's no one else around. Not a soul. I have a better chance of getting to the hostel or at least an open store of some sort before I get to the train station.

I should at least cross the road. If he follows me, then I know to start running. The last thing I want is to start freaking out for no reason and look like an idiot, but that would definitely be a solid sign that *You need to run, bitch.*

I look down the street and see a car turning onto it, the headlights illuminating the dark street just enough. I take a chance and glance down the street, hoping to get a good look at this guy just in case something happens to me.

All I see is a large bald man running toward me with his hands out, and then a glimpse of his wild eyes.

It all happens in a blur.

I cry out and turn to run from him, but just as I'm stepping off the curb, he grabs the back of my pack, yanking me to the side.

My left foot lands at an unnatural angle.

I cry out as sharp pain shoots up from my ankle, jagged bolts of hot lightning that run along my thigh, all the way to my heart, freezing me on the spot, both in terror and in pain.

And yet I'm falling anyway, my shoulder striking the pavement, my skin on fire, as the man tries to get my purse over my head, the cross-body strap digging into my windpipe.

I'm screaming and yelling, but it's coming out garbled, and I'm trying to kick with only one leg, because my other one is exploding with pain. Through my cries and the man's hoarse grunts as he fights for my purse and pack, I hear the screech of brakes—and then suddenly there's another man on the scene.

As I scramble, frantically trying to get away, I see this new man tackle my attacker, bringing his gargantuan frame to the ground, and then I'm free from his grip.

But I can't run; I can barely move. I only scramble so far, my palms and elbows scraping along the rough pavement, before I collapse onto the street in the fetal position, feeling pain run in sharp rivers all throughout my body.

The men continue to tussle—it's like two wild beasts in a fight to the death—and then the new guy is throwing heavy, savage punches at my attacker. I hear the breaking of bone, see the spurting of blood, and I close my eyes, wishing I could wake up from this violent nightmare.

Then everything seems to grow quiet.

When a hand touches my shoulder, my eyes fly open, and I let out a high-pitched cry of pure fear.

"*Est-ce que ça va?*" the man asks, crouched beside me. "Are you okay?" He switches to English, his accent like velvet.

I shake my head, letting out a whimper as tears rush to my eyes.

"Where does it hurt?" he asks, looking me over. "Can you get up?"

"No," I whisper. I don't want to get up. I don't want to move. I want to lie here, alone, without this stranger by my side, even if he did beat the shit out of the other guy.

Oh shit, what if my attacker is dead? Those punches were ruthless.

I raise my head to look. With the headlights half illuminating the giant of a man, I can see his chest rise and fall. His face is bloody, but he's stirring slightly. Not dead.

"Did you know that man?" the guy asks me, following my gaze.

"No," I whisper. "I was just walking to the train. I thought he was following me for a few blocks and—" *Shit, my train.* I glance at the guy with wide eyes. "I have to catch my train."

Though I can't make out his face properly in the shadows, I see him frown. "Train?" he repeats incredulously.

"I have to go," I tell him, trying to roll over to push myself up, but my backpack holds me down.

The man moves more into the light, blinking at me in disbelief as he grabs my shoulders to keep me still and then slips the straps off me until I'm free of the backpack. "You're not catching any train," he says. "You're going straight to the hospital."

It takes me a moment to really look at him, and I'm momentarily stunned. Dark mussed-up hair, darker eyes, perfectly groomed facial hair over a wide jaw and dimpled chin. He looks like he could be in his late twenties or early thirties. I must be more fucked-up than I thought, because there's no way this guy is real. This might be the most handsome man I've ever seen.

It figures this is how I'd meet him.

Somehow I manage to tear my eyes away. Actually, the throbbing pain around my ankle makes it easier. I close my eyes tightly as I wince.

Son of a bitch.

"I can't go to the hospital," I say through gritted teeth.

"Why not? You're hurt. You need to go to the hospital, then to the police station to file charges against this man." He gestures to the beaten man with disgust before he reaches into the front pocket of his crisp, white shirt that's now dotted with blood and pulls out his phone. "I'm calling you an ambulance."

"Please, no," I say quickly. "Don't. I'm fine." I manage to pull away from his grasp, trying to get to my feet.

His frown deepens, creating a sharp line between his low, dark brows. He tucks his phone away. "You're not fine. *Allons-y.*"

He comes around behind me and puts his arms under my back, holding me tight as he lifts me to a sitting position. I'm aware of both how useless I feel and how close this stranger is to me. He smells amazing—a faint trace of cologne I can't place—like he was born in the sea. It brings an image of a calm blue ocean, like the color the water was this morning on my jog.

That's it, focus on his smell, I tell myself. *Don't think about that ankle. Don't think about the pain. Calm blue ocean, calm blue ocean.*

Then he hooks his elbows under my arms and gently hauls me up to my feet. My left ankle screams with pain in protest, and I let out a yelp.

"Don't put pressure on it, lean on me," he says, pulling my arm up so it's over his shoulder. Hell, he has broad shoulders built like a rock, and yet his movements are completely fluid, elegant.

I put my weight on him just as I hear a grunt and a stirring sound from behind us. We both turn to see the attacker staggering to his feet.

"Arrête!" the man yells at him, but the attacker is getting the fuck out of here. Without a glance at us, he starts stumbling down the street.

"Fuck," Sexy French Guy swears, and I can feel him start to pull away as if he's about to run after him.

"Go," I tell him. "I'll be fine."

As much as I don't want him to leave me here all alone, I also don't want the attacker to get away with what he did.

But he takes one look at me and shakes his head. I see the tension in his jaw, the sharpness in his eyes. "No. I'm not leaving you like this."

"He'll get away."

"No," he says in a hardened voice. "He won't."

I frown. No? The attacker literally just got up and ran. What is he going to have the police do, follow the drops of blood throughout the city?

"Come on," he says, turning us toward the car that's stopped in the middle of the road. "If you don't want an ambulance, then I'll take you to the hospital myself."

"No," I plead. "The train station is fine."

He takes a long look at me, and my eyes are momentarily caught in the depths of his. At first I thought maybe they were brown, but the closer we get to the headlights, the more I can see they're a stunning dark green.

"Where are you trying to escape to?" he asks.

"Escape?" I repeat, trying to keep my voice low, considering his face is just inches from mine. The last thing I want is to breathe BBQ breath all over him.

"How is getting on a train more important than seeing a doctor? Where are you going, *lapin?*"

Lapin? I don't follow.

"Barcelona," I tell him, grunting through the pain as he helps me hobble closer to the car, which I now notice is a shiny, new Mercedes. "Is this your car?"

"Oui," he says. "And what is so important in Barcelona?"

"I don't know," I say, feeling strangely defensive. Why is this stranger all up in my grill about my business? And what was a sharply dressed, insanely handsome man with a fancy-schmancy Mercedes sports car doing in this neighborhood?

"Where are you from?" he asks, after further inspection of my face. It's rather unnerving, the way he's looking at me.

"Seattle," I say automatically. "America," I add.

"Yes, I've heard of it. And you're alone?"

"Yes," I tell him. Unfortunately.

"You're not going to Barcelona to meet anyone?"

"What? No, why?"

He takes me around to the passenger side. "Then I'm most definitely not putting you on a train. Alone."

I sigh heavily, hating to admit what I'm about to, especially as he's opening the door to his spotless leather seats. "Look, I'm broke, okay? I'm just a backpacker and a college student, and long story short, I ended up with fewer funds than I needed, and I can't afford to go to the hospital, nor can I afford to miss this train ride. I've already booked and paid for it."

He nods slowly. I don't think this guy has ever been in my shoes. From his watch to his shirt to his car, everything about him screams *money*.

"Don't worry about it," he says. He gestures to the seat. "Get in."

"Easy for you to say."

"Because you're having trouble moving?" He takes my arm and tries to help me inside. I resist.

"No, because it's easy for you to say I don't have to worry about losing money on that train ticket."

He tilts his head back, examining my face. "Are you always this stubborn with people who've just saved your life?"

"Saved my life?" I repeat, almost laughing. "That guy was just trying to mug me, right? Saving my life is a bit of a stretch."

I realize how ungrateful I sound as he shrugs faintly. "Maybe, but if you fought back or made a scene, I don't know. Nice is a safe city, but you can always be an exception. You're lucky I was here."

I guess all the pain and adrenaline of the situation kind of tempered that reality for me. All I could think about was making that train—the train that I'm sure has already left without me on it. It kept me from focusing on the terrifying and brutal truth that I was just attacked on the streets of Nice. If it hadn't been for this guy, who the hell knows what might have happened to me? There's a chance the attacker wasn't even trying to mug me to begin with. He could have dragged me into an alley, and I would have been completely powerless.

Jesus . . .

"Hey," Sexy Rich French Guy says after a moment, his voice growing soft. He gives my shoulder a light squeeze. "You've been through a lot. Let's get you to the hospital. I promise you, you don't have to worry about money for the next while."

I swallow hard, arching a brow at him. After what I've just been through, I should be on guard with this guy, too, offering to pay for me and all. He might have saved me and fought off my attacker, but I'm not sure I can trust him either. Who knows what his agenda is?

"If you want, I can call an ambulance like I said I would," he says after a beat, taking out his phone. "You certainly don't have to get in this car."

He means it. I don't know how I can tell, but I can, and it's nothing to do with how well put together and respectable he seems. It's something in his eyes, some kind of softness and understanding.

And, okay, maybe the fact that the longer I stare at him, the more my heart starts to flutter.

I really should get my head on straight, because these kinds of thoughts are pretty fucking trite after what just happened, but this is also the first time I've found any man attractive after Tom, so I'm just going to go with it. It's better than thinking about how royally fucked I am.

"It's okay," I tell him. "Let's go get me fixed up."

I let him help me into the car and buckle up as he gently closes the door, then runs over to the curb where my backpack is. He hoists it up like it weighs nothing at all and then tosses it in the trunk. After he gets in and starts driving, I lean my head back against the seat and try to figure out what I'm going to do about Barcelona, but before I can form a single coherent thought, I slip away into a dark, cold sleep.

When I wake up, we're in the parking lot of a hospital, and Sexy Rich French Guy is gently shaking me.

"We're here," he says softly, peering at me. "Did you hit your head when you fell?"

I'm so groggy I can barely speak, and the longer I stay awake, the worse the pain gets. "No, my shoulder took most of it," I manage to say.

"I just want to make sure you don't have a concussion," he says. "You were passed out cold for the last ten minutes."

"It's been a hell of a night," I tell him, trying to smile.

He doesn't smile in return. "It's not over yet," he says. Then he opens his door. "I'm going to get you a wheelchair. Stay here."

Before I can tell him both not to worry and that I won't be going anywhere, he's jogging over to the doors to the emergency ward.

I realize I don't even know this guy's name.

CHAPTER TWO

OLIVIER

"Can I get a wheelchair?" I ask the sullen woman behind the counter in the emergency room.

She raises her brow slowly. You'd think she'd be used to dealing with emergencies. "What do you need it for?"

What do you think?

"I have a woman in my car; she was attacked tonight. I think her ankle might be sprained or broken," I tell her.

The woman's expression doesn't change. "Attacked?"

"Yes," I say impatiently, tapping my fingers on the counter.

"By who?"

"I don't know. A man."

"You'll have to call the police."

"I will," I tell her, "as soon as you admit this girl, and for that I need a damn wheelchair."

The other brow arches. She's obviously not used to being spoken to this way, but I'm not used to being treated this way either.

"What is her name?" she asks after a beat, looking down at her sheet.

Fuck. I have no idea.

"Jane," I say quickly, thinking of the most American name I know. "Jane Doe. Now can I have a wheelchair, or do I have to steal one?"

She narrows her eyes at me, and they momentarily flit over my shoulder. I turn around to see a couple of wheelchairs folded and stacked against the wall.

"Thank you," I tell her and run over to grab one before she can protest.

This certainly wasn't how I thought I'd be spending my Friday night.

Then again, my night wasn't shaping up like I'd planned to begin with.

First, there was my date, Celine, whom I knew was using me. They all do; I've known this since I was a teenager, and models are the absolute worst about it. Doesn't seem to keep me from fucking them, but it does get tiresome after a while when I have to pretend that I didn't see it coming.

In this case, today I was supposed to pick up Celine from her train arriving from Paris, then take her out to dinner in Cannes at one of the newest, hippest restaurants. Which, of course, is pointless, because I know models, and I know how much they only *pretend* to eat. Instead of taking one out to dinner, it's best to save your money and let them have limitless champagne and coke in your hotel room, along with a couple of olives to kill their hunger pangs before you screw them senseless.

Not that wasting money matters much for me, but it's still the principle of the matter. And in this case, not only was I taking Celine out for a meal that she'd only pretend to eat, I was unknowingly being used as a pawn in some jealousy scheme. Turns out the owner of the new restaurant, a hotshot chef fresh from London, is Celine's ex-boyfriend.

Suffice to say, things got a bit awkward, and I'm fairly certain that there was spit in my leek-and-scallop soup. I managed to get out of there without getting into a fistfight—which is what I'm pretty sure Celine was gunning for so that she could be front-page news with these two men brawling over her—and dropped her right back at the train station. There was no way I was taking her back to my hotel.

So I was a bit rattled and disoriented after that, especially since Celine started crying big, fat crocodile tears just as I put her on the train, and I ended up driving down the wrong street.

Or maybe it was the right street. I've given up on fate at this point in my life, but I shudder to think what could have happened to this girl had I not been driving through at that time.

I glance down at my bleeding knuckles as I push the wheelchair toward my car. I guess I did get my fistfight after all.

I wheel it over to her side and open the door. The American girl has fallen asleep again, which makes me a bit nervous for her. I'll make a point to mention it to the doctor.

I clear my throat. *"Lapin?"* I ask, leaning over to gently shake her awake.

"That's the second time you've called me that," she says, her voice groggy, and I breathe a sigh of relief. She gingerly opens her eyes and looks at me.

Her eyes do the same thing to me as they did when I first looked into them on that darkened street. I've never seen such big, round, and impossibly blue eyes before. They're mesmerizing, giving her an otherworldly quality, like she's straight from a fable my mother used to read to me.

The way they look at you, full of wild innocence, makes something in my chest catch. And combined with her round face, full cheeks, and, well, large, somewhat pointy ears, she reminds me of a pet rabbit I had growing up, before the cook slaughtered it for dinner one evening. I loved that damn bunny.

But I'm not tactless, and I'm not about to tell this poor girl that she reminds me of a beloved pet rabbit. I give her a gentle smile instead and say, "What is your name, then?"

She clears her throat and slowly sits up straighter. "Sadie. What's yours?"

Sadie. I like that name too. It could be French. So much better than Jane Doe.

"Olivier," I tell her, holding out my hands and grabbing her by the elbows to haul her out of the car.

She's quite short, and while she's got an ample amount of curves on her—a refreshing change from the skin-and-bone runway models—she's still light. I practically pick her up and carefully place her in the chair.

She's wincing from all the movement but then covers it up as soon as she catches me looking. "I'm fine, I'm good."

"I'm sure the doctor will prescribe you a generous amount of drugs to take the pain away," I tell her, placing my hands on the handles and wheeling her toward the doors. "And if he doesn't, I know where I can get you some."

She glances up at me over her shoulder. "Money talks, huh?"

Normally I would be more on guard, but I have the feeling that she has no idea who I really am. How could she? She probably just thinks I'm some rich French man with a new Mercedes who was in the right place at the right time.

"Knowing how to speak French talks," I tell her. "I'm guessing you don't know any."

"I know *merci* and *bonjour* and '*Zut alors!* I have missed one,'" she says in a ridiculous accent. "That last part is from *The Little Mermaid*," she adds.

"I think you're a bit young to know that movie."

"I'm twenty-three," she says stiffly, "and I grew up watching cartoons. Animation is so much more interesting than reality."

That explains some.

Once inside the emergency room, I take her back to the nurse at the front desk.

"Is this Jane Doe?" the nurse asks.

"What is she saying?" Sadie asks me with those big eyes. "Jane Doe?"

I give her a quick smile and turn my attention back to the nurse. "Her name is Sadie."

"Sadie what?"

I glance down at Sadie. "Your surname?"

"Reynolds."

"Sadie Reynolds," I inform the nurse.

"And she's not French?"

"No, she's American. From Seattle."

"Does she have insurance? This isn't free for everyone, you know."

"Don't worry about that, I'll cover it."

Another brow raise. "And who are you?"

"Why does it matter?"

"Because I need your credit card."

"Already? Can't she see a doctor first?"

"It's to hold it. It's the weekend. Many tourists get treated here for God knows what and skip out on the bill."

I sigh and reach into my pocket, pulling out my wallet.

"Seriously, you don't have to pay for me," Sadie says.

"Don't worry about it," I say, not wanting to explain that it's not paying that's the problem here.

I hand the nurse my American Express Black Card, and she stares at it.

"Olivier Dumont?" she repeats.

"That's me."

She squints at me, but there's something changing in her expression. She's softening, and not in a good way. "You mean *the* Olivier Dumont? Son of Ludovic Dumont. Of the Dumont family. The handbags."

Handbags, perfume, haute couture. The Dumont brand is on par with Chanel and Hermès in terms of the billions of dollars in revenue

23

and being intrinsic to French culture and society. Outside of France, no one really knows we're behind the label, thanks to my father's wishes to remain as discreet as possible. Inside of France, though, everyone knows who we are.

You buy a Chanel to show the world you've made it. You buy a Dumont to show yourself you've made it.

At least that's how my father spins it. It's worked for him.

"Yes," I say to her tightly, not wanting her to go on, "that's me."

"What's going on?" Sadie asks, brows furrowed, and I realize she can't understand a word we're saying. Thank God. "Is there something wrong?"

Not yet, I think. The thing is, I don't even have a problem with being recognized. It's just that, for what it's worth, I'd rather Sadie keep thinking I'm some random guy, and I want to keep her out of the tabloids. She may be a stranger to me, but she's been through a lot, and the last thing she needs is to be splashed across newspapers as the mystery girl I "saved."

As for me, well, this might be the last chance I have to remain as I am in the public eye. The clock is ticking, and I only have three weeks until I need to make a choice. If I choose wrong, the world won't smile very kindly on me—my uncle will make sure of that.

"Nothing is wrong," I tell her. Then I open my wallet, take out a wad of hundreds, and slide them toward the nurse. "This," I say, lowering my voice and leaning in, "is for you to keep quiet about this. I don't know this girl, I saw her being attacked on the street. She's a poor American student. She doesn't deserve to be sold out in any way, nor do I, you understand me?"

The nurse stares wide-eyed at the cash and then quickly nods. She goes to grab it, but I don't let go. I give her a hard look. "I mean it. Tell me you understand me."

"I understand," she says.

"And I want to see a doctor right away," I tell her, letting go. She quickly takes the money and tucks it in her uniform. Now she's all smiles.

"Of course," she says. "Let me see what I can do."

She gets up and leaves her position, passing through the waiting room full of sick and miserable-looking people.

"What was that all about?" Sadie asks.

"I just made sure we could see a doctor as soon as possible," I tell her, giving her an easy smile.

"You handed her like five hundred euros!" she exclaims softly.

I shrug. "You get what you pay for."

Sadie frowns, seeming to sink back in her chair, and I can tell she's extremely uncomfortable with all this. Too bad. Once I decide to do something, it's hard for me not to see it through. It's the only reason why I've gotten as far as I have in life.

But money does talk, and it's not long before we're being ushered into an examination room, where the doctor does a thorough once-over, complete with X-rays. I stay outside for most of it, checking emails on my phone, because even though it's Friday night, the work never really stops. A proper vacation should be in order, just a few days without having to do any business, but I always think that when I come down to the Riviera, and it never happens.

Then, just as Sadie is being bandaged up for her sprained ankle and prescribed meds for the pain, the police show up, and the two of us have to give statements.

Naturally, the police are more interested that it's Olivier Dumont who saved the American stranger than anything. But in this case, it works in our favor, because now they have more reason to track down this man, and, with my penchant for remembering faces, I give a pretty good description of him. If I had to spot him in a lineup, I could with ease.

"Did the police think I was faking the whole thing?" Sadie asks me afterward as I wheel her out to the car. She's just taken the painkillers, but they haven't kicked in yet, and I'm carrying her crutches under my arm.

"What do you mean?"

"I don't know. They were acting weird."

"It's probably because you don't speak French."

"They were wary of you."

I cock my brow. "Is that so? I hadn't noticed. Come on." I open the car door and bend over to help her out of the chair.

"They were. The doctor was too. And the nurse. They treated you differently."

"Maybe they're not used to seeing someone as handsome as me."

She bursts out laughing, and I try not to feel insulted. It's not that I doubt my looks for a minute, but it wouldn't hurt if this pretty little girl thought of me in such a way.

"Maybe," she says with a wry smile, and she slowly eases into the seat.

While she buckles in, I toss the crutches in the back seat. Then I leave the wheelchair just outside the hospital doors and get in the car. As I start it, I glance over to her and say, "Where to?"

She blinks at me. "I guess it's too late to catch a train."

"It is."

She nods, determination setting over her face. "Well, okay. I guess you can take me back to the hostel. No one took over my bed all day, so it should still be available. Ryan might even let me stay for free."

For some reason my chest feels hot at that. "Who is Ryan?"

"Oh, no one. He just works the front desk at the hostel."

"So you want me to drop you off at a hostel?"

"If it's not too much trouble," she says, fixing her big blue eyes on me. *Merde.* She's serious. As if I would drive her back to a fucking hostel, of all places, so she can fend for herself with a bunch of dirty backpackers.

"I am not taking you to a hostel," I tell her. "Not even if you weren't in this condition."

She snorts loudly. I'm not sure if she meant it to come out that way or if it's the drugs kicking in, but it's rather adorable. "Please, I'm used to it. Believe me, I have no problems with slumming it. Been doing it all my life."

"I'll put you up in a nice hotel."

She shakes her head, pressing her lips together for a moment. "I'd rather you didn't."

"And I'd rather I did, *lapin*."

She rolls her eyes and reaches into her purse for her phone. "*Okay*, I need to know what the hell *lapin* means."

I reach over and put my hand over her phone, holding it. "It means you remind me of something good."

I want to say that it means she's cute, but I have a feeling she hears that a lot, and in my experience, girls don't seem to like that word. I also want to say she's unbelievably sexy, but I know at some point she's going to figure out I'm calling her a bunny, and she's probably going to think I've got a few screws loose.

A flicker of something dances in her eyes, making them seem lighter. "As long as it's a good thing," she says softly. Then she clears her throat. "Who the hell knows what I've been called so far on this trip. Men yell at me in French, Italian, German. I doubt any of it's something good. Probably always to do with my knockers."

I laugh at her phrase and fight to keep my eyes glued to the road and not her knockers, which are pretty fucking fantastic from what I've seen.

"I guess it comes with the territory of backpacking alone," I offer.

She shrugs and lets out a heavy sigh before leaning her head back on the seat rest. "Yeah. I mean, they did it when I was with Tom, too, but of course he didn't fucking care. Now I know why."

Again, heat in my chest. "Who is Tom?"

What other guy's name is she going to mention?

"Tom is my . . . my *ex*-boyfriend," she says. "Fucking asshole supreme."

At least he's her ex. "What happened?"

"Well, to give you the bullet-points version, he and I were together, we planned this trip together, we started on this trip together, and then, a month into it, we broke up. He's back at home. I'm here."

"You know you're going to have to give me more than that. What happened?"

"Ugh," she says in a moan. "Let's just say I got screwed over. What does it matter, anyhow? We're done."

"How much longer do you have left in Europe?"

"I was planning on spending my last three weeks in Spain. I fly out of Madrid. Hoping I can survive grazing on tapas all day, but who the fuck knows if I'll even make it out of my hostel since I can barely walk."

I feel bad for her. Not just going through a breakup but having to deal with her injuries as well. "You can't get an early flight back?"

"No. There's no changing it. My flight was bargain-basement bin. I'm probably seated on the toilet."

"You can book another flight back."

"With what money?"

She stares at me, and I know she's almost daring me to say, "My money." But I have a feeling she's going to see that as charity and get defensive again. "Don't you have parents or someone back at home to help you out? This is kind of an emergency."

With a shake of her head, she snorts again. "Parents? No, my dad left when I was young. My mom is broke as fuck. I help her out when I can; it's not the other way around."

We drive in silence for a few moments as I pull onto the motorway, heading south. "Your foot will heal fast. The doctor said it was a very light sprain. You'll be walking in no time."

"Mm-hmm," she says, and seems to be dozing off. Suddenly she lifts her head. "Where are you taking me?"

"To a hotel. As I said."

"Where? We're leaving Nice. Right? That was Nice back there, wasn't it?"

"The hotel isn't in Nice."

She tenses up and stares at me with wide eyes. "Where is it?"

"Relax," I tell her.

"Are you abducting me?"

I give her a steady look. *"S'il vous plaît."*

"I don't know. I don't know you. I know your name is Olivier, and you've done nothing but be nice and gracious so far, but being taken out of Nice wasn't part of this whole charity mission."

"It's not a charity mission," I say patiently, even though she's trying mine. "I'm taking you to Antibes, to the hotel I'm staying at. I can get you a room. You won't have to worry about a thing."

She grows quiet after that, and I think she may have fallen asleep. I'm starting to wonder what I've gotten myself into. It's already two o'clock in the morning, and I have a feeling those drugs are going to hit her really hard, really soon.

That said, she might be easier to handle.

"Why are you doing all of this?" she eventually says, her words slurring slightly. "What do you want from me?"

I can't help but bristle at that. This girl seems to know how to get me where it stings.

"I can't just be a concerned citizen, no? A nice guy?"

"There are no nice guys," she says. Her voice is low, and she stares out the window at the darkness. She's *definitely* been fucked over.

"Maybe you've been looking in the wrong place."

"I'm not looking for anyone," she says sharply. "And anyway, there are no nice guys with money."

I don't know how to argue with that. I think of Pascal and Blaise, my cousins. I think of Uncle Gautier. They're worse than Sadie can probably even imagine. I've spent most of my life trying to take after my father, trying to differentiate myself from them. I've tried to be seen as the nice guy, but it's a hard fucking line to walk, and it's a dirty world.

"You'll just have to trust me," I tell her after a moment. "That's all you can do. If you really want me to turn this car around and take you back to Nice, to that hostel, so some Ryan guy can take care of you, then I will."

She seems to shut up at that.

"If it helps," I go on, "the police have seen us together. Believe me, if anything were to happen to you—and it won't, but you do seem to be terribly suspicious—they would look for me first. They know who I am."

"And who are you?"

"Olivier Dumont," I say simply. "And I'm trying to be a fucking nice guy, *d'accord*?"

The name does nothing to her. She doesn't know me. I feel a well of relief inside.

"I have a right to be terribly suspicious after what just happened to me," she says after a moment.

I sigh, my hands squeezing the steering wheel. "You're right. You're absolutely right."

"But I am choosing to trust you," she adds quietly.

I glance at her. Her eyes are heavy lidded, her smile weak.

She's passing out.

Luckily, the drive to Antibes is only thirty minutes, especially in this car and on a near-empty motorway. It's not long before I'm pulling up to the Hôtel du Cap-Eden-Roc. I park the car right in front of the doors and run around to her side.

"Mr. Dumont," Felix, the valet, says to me as he trots down the stairs. He pauses once he sees me attempting to get a very drugged Sadie out of the car.

"Can I help?" he asks.

I get her arm around my shoulder, her head lolling from side to side like a rag doll. This isn't going to work if she can't walk.

"Just get the backpack and crutches," I tell him. "I'm taking her to my room."

As Felix does that, I stoop and pick Sadie up in my arms, climbing the stairs to the hotel with her. I stride through the lobby, glad that no one is about—not that anyone here would dare report on anything about the guests. Absolute discretion—along with luxury amenities and the sea—is the reason why so many celebrities and politicians stay here.

"Marie," I say to the night receptionist as I pass by her, "do you have any of the villas available tonight?"

She stares at the passed-out girl in my arms for a moment before remembering her manners, shaking sense into herself. "Let me check." As I wait for the lift, she does a quick search in the system. "Villa Eleana is free. That K-pop band left this morning." She trails off, staring again, this time at Sadie's bandaged foot. "Is she . . . okay?"

"She's fine. Just a sprain, and the doctor gave her drugs," I say quickly, not wanting her to pry any more.

"And the villa is for . . . ?"

"It's for me," I tell her as the lift doors open and I step in. "This is Sadie. She'll be staying in my room."

She makes an O motion with her mouth just as the doors close. It's the first time Marie has seen me bring a girl to the hotel only to get her a separate room.

There's a first time for everything.

CHAPTER THREE

SADIE

Pain invades my dreams.

Then light behind my lids.

In the moments before I open my eyes, I try to figure out where I am. There's a bit of a delay to my thoughts, and for that I'm grateful. I know normally I would be panicking because—

Wait.

Wait.

I *should* be panicking.

Flashes of last night come back like a hailstorm.

Walking to the train station.

The man following.

The wild look in his eyes as he attacked me.

The pain from my ankle, my shoulder striking the ground.

Then . . .

Olivier.

Swooping in to beat the shit out of that man.

Did that really happen?

Did he really . . . save me?

Who is Olivier, really?

Where am I?

I open my eyes and blink hard at the light streaming in through gauzy curtains. The light is soft, and there's a breeze coming through the French doors. It smells mineral-fresh. The sea.

I slowly lift my head and see the Mediterranean glinting blue in the distance, the surface shimmering like diamonds. But closer still is a large terrace with lounge chairs and a giant, round hot tub built right into the teak floor. It almost looks like I'm on a ship.

I glance down at myself and, with some relief, see that I'm still in the same clothes as last night: bateau-necked tank top, linen pants— both shredded in places and looking worse for wear, but at least I'm clothed.

Not that I suspected Olivier would do anything. I know I really shouldn't trust anyone at the moment, but at least until we part ways later today when I get the next train, I'm going to give him the benefit of the doubt.

Besides, it seems like he's put me up in a wildly expensive hotel. I gingerly turn my head and look around the room, which is about three times the size of the last dorm room I stayed in that housed six bunk beds.

I let out a whistle under my breath as I take it all in. From the four-poster king bed to the embroidered chairs and the chandeliers, it looks like I've been holing up in some luxurious seaside chateau.

Jeez Louise.

For a split second, it feels like getting attacked was the best thing that could have happened to me—until the slightest movement brings shooting pain back to my ankle.

Shit. Ow, ow, ow.

I roll up my pant leg and stare at the bandages. I don't remember what the doctor said about them. Do I change them? Tighten them? How long do I stay off my foot? I don't even remember using crutches.

And yet there they are, looking woefully out of place, resting against an antique white wardrobe across from the bed.

"Okay," I say out loud, taking in a deep breath. "Think, Sadie. What did the doctor say?"

But I've got nothing. I'm just crippled and talking to myself and cursing myself for not understanding French. I should have asked more questions. Now Olivier is probably gone and I'm alone and—

A knock at the door.

My heart leaps.

"Hello?" I cry out, trying to figure out how to hobble to the door to open it. I move to swing my legs over the edge of the bed, but it's already so painful I have to stop.

"Sadie?" Olivier's voice comes through the door. "Are you decent?"

"Yeah," I say, and before I can force myself to get up and limp over, the door starts to unlock.

What the fuck? How does he have a key?

The door swings open, and his head pops around the corner, brows raised in concern. "*S'il vous plaît*, don't get up!"

Then the door opens wider, and suddenly what looks to be a butler is pushing in a cart topped with metal-domed plates.

"*Merci*, Marcel," Olivier says quietly to the butler, who exits as quickly as he came in. The door closes behind him, and I'm left in the room with Olivier, my eyes jumping from Olivier to the cart and then back to Olivier.

Of course, there's no secret why my gaze keeps going back to him because, Christ on a cracker, now that it's the light of day and I'm out of danger and the pain is only somewhat excruciating, I'm really seeing him for the first time.

The man is fucking *gorgeous*.

I mean, like the kind of guy you see on an ad for Hugo Boss or something. The kind of guy God definitely didn't make enough of. The kind of guy you can probably only find in the South of France.

And he's here. In my hotel room.

Or maybe this is his hotel room?

"How did you get in here?" I ask after I find my voice.

He holds up a room key. *"La clé."*

"I assume that means key? Why do you have a key?"

He tilts his head as a small amused smile teases his lips. "Why wouldn't I? This is my room."

"Your room?" I exclaim, looking around. My God, did he sleep here with me?

I feel a shot of warmth between my legs. Holy hell, the mere thought of that shouldn't be turning me on.

"No," he says matter-of-factly. "I slept in the villa. I would have put you in there, but it's a bit out of the way. Usually occupied by royal families or celebrities on getaways, but it was free last night."

I stare at him. "I don't understand."

He gestures to the cart. "This is your breakfast. I didn't know what you wanted, so I ordered pretty much everything on the menu."

Get. The fuck. Out.

I shake my head, scoffing. "No. This can't be real. You are not real."

"I'm very real."

"I'm dreaming then."

"I can pinch you if you want," he says, his silken voice dropping a register, a devious glint in his eyes. The kind of look that increases the heat between my thighs. Oh, fuck me, I'm in trouble. He should know how dangerous those looks are when they're coming from him. Or maybe he does know.

I take him in again, the V-neck white T-shirt that looks especially soft, showing off his olive skin, darkened from the summer sun. He's taller than I remember, at least six foot, which makes him a giant compared to my five-foot-two frame, and he's all muscle. Not the big and bulky kind that one would get from hours in the gym, the kind that seems to come naturally—strong forearms, wide, firm chest, broad shoulders, slim hips.

Okay, I need to stop staring.

I sit up straighter, trying to make sense of everything and knock some reality into myself. On top of everything he's already done for me, I've taken his hotel room, which probably costs a small fortune, *and* he's brought me room service.

Every fucking thing on the menu.

"What's your endgame in all of this?" I can't help but ask. I know I should just be grateful, but still, this is so much to do for a stranger.

"Endgame?" he repeats, folding his arms, his watch gleaming.

Wow. Wow, yeah, I'm a sucker for those forearms.

"Uh-huh," I say slowly. "Are you trying to, I don't know, seduce me?"

I regret it the moment I say it.

He breaks into a devastating grin, the kind that could steal my breath away and never give it back. "Do you want me to seduce you?" he asks, running his long fingers down the length of his jaw, like he's now considering it.

"No," I say quickly.

I'm pretty sure I'm lying.

"Good," he says, still smiling. I see a hint of pink tongue as he bites his lip. "Because, believe me, *lapin*, you wouldn't be able to handle it."

Okay, that reminds me—I need to figure out this *lapin* shit pretty quick. We don't know each other enough to have nicknames.

Yet you're in his fancy-schmancy hotel room, about to have breakfast in bed while making innuendos.

With my cheeks flaming, I clear my throat and promptly change the subject. Unfortunately, everything I want to talk about involves us.

"So, uh, I can't imagine how you got me in here last night."

"I carried you," he says, lifting a dome. "This is an egg-white omelet."

I wrinkle my nose. "I need me some yolks."

He laughs at that, his eyes squinting delightfully. "My kind of girl."

Oh boy, I don't like how tingly that comment made me feel.

"You seriously carried me?" I ask. "What did the hotel staff say? Weren't you—uh, we—caught?"

He nods and lifts another dome. "I explained what happened. Crêpes, if you want something sweet." He shows me the plate—blueberry and what looks to be Nutella. My stomach rumbles even though I'm not a sweets-for-breakfast person.

"I'd think the staff would maybe be suspicious since I was, oh, unconscious and in your arms and all."

"They trust me. As should you."

"Why should they trust you? Do you come here often?"

He just grins and lifts another dome. "Avocado toast. All the young Americans here request it. This one has truffles and radishes."

"You mean millennials. Of which I am one. And, no, I don't take it as an insult."

"No insult intended," he says smoothly. "And finally, bacon and eggs," he says, lifting another lid.

My stomach literally groans at the sight of the crisp bacon and perfectly poached eggs. The sound fills the room, and I wince inwardly.

His eyes light up. "I think your stomach would like this one."

He takes the plate of bacon and eggs, plus napkin and cutlery, and brings it all over to the bed, handing it to me.

"I'm guessing you want coffee too?" he asks as I take the plate from his hands, still dumbstruck by what's happening. "With milk?"

"*S'il vous plaît,*" I tell him as he heads back to the cart.

"Ah, now you know another saying in French," he says, pouring me a cup. "I had the cook make it an Americano since I know you're probably missing the coffee from back home."

He hands the cup to me, but I'm already a bit off-balance with the plate on my lap, and the coffee spills onto the pristine white bedcover.

"Fuck," I say. "I'm so sorry."

I can't imagine how a fancy hotel reacts to shit like this.

"Don't worry about it."

"But won't you get a cleaning bill for it or something? I spilled coffee on my favorite shirt once, and that never came out. I still wore it because I couldn't afford to buy another one, so for weeks it looked like someone had shit on me."

"I said don't worry about it," he repeats, picking up an espresso cup and sitting on the corner of the bed. He does this with ease, as if the two of us do this every morning.

Lord, one could only imagine.

"Aren't you having anything to eat?" I ask him as I start to dig in.

"I ate earlier," he says before taking a long sip, his eyes never leaving mine.

Great. Nothing I want more than the world's sexiest man watching me intently as I stuff my face with food.

"But this must have cost a fortune," I tell him in between the most delicate bites I can muster.

"It's fine."

I give him a loaded look. "It's not fine. You put me up in a hotel room with a goddamn sea view and its own terrace and Jacuzzi, you order me everything on the breakfast menu, and then I proceed to spill coffee all over the bed. This is going to be a hell of a bill for you."

Not that I could really do much to offset it with my dwindling savings, but it doesn't feel right that he's forking out for all this, no matter how much money he appears to have.

He finishes his espresso and stares down at the empty cup, seeming to ponder something, perhaps the bill. His dark brows come together, and somehow he looks even sexier.

Suddenly he gets up, takes the espresso cup and saucer, and walks over to the tiled part of the floor. Then he raises them in the air before throwing them down on the tiles, where they smash into pieces.

I let out a yelp, spilling my coffee again, this time all over myself.

"What the fuck?" I cry out. "What are you doing?"

"You know Alfred Hitchcock?" he asks, staring at the broken pieces scattered on the tiles.

It's scary that I know exactly what he's about to say. "Yes. He used to smash his china on the floor every single day because it made him feel better."

He stares at me for a moment, brows raised. "You impress me, Sadie."

"Well, I love the man's films, but he himself was actually a monster."

"Quite true. Shows how monsters lurk within even the most respected people."

What on earth is he talking about?

"So this is what you do, just break things in hotel rooms? Do you want to get kicked out? Are you living out your nineties Johnny Depp fantasies?"

I mean, he kind of has the facial hair going.

"Sometimes this helps," he says.

"Helps what?"

Do I want to know?

He shrugs. "It doesn't matter. I'll have someone come clean it up."

He strides over to the phone and dials. He speaks in French and then hangs up. "Marcel will be up soon."

The way he's just doing what he pleases and ordering people around makes me think he's more of a permanent guest. "Do you, like, live here or something?"

"Sometimes," he says, his dark gaze wandering to the sea view and the billowing curtains. "Only when I want some sunshine and a change of pace."

"Where do you normally live?" I ask before munching on a piece of bacon. As much as his theatrics with the china shocked me, I can't deny how damn hungry I am.

"I have an apartment in Paris," he says. "Properties in Bordeaux, Cannes, Lyon, Biarritz. No, wait, we just sold that one."

"We?" I repeat. I ignore the fact that he just rattled off a list of properties and focus on the *we*. My God, does Olivier have a wife?

I never notice wedding rings, but at second glance, he doesn't have one. Still, that doesn't seem to mean much in Europe.

"Well, the company," he explains.

"What company?"

"My company," he says just as there is a knock at the door.

He walks over and opens it, and Marcel enters the room.

"Monsieur Dumont?" Marcel asks him questioningly.

Olivier just points to the mess on the ground, and Marcel starts to clean it up.

"*S'il vous plaît. Merci*, Marcel."

I'm not sure if I should keep asking him questions while Marcel is here, but everything about this has gotten so weird.

"What, uh, what company?" I prod. I can't help it.

Olivier walks over to the bedside table and tosses me the hotel's notepad so that it lands right beside me.

I pick it up with my greasy bacon fingers. There are two things on it that make me gasp.

One is that the hotel I'm staying at is the Hôtel du Cap-Eden-Roc, and even I know that this is where all the world's celebs and royals stay. I can't believe this, of all places, is where I am.

The other is that above the name of the hotel is a logo that says, "The Dumont Collective."

Dumont.

As in . . . *Olivier Dumont?*

I glance up at him sharply. "Is this *your* hotel?"

He nods with just a touch of a smile on his full lips. *"Oui, madame."*

And now it all makes sense, everything sliding into place. His money, his access to this hotel, his villa, the way the staff seems to know him, the way he doesn't care about the bill or the spilled coffee. Still doesn't explain the whole Alfred Hitchcock imitation, but I gloss over that.

He adds, "And you're free to stay here for as long as you want."

I blink at Olivier for a moment as his words settle in the foggy confines of my brain. For a split second, I imagine a different version of myself. One that will take what he's saying seriously, that will end up shrugging off school and the responsibilities I can't escape for a life of wine and lavender-scented linen and the bright blue of the Mediterranean, my skin tanned and glossy, my smile as carefree as the sea breeze that blows my hair around me.

But that version of myself disintegrates as quickly as it appeared.

"What do you say?" he asks.

"About the fact that you're suddenly the owner of a very famous hotel chain?"

He smirks, the corner of his lips curling up just so. He always seems to be amused by me, which I honestly don't mind.

"No, not suddenly. I'm afraid I've been working at this a long time, and sometimes it feels longer."

"But you're . . . young," I tell him.

"Thirty," he says. "Which, yes, is young. I've heard that a lot. But I was pretty much groomed for this from the day I was born."

I begin to go over everything I know about these hotels, which isn't very much, except that the rich and famous stay here. And judging by the way the front-desk woman at the hospital and the cops treated him yesterday, I'd say it's not just the rich part that he has down pat.

"Dumont," I say slowly. "Wait, don't you have something to do with the handbags, like, the French clothing line?"

The smirk on his face falters, just for a second.

"*Bien sûr,*" he says, but now his easy casualness seems a little bit forced. "But my father and sister run that side of the company."

"No interest in fashion?" I find that hard to believe since he's so impeccably put together.

He shrugs. "I care. I care in general about it and especially about the Dumont brand. But not the business side of things. Being a hotelier is more—what's the expression—up my alley." Olivier strikes me as the type of man who has many alleys, none of which I would mind exploring. "I promise I can tell you more about it . . . if you stay."

Marcel exits just as Olivier says this, leaving the two of us alone in the room again. The air feels heavier now, like it's laden with promise and possibilities. It doesn't help that Olivier's stare has intensified with every long second that ticks by.

"You're joking," I tell him.

"I'm not," he says softly. "Stay with me. Just for a few days. Just until you heal."

Even though I can feel a smile spread across my face, it's wavering with disbelief. "I can't do that."

He tilts his head. "*Pourquoi pas?* Why not?"

"Because of a million reasons."

"Which are?"

He doesn't seem to get it.

I gesture to the room. "For one, I can't afford this place."

He seems to fight the urge to roll his eyes. "Quite obviously, you don't have to worry about that."

"I don't want to take your charity."

"*Charity* implies that I'm helping you out of my selfless heart. I assure you that I have a very selfish reason for wanting you to stay."

Don't say it, don't say it, don't say it.

"Because you want to sleep with me."

Ugh. I said it.

He grins, and once again my world tilts on its axis. "I never said that. I won't say that you're wrong, but perhaps a better way of putting it is that I'd like to get to know you."

"I'm sure you have many people you'd like to get to know."

"Not particularly."

Okay, I've already blurted out what should have been filtered, and I don't want to get all insecure and whatnot right now with him, but honestly, I have no idea what this guy could even want with me. I'm not some model; I'm not French; I'm not rich. I'm anything but those things, and yet this guy wants to spend time with me and get to know me? He has no idea how boring I actually am.

"You don't seem to believe me," he says with a shrug. "I'm not sure what to say to that. All I know is that you don't have to be anywhere. You've already missed your train. You're going to need to take it easy for the next few days with your ankle, and I hardly think you should travel in your condition. So why not make things easier on your health and your heart by just staying here?"

Heart?

He reads the confusion on my face and explains, "Stress affects your heart. You've been stressed. I can tell. Not just because of the terrible thing that happened to you last night, but other things as well. Let your heart beat freely for a while, nothing weighing it down, nothing holding it back." He gestures to the doors and the bright-blue sky outside. "Out there is the sea. The waves come in, the waves go out. Slip into its rhythm for a while."

It all sounds so tempting and nearly too good to be true—which is why I think I need to keep my guard up, despite all the poetic things that keep pouring out of Olivier's mouth.

God, that mouth.

I tear my eyes away from his face.

"Have you seen the movie *Vertigo*?" I ask him.

He blinks at me. "Of course. You just saw me smash the cup. I've seen everything Hitchcock has done."

"Then you probably won't blame me for thinking you're getting a little Jimmy Stewart with my Kim Novak."

"Because I think you're a ghost?"

"Because she jumped into San Francisco Bay, and he saved her life. And what was the line he used? 'The Chinese say that once you've saved a person's life, you're responsible for it forever.' So, as he said, you're committed."

He folds his arms across his chest, amused again. "Actually, the Chinese have no such saying. It was invented for the film. And if I do recall, last night you acted like you were never in much danger at all."

He's right, and I feel awful for it.

"Well, let's just say I was in shock. But I mean it when I say I do owe you my life. I'm trying to just ignore what happened but—"

"Don't ignore it. Never ignore trauma. It will only traumatize you from the inside out. You had quite the ordeal, and it's going to take you some time to come to terms with that. So you might as well come to terms with it here. With me."

My God, he's persistent. I can't believe I'm putting up as much of a struggle as I am. My friend Chantal would be hitting me upside the head right now if she knew how stubborn I was being, especially since she's been harping on me to just find some hot European guy and sleep with him as a giant "fuck you" to Tom.

But that's not in my nature. I didn't have any boyfriends in high school. I lost my virginity at seventeen with my best guy friend, just to get it over with. I'm uncomfortable and shy with men, especially with anything sexual, since Tom has been my world for so long.

And yet, here I am feeling a level of familiarity and comfort with Olivier that I haven't felt with anyone before. Not with a stranger, anyway.

It probably has everything to do with the fact that he saved you, I tell myself.

But so what?

Why not just go for it for once, even if it's against my nature?

I glance at him and really take in his face, pushing past all those handsome barriers that take my breath away to really get a feel for who he is. It's in the curve of his lips, the warmth of his eyes. And, yeah, the fact that he's probably a billionaire.

"Okay," I say softly.

"Okay?" he repeats, brows raised.

I nod and bite back the grin on my face.

"I'll stay," I tell him, then add quickly, "but only until I'm better, and even if I'm not, I'm not missing my plane back home. I've got school; I've got my mother; I've got . . . a life I need to get back to."

"But that doesn't mean you can't live another life until then," he says, like he already knows this isn't something Sadie Reynolds normally does.

Another me, another life.

Just for a bit.

CHAPTER FOUR

Olivier

I don't think I've ever met any girl so stubborn before, though that's probably part of the reason why I'm so taken with Sadie. As callous as it sounds, I'm used to snapping my fingers and having a lineup of women at the ready, so the fact that now she knows who I am and still needs extra convincing to stay makes her an even more enticing challenge.

But I don't want to come on stronger than I already have. After she agreed to stay, I decided to let her have some time alone while I took care of some business.

Unfortunately, it wasn't my usual business. It was a text from my sister, Seraphine, wondering if I wanted to meet for a drink in Paris tonight. I'm fairly close with her and see her at least once a week when I'm in town, but I know tonight she would be talking about business. Our father's business. With Paris Fashion Week around the corner and the fall releases coming up, she does everything she can to try to rope me into that side of things.

I wasn't lying when I told Sadie that I wasn't interested in that part of the Dumont brand. I'm quite happy being a hotelier, rather than worrying about the changes that happen with the label several times a year. It's cutthroat, stressful, and far too complicated when you combine everyone in my family who has their fingers in the pie.

I also know that I would be good at it. I would be very good at it. I know that my father wishes for nothing more than for me to follow in his footsteps, and I've spent the last ten years trying to distance myself in every single way possible. Not because I necessarily want to—because I have to.

What puts me in even more of a tough spot is that I know Seraphine needs me on her side. It's always been her and my father versus Pascal, Blaise, and Gautier. It's been more unbalanced than it should be, and I only have myself to blame.

But my sister and father don't know the truth. They don't know what I did; they don't know what I signed. They don't know that the end is coming near, and I'll have to give up my shares of the company to Gautier, or the world will know of my indiscretion. They only know the lie, and I've got to do everything in my power to keep that lie alive.

It's almost noon when I return to the villa to check on Sadie. Naturally, I'm not empty-handed—I've got two cold bottles of Dumont champagne nestled in a gilded ice bucket. Even though neither of us has had lunch yet, I think we both deserve a little something to ease into the day.

I knock on her door and call her name softly, and when she doesn't answer, I use my key card to unlock it. I have to admit, I do feel like I'm overstepping my boundaries a little by doing this.

"Sadie," I call out, slowly opening the door. I peer inside and see her bed neatly made, the trays of food stacked beside the door. I should have reminded her that she could call Marcel at any time, and he would have dealt with it.

One of the doors to the deck is open, and I can see Sadie outside, sitting on one of the lounge chairs. She's wearing a plain black tank top and denim shorts, her hair pulled back into a messy bun as she leans over and fidgets with the bandages around her ankle.

"Good afternoon," I say to her, and she jumps a little at the sound of my voice, her eyes landing on me. She smiles when she meets my gaze, and her demeanor grows more impressed when she sees the champagne.

"I didn't hear you come in," she says sheepishly.

I cross the deck and pull up the lounge chair beside her, placing the bucket on the small teak table between us.

"I guess I'm used to sneaking around," I tell her.

"I bet you are," she comments, but despite the knowing tone of her voice, there's no malice in her eyes.

"I'm the youngest," I explain. "While my father was always occupied with my brother or sister, I was the one climbing out of my window. Sometimes I'd go right through the front door. No one would notice."

"Oh, see, I would have thought that maybe you would have had to sneak your women around," she says.

I cock my brow. "Women?"

The corner of her lips twist into a smile, making something in her eyes dance mischievously. It's a look I want to see more of. "I may have spent the last few hours Googling the hell out of you."

I roll my eyes and sigh. *"Mon Dieu."* There's no telling what information she's managed to unearth in that time. I hardly know what's being said about me. Even with my public persona of being a serial dater, I still manage to keep things about my personal life fairly discreet. If I'm photographed with a different girl every week—or every night—that doesn't matter much to me. I know people will never know just how I feel about any of them. The only thing I really talk about with the press is my hotels. I don't comment on the Dumont line at all, leaving all that to my sister and father.

But the more private I am, the more the press tends to run wild with rumors. They have to print something, after all, and if any of my cousins happen to have a slow news day, the media often turns on me.

"Well, rest assured, I don't believe everything that people say," Sadie says. "Especially when it contradicts what I've seen so far."

"It comes with the territory," I admit and then gesture to the champagne. "I guess me bringing you some champagne is no surprise."

"Oh, believe me, everything is still a giant surprise," she says, looking around with big eyes. "I've wanted to pinch myself a few times to find out if I'm dreaming or not. Luckily, my ankle has taken on that role quite well."

I glance down at it. "Does it hurt? Did you take off the bandage?"

She shakes her head. "I attempted to, and then I worried I wouldn't know how to wrap it up perfectly."

"Do you mind if I take a look?"

"And you're a doctor now?"

I grin and get to my feet. "You didn't read that about me?" I joke. "Stay there. I'll get something for the pain first."

I disappear back into the room, pluck two champagne glasses from the cabinet, and come back out with them. "Here we go."

I expect her to tell me she doesn't want any, but instead, her eyes never leave me as I pop the champagne cork and send it sailing over the balcony railing.

"You probably won't be too shocked, but I've never had Dumont champagne before," she says as I carefully pour her a glass. "Or Dumont anything, for that matter."

That's going to change, I think to myself, and when she meets my eyes, I swear I see a flash of heat burn behind them, as if she knows exactly what I'm thinking.

I pour myself a glass and hold it up to hers, clearing my throat before I say, "Here's to being in the right place at the right time."

She gives me a loaded look. "I think it's more wrong place at the wrong time, wouldn't you say?"

"Yes, but I was thinking about me."

She scoffs, lets out a dry laugh. "Okay, well then I'm toasting to how lucky I am that it was you, of all people, who happened to save me. I doubt I would have ever experienced a place like this otherwise."

"*Santé!* You never know," I tell her as I clink my glass against hers. "Perhaps we would have found each other some other way."

Her eyes flash at that, and I know perhaps I'm being a little presumptuous, but I've found it impossible to be anything but that around her. I take a sip of my drink, and when she pauses with hers, I tip up the bottom of her glass so that she finishes most of it in one go.

"For the pain," I remind her.

She smiles, licking her lips in a way that nearly undoes me. "That's what the painkillers are for. If I didn't know any better, I'd say you were getting me drunk."

"Drunk?" I repeat. "No. We don't get drunk here in France. We get happy. Now, let me take a look at your foot."

I put my glass on the table and sit down beside her on the lounger, gently taking her calf in my hands and placing her ankle over my thighs. Her breath hitches, and she tenses as she moves back to accommodate me. I give her a reassuring glance, reading the trepidation on her face. "I won't hurt you, I promise."

"How can you be so sure?" she asks after a beat, and there's a weight to her words, as if she's talking about something else.

I don't let my mind go there. Instead, I slowly and carefully start to unwrap the bandages around her ankle. I obviously have no medical training, but Seraphine used to do ballet, and I have memories of my mother helping her with her feet on particularly rough days.

Sadie gasps when I pull apart the final wrap, but her ankle isn't as bad as I thought it would be. It's just puffy and swollen, with very light bruising.

"It looks fine," I tell her.

"It's not fine," she says. "It looks gangrenous."

I laugh. "It isn't gangrenous. It's just inflamed. Another few days of plenty of rest and keeping your weight off it, and you should be fine. I didn't hurt you, did I?"

"Well, no. But you have to wrap it back up, so there's always another chance."

I can't help but grin. She can be so prickly. I nod at her drink. "Pour yourself another glass and drink up."

"Back to getting me drunk."

"I'll join you in a second."

And I'm not lying. With the same care as when I took off her bandage, I wrap her ankle back up. "Not too tight?" I ask, her ankles still resting across my thighs.

"I'm impressed," she says, taking a sip of her drink. "Just as I'm impressed by this champagne, this hotel, you, and everything else that you happen to touch in some way or form."

"Well, I'm glad I can impress you by the things I do and not by the things you've read about me."

"Oh, believe me, I was still impressed. Even by the blatant lies. I had no idea you had a secret baby with the princess of Monaco." She pauses, narrowing her eyes. "Unless . . ."

"Blatant lie," I tell her. "Though I do think my cousin has had a few dalliances with her."

"Which one?"

"You know about them?" I practically bristle.

"It's hard to do research on Olivier Dumont without learning about the rest of his family."

"What did you learn?" I ask carefully.

She shrugs. "A lot, but who knows what's true and what isn't? Your family does seem to be at odds with each other, though. They seem so different from one another, your father and your uncle."

"How so?" I ask. Of course, I know the truth, but I'm always curious to see how we appear to others, particularly to people from outside of France who weren't brought up with my father and uncle dominating the news from time to time.

"The gossip sites like to paint you like you're in a family feud. There's the so-called good side with you and your sister and brother and parents. And then there's your uncle and aunt and their sons. The so-called bad side. Though sometimes they just called them progressive, so I guess 'bad' is just a relative term. So to speak."

She has no idea. "You're right. They are more progressive," I admit. "My father has always believed in running everything Dumont the same way that our grandfather did. He sees only harm in changing things to fit with the times."

She stares at me inquisitively, which makes me want to drink. I quickly finish my glass. "And what do you believe?" she asks. "Do you agree with your father?"

I nod. "I do. I adapt in my own way when it comes to my side of the business. My hotels will always have an old-world feel about them in terms of service and location, the things people think of when they think of a place like this. But obviously I adapt, like all hotels do. The online marketing world to individuals is everything. Using Instagram, social media. If I didn't adapt and utilize them, I couldn't sustain the momentum."

"And your father? He doesn't even have an online store."

"Well, the products are online. He just doesn't let you buy them that way. You have to go into a store."

"You don't think that's inconvenient?"

I've heard this argument so many times, and I know every way it can pan out. "It may be inconvenient, but it keeps the brand from becoming cheap and fast fashion."

She bursts out laughing. "Cheap? I looked at your handbags. They're five thousand dollars."

"So is Chanel, and you don't see anyone balking at the price."

"Oh, I'm balking at that too. It's ridiculous. My whole trip here cost half that much."

She's got a point. For once I'm at a loss for words.

"Look," she says after a moment. "I don't mean to, you know, insult you or your father. I'm sure it's all worth it. It's just a totally different world, and it's one I doubt I'll ever understand. Our worlds couldn't be further apart."

"And yet here we are. You and me. Sitting on the deck of my villa at the Hôtel du Cap-Eden-Roc, drinking champagne. It looks like our worlds have collided very well."

"It's temporary," she says. "And it's only because of your generosity."

"I guess I should be flattered you didn't call it charity, for once."

"I'm trying to mind my manners," she says. "And I don't know if I'm doing a good job."

I reach out and put my hand on her knee, feeling her warm skin beneath my palm, conscious of how close we're still sitting with each other, her legs up on my thighs, exuding a familiarity that probably shouldn't exist yet. "You're doing a good job. You're being honest. We all need honest people in our lives, otherwise we're going to keep on making the same mistakes. And whether you think the bags are overpriced or not—even with the labor and materials that go into them—we could definitely be more progressive. But I also see great value in holding on to the past. It keeps us accountable. Sure, maybe my uncle would be happier if we could go online and start cutting corners to turn a greater profit, but I admire my father for sticking to his guns."

And now I think I've said too much. I can't remember the last time I really opened up about my family or the business, even for a minute. My family is so complex and layered as it is, it's like opening a can of worms, and that's a lid that needs to be permanently sealed.

I clear my throat. "But I don't want to bore you with my business. How about we talk about lunch instead?"

"Honestly, it's not boring at all," she says, just as her stomach erupts into a loud growl.

I laugh, finding it particularly cute how embarrassed she seems by it. "I think your stomach would beg to differ."

"I thought I ate too much at breakfast, but I guess I was wrong."

"Well, having an appetite is a good sign. Would you like to go into Cannes for dinner? Antibes? We could also eat at the restaurant here or order room service."

"Aren't I supposed to stay off my feet?"

"I can assure you, you won't be walking anywhere. We could even have lunch on the boat."

"Of course you have a boat," she says dryly, but she's smiling. And the more she's smiling, the more I find myself wanting to keep that smile going, no matter what it takes. Don't get me wrong, I always show a woman a good time, something to be remembered, but I can't recall the last time I even had the urge to pull out all the stops like this. The funny thing is, it takes almost nothing to impress Sadie.

Actually, that's the wrong way of looking at it. It's not that she's easy to impress, more that the things that impress her come from a different, more sincere kind of place.

Once again, a challenge.

But as much as Sadie is a challenge to me, when it comes to lunch, she doesn't put up that much of a fight. She thinks she's terribly under-dressed for being seen in public, but even though she's wrong, I can tell the idea makes her uncomfortable. So we decide to order in room service for lunch, and I have the chef craft her something off the menu, anything her heart desires.

Her heart's desire is a simple American hamburger, which she scarfs down in a second. Sure, it was made with Wagyu beef, but I don't need to tell her that. We follow with more champagne, this time mixed with cassis liqueur to make Kir Royales, and soon we are stuffed and tipsy and feeling pretty good.

At least I am. It's nice to have a day where I don't have to worry about anything, where the future is only the horizon: a thin, faded line in the distance.

The horizon right now is a rich blue, wavering ever so slightly from the waves. We're both leaning against the railing and staring down at the large lap pool perched by the rocky edge of the shore. The loungers are all occupied, some people splashing around in the water, some being served drinks by the waiters. It's peak season and prime for people-watching.

But my attention is on the girl beside me, the breeze blowing back a few loose strands of hair from her ponytail, a reddish-gold gleam catching in the sun. The few freckles across her face seem even more pronounced, like she's blossoming right in front of my eyes.

Her gaze is locked on a sailboat cutting smoothly across the water, the white sail stark against the vibrant Mediterranean blue, but then she swoops her eyes over to me. I'd never noticed how the blue of her irises matched the sea so well.

"What are you staring at?" she asks, her voice taking on a shy tone.

Once again, I know I'm probably making her uncomfortable, but I can't seem to help myself. "Your eyes. They're marine blue. Same as the sea."

She smiles, the color of her cheeks deepening as she averts her eyes. "You know, when I was doing research on you, it wasn't the only thing I was Googling."

"Oh?"

"I learned what *lapin* means."

I should have figured this would happen. To her credit, though, she doesn't look mad. Just amused.

"I can explain," I tell her.

She laughs. "You'd better explain why I look like a rabbit."

"You don't look like a rabbit," I tell her, reaching out briefly to touch her arm, her skin seeming to grow hot under my touch. "It's just—"

Her hands fly to her ears. "Yeah, my ears. I know they stick out. Believe me, when I was a tween I was called 'Arwen' by everyone in my class."

"Arwen was beautiful," I point out.

"Yeah, when she's played by Liv Tyler. Trust me, no one thought they were being complimentary when they said I looked like an elf."

I should have figured this was a sensitive subject. "It will probably sound weird if I explain, but just trust me when I say it's a compliment."

She eyes me for a moment, her gaze narrowing before she shrugs. "I guess I have to take your word for it. The French sure have a weird way of phrasing things."

"Don't blame the French. Just blame me. I'm not exactly up to the country's standard when it comes to romanticisms."

"You'd think you would have had enough practice by now," she says lightly.

"You'd think," I tell her. "But perhaps we need to even the playing field, just a little. You seem to know so much about me, but I, well, I know practically nothing about you."

"There really isn't much to say," she says, trying to brush a strand of hair out of her eyes.

I reach out and tuck the strand behind her ear. To my surprise, she doesn't flinch at my touch this time. "Everyone has a story. I bet yours is far more unique and interesting than you think. Tell me about where you grew up."

She grimaces, scrunching up her nose. "It's nowhere you would have heard of."

"Tell me anyway."

She lets out a long breath of air. "Okay. Well, I was born in a place called Wenatchee in Washington State. It's like the interior of the state, so not close to Seattle at all. It's very dry and desertlike, but there are some nice lakes around, and we're famous for our apples."

"Sounds very nice."

"It's okay. I'm painting you a nicer picture than it is."

"And what did your parents do? Grow apples?"

She laughs. "That would have been nice. No, my father was a bank manager; my mother was a waitress. They didn't make a lot, so we lived in a trailer park. But it was a nice trailer park, at least. I had my own room, so I was happy . . ." She trails off, looking the opposite of happy.

"Any siblings?"

"No."

"Are your parents still together?"

She shakes her head, looking down at the people by the pool in a rather blank way. "My dad left when I was young. Don't know where he is now. Don't care."

I know better than to ask any more about him.

"So I take it you're close with your mother?"

"Yeah," she says, and her voice goes quiet.

"Was she worried about you coming over here? Traveling?"

"A little. I think . . . I think she misses having me around. I live with her in Seattle, near the university. I know she's extra worried now that I'm alone."

"You mean you're no longer with your boyfriend. What was his name again? Dom?"

"Tom," she says quickly and shivers, as if even saying his name is too much. "She liked him enough, but it gave her peace of mind to know that he was looking after me. Well, you know what I mean."

"Will you tell her about me?"

She raises her brows. "About you? And what am I supposed to say about you?"

"That you met a very handsome French man who promised to take care of all your needs."

She slowly shakes her head, a smile spreading across her face. "You are unbelievable."

I lean in close to her, breathing in her sweet vanilla scent mixed with the fresh minerals of the sea. "*Lapin*, you have *no* idea," I say softly into her ear.

CHAPTER FIVE

SADIE

"So tell me all about Spain," my mother says. "How is Barcelona? Or are you in Madrid? It's hard to keep track."

"I'm in Barcelona," I tell her. I hate lying to my mom, but there's no way around it right now. If I were to tell her the truth about what happened to me, it would only make her worry, and she's so stressed out as it is, that's the last thing she needs. Best to just let her think everything is fine.

There's a long pause over the line. "Are you okay?" she asks.

I clear my throat and try to sound more chipper. "Oh, yes. For sure. Just a bit tired from all the traveling, you know."

Another lie. I'm a bit hungover, plus groggy from all the painkillers. Yesterday I drank a little too much during the day with Olivier, which resulted in me going to bed around dinnertime. In fact, I think I was nodding off just as he was about to order in food, and I have vague memories of him bringing me to the bed, after which he left, and I got under the covers and passed out.

I've been nothing but a class act with this guy.

"I knew I should have waited another hour or so to call," she says. "I just hadn't talked to you in so long, and you'd said it was impossible to sleep late in a hostel anyway."

"No, you're right. I'm glad you called. So how was work?"

My mom would have just come off her late shift at the diner, her job at the moment. Normally, my mother goes through jobs every few months, unable to hold one down for long, thanks to her constant battle with bipolar disorder, but it seems like this one has been good to her.

"It was all right," she says with a sigh. "I had a tough go the other day . . ." She trails off, and I know she doesn't want to tell me what happened. But at the same time, I know she will. She has no one else but me to confide in.

"And?" I prompt her.

"Well, the good news is that I still have a job." She laughs nervously and then groans. I can picture her now, rubbing the heel of her hand into her forehead as if she could break through to her brain that way. "But, darling, I was in a bad way. I just couldn't get out of bed. That black hole, that void, it had me, and I honestly didn't think I'd ever get out of it."

My heart squeezes. I know what she's talking about. I've been in that void myself. But I know it's nothing compared to what she feels and deals with on a daily basis.

I'm afraid to ask, but I do. "How many shifts did you miss?"

"Two," she says after a beat. "But they were very understanding. In fact, Agnes who works here—I think I told you about her in an email I sent you—she's very eager to take on any missed shifts. So if I ever have a hard time, I can always call her, and she'll cover for me."

I breathe out a sigh of relief. She's never had this level of support before at her jobs. I know my mom tends to keep everyone at arm's length, and for good reason, but maybe because I've been gone, she's actually been able to branch out. She's relied on me for so long for company and emotional support, and as much as I'll never ever turn my back on my mother, it does take its toll on me. I've been shouldering her burdens for as long as I can remember, even before my father left us.

"I thought I saw Tom the other day," she says, switching the subject in the most horrible way.

I groan out of habit, though I have to admit that ever since I met Olivier, Tom hasn't been on my mind like usual.

"I was tempted to run him over," my mother adds. "I'll never forgive him for what he did to you."

"Me neither. But it doesn't matter."

"He ruined your vacation, sweetie."

I'm smiling, just a little. "It's getting better. I promise."

I stay on the phone for a few more minutes while my mom makes herself Sleepytime tea and gets ready for bed. Then I hang up and try to summon the energy to get myself out of my own bed.

It doesn't help that it's insanely comfortable, and lying here is like being held in the palm of heaven. Even my pounding head and the faint throbbing in my ankle seem to take a back seat in this bright-white room—clean and pure and luxurious all at once.

Now that I'm fully awake, my mind naturally goes to Olivier.

How can it not?

I mean, good Lord.

I don't know if this is karma for having a pretty shitty childhood, or Tom dumping me, or what, but I know I should stop questioning it and start enjoying it. The man is just too unbelievable to be real, starting off with the *Pretty Woman*–style breakfast in bed, followed by day drinking bottles and bottles of his own champagne while lounging in the Mediterranean sunshine. The conversation flowed easily, as long as we weren't talking about me, and there were numerous occasions when he reached out and touched me in some way. Every time his skin made contact with mine, I felt like we were connecting on some cellular level, like something deep inside me recognized something deep inside him.

But that's all just crazy talk. I'm obviously smitten with the fact that he's completely gorgeous, totally French, and obscenely rich and successful. Anything else is probably a product of my very active imagination. I mean, other than his touching my ankle, or my thigh, or pushing a strand of hair off my face, he's made no real moves on me.

I thought he was going to. Especially when he got this heated look in his eyes more than once and leaned in just a little closer. Normally, I would freak out, and even though I was internally, I didn't jerk out of the way or anything.

But, no. Either the man is a tease, or I'm picking up on the wrong signals.

Or maybe he's a gentleman who doesn't believe in going after injured young women, I remind myself.

It could be that. There's no denying there's chemistry between us; it's just a matter of acting on it, and I sure as hell won't be making any moves over here. Not when I can barely move to begin with.

And yet, as I manage to get out of bed, my body does feel less stiff and sore than it did yesterday. Maybe Olivier was right, and the champagne really was best for my stress levels. And what had he said about the sea? That it was good for my heart?

I carefully get up and see there's an envelope underneath the door. I hobble over to it, too afraid to put any real weight on my ankle yet, and pick it up.

Scrawled in elegant handwriting on the hotel stationery is a note:

Mon Lapin,

I hope you were able to get some much-needed rest. I will be working for most of the day, so I hope you'll feel free to entertain yourself. If you want food or drinks, please order to your heart's desire. If you wish to go to the pool, to the restaurant, anywhere you like, please

*dial the concierge, and Marcel will be at your beck and
call. I will be back for you at seven o'clock tonight for
dinner. There are some dresses outside the door, in case
you want to wear one for the occasion.*

Olivier Dumont

Oh. My. God.

I open my door and peer outside. I gasp. There is a legit rolling rack outside the door with numerous garment bags hanging off it.

I manage to keep the door open and pull the rack inside the room. I quickly get to work unzipping the garment bags and discovering each dress hidden inside. They're all black—I suppose it's the safest and most elegant choice—all in my size, and all with the Dumont label. My stomach flips, knowing each dress has to be worth at least $1,000.

Shit. He wants to take me out for dinner tonight, with my bungled-up ankle and lack of decorum? He might be able to fit me in a flattering and beautiful dress, but it might be akin to putting lipstick on a pig. Or at least designer clothing on a girl from a trailer park.

I carefully try on each one, trying to play the part of princess, even if just for a day. I eventually settle on a billowy lace number with a low-cut neckline that shows off my chest and flares out toward the knee. Bonus points for not having to wear a bra with it.

The biggest challenge is trying to occupy myself for the next ten hours or so. Luckily, the time passes easily. I order in a big enough breakfast, with copious amounts of coffee, so that I don't need anything for lunch, then spend the afternoon lying by the private hot tub and getting some sun.

By the time seven o'clock rolls around, I'm slightly burned, light-headed, and nervous, but the dress looks great on me, and I've managed to make some faint waves in my hair so that it fans out on my shoulders. I haven't bothered with makeup much while traveling, since it all seems to melt off my face, but I do what I can to make myself look fairly pretty and presentable.

If it's pretty enough for Olivier Dumont, well, that remains to be seen. But fuck it. I can be insecure some other time. I'm going to take advantage of tonight—this once-in-a-lifetime, fairy-tale kind of date, this other life I'm living—and I'm going to believe I deserve every single minute of it.

Olivier is punctual. There's a knock at the door at exactly seven o'clock, and it takes all my concentration to keep myself from freaking out.

I hobble over to the door, with my flip-flop on one foot and the bandage on the other, and open it.

Fuck me.

Olivier is standing there with a bouquet of pink and coral roses in his hand, but it's the rest of him that takes my breath away.

First of all, he's dressed in a freaking tuxedo. I mean, this is a slick suit, complete with bow tie and shiny shoes. Second of all, his hair is all artfully mussed up with some kind of product and pushed off his face, letting those gorgeous eyes of his shine. And, of course, that cocky as hell smile that I could stare at all night long.

"You look beautiful," he says to me, letting his heavy-lidded eyes slowly coast up and down my body, pausing ever so briefly at my breasts. "You made the right choice with that dress."

I'm blushing. Damn it.

"They were all so lovely," I tell him, feeling all sorts of awkward all of a sudden, because now he's here, and this thing is so real. "I had a hard time choosing. Sorry I don't have the right footwear to complement it, though." I point my mangled foot at him.

"I won't be staring at your feet, don't worry," he says. "May I come in?"

"Of course, it's your room."

He grins at me as he strides into the room, and I catch the fresh scent of his aftershave. Mint and cedar and something clean. "It would be very dangerous for me to think of my hotels that way," he says as he takes a vase from the corner of the room and fills it up with water in the bathroom before artfully arranging the roses in it.

"Oh, I'm sure plenty of women—and men—wouldn't mind if you barged in on them."

"You seem very preoccupied with the idea of me and other people," he says to me, placing the roses by my bed. "For as long as you see me standing before you, other people don't exist. It's only me and only you." The way his eyes are latched on to mine is so intense, I can feel my core grow hot. "Especially only you. *Tu comprends?*"

I feel a little sheepish at that. I'm not sure why I keep bringing it up; I guess it's because it's really the only thing I know about him. And, I mean, just look at this guy.

"Okay," I say quietly, giving him a shy smile. "It's just me and just you." I clear my throat, changing the subject. "So where are you taking me tonight?"

His eyes go to the French doors and the setting sun beyond, which is painting the sky shades of lavender and peach. "I hope you don't get seasick."

"You're taking me on the boat?"

He nods. "Just you and just me. Oh, and Marcel and Philippe. He's an excellent chef, won many awards."

I can only blink at him.

"So I can still surprise you," he says. "That's good to know." He comes over to me. "Now if you don't mind, we have a boat to catch." He holds his arm out to me. "You can use me as a crutch, or I can carry you in my arms."

"Sure you don't want to put me in a wheelbarrow? I'm sure that will turn a few heads."

"People here have seen stranger things, I'm sure."

Since I've been resting most of the day, I find I can get along pretty well with pressure on the ball of my foot, so luckily the wheelbarrow is out of the question. I take his arm and grin up at him, my nerves dancing at how close we are, making my skin feel flushed and tingly.

"Shall we?" he asks, his voice taking on this throaty, silken quality that makes me bite my lip. I nod.

The journey down to the boat is fairly painless. The path is level and well groomed, making it easy to just lean on him. The sounds of birds and cicadas fill the candy-colored air, and I breathe in the smells of rosemary and cypress.

"God, it's beautiful," I tell him. "It feels so good to be outside of the room."

"I can imagine," he says.

"Why do you live in Paris? I'd live here if I could."

He chuckles softly, and when I glance up at him, I can see the fiery skies reflected in his eyes. "I'm too young to live here. This is where you go when you retire."

"But I mean, I'm sure you could retire tomorrow if you wanted. You don't have to work a day in your life if you don't want to."

He nods, his lips pressed together. "You're right. I don't have to work. But I want to. It's . . . what gives me life. And Paris is where the work is, where the life is. When I feel I've taken on too much, maybe then I'll come down here and relax for a few days."

"But I bet you don't. I bet it's always business for you."

He shoots me a quick smile. "Are you making guesses, or are you just observant?"

I shrug. "A little from column A, a little from column B."

He frowns. "I don't understand the reference."

"You don't have to."

The boat is actually a massive sailboat situated along a dock with a few other ridiculously large ships tied to it. Olivier lets it slip that one of them belongs to a very famous couple I have no doubt is Jay-Z and Beyoncé.

But before I have time to marvel over their impressive motorboat, I'm scuttled aboard Olivier's, which is all teakwood and cream colors, both modern and vintage. I don't know a damn thing about boats and have been on only one, during a field trip in tenth grade, but I know this thing is top of the line.

With Philippe the chef cooking up a storm in the galley kitchen, Olivier and I settle into the plush seats by the cockpit, with Marcel at the wheel of the boat as it pulls away from the dock and heads out to sea.

"Is there anything you can't do, Marcel?" I ask the concierge teasingly.

"*Absolument pas,*" Marcel says with a wink.

"But seriously," I say, turning to Olivier, who has his arm along the back of the seat. With his tux and the sunset skies and the dark waves glittering with gold behind him, he looks every inch a French James Bond. "I didn't peg you for a sailor. Don't you need to have a lot of time on your hands for that?"

He gives me a lopsided grin. "You do. And Marcel is a far more capable sailor than I am. This boat actually belongs to my brother, Renaud."

"Where is Renaud now? He doesn't mind you using his boat?"

"So many questions." He reaches out and gives a few strands of my hair a light tug.

I swallow. "I like to know things. I'd like to know you. The real you, not the one I read about."

His gaze drops to my lips, and for a heady moment, my world starts to spin, and I think, *This is it, he's finally going to kiss me.*

But the spell is broken when he looks away at the darkening horizon, clouds spreading through the sky like an inky bruise. My heart is beating loud in my chest, waiting, waiting . . .

"Renaud lives in California," he finally says, his voice growing quiet. "He started out with a few of our wineries here in Bordeaux and then kept expanding and expanding. He now stays at his biggest winery in Napa. Actually, he's been trying to get me to develop a hotel there for a while, but . . ."

"You don't want to leave France."

"It's not that. I love California, and I haven't expanded to the States yet. But . . . I think I need to stay near my family. For now."

I don't want to pry more than I have already. I read that his mother died in a car accident about four years ago, so I figure he may be supporting his father in more ways than one, even if he wants nothing to do with that side of the business.

"Have you been to California?" Olivier asks me. The question sounds natural, but I can already tell that he's just trying to change the subject. I tell him I've been there with a friend—to Universal Studios to see Harry Potter World. Actually, I went with Tom, but I don't want to bring that loser up—and we get onto the subject of traveling, which is something I can now talk his ear off about, letting him off the hook.

Can't say I blame him for being a bit cagey about his family. In many ways, we're still total strangers, and I know it usually takes a long time before I start opening up to people about my life. And I mean the real, nitty-gritty, not-so-pretty parts of it. On the surface we might seem like two completely different people from totally different lives, but perhaps we're not so different if you dig a little deeper.

But, as usual around Olivier, I'm getting a little ahead of myself. I don't know why I keep trying to make this something it's not, when it's not even anything to begin with.

And yet, here I am on his family's yacht, under a twinkling night sky, floating on the Mediterranean, while a Michelin-starred chef serves us a seafood feast the likes of which I've never experienced before. The Dumont wine is at the ready, and Olivier is giving me his undivided attention, as if he's feasting on me with his eyes and ears.

I wish he would feast on me in other ways.

I wish I had the nerve to touch him, kiss him, do something.

I'm growing afraid.

But I'm no longer afraid of what might happen—I'm afraid of what might not. When I first saw Olivier, when he first took care of me and brought me here, I was so sure that his main goal was to seduce me. I couldn't explain why, because, let's face it, I'm not his usual type, but that's honestly what I thought. Then, as the days started to tick by and we got to know each other in a purely platonic way, well, then that little theory of mine started to melt away.

If I started out with jitters and butterflies in my stomach over the idea of Olivier and me together physically, then those butterflies inside me have now morphed into desperate, voracious beasts.

I want to consume this man, and I want him to consume me.

I want to feel this part of him before we say goodbye and the fairy tale ends and my old life begins again. I want Olivier before it's too late.

It's just after dessert—a meringue-and-almond dish with a raspberry coulis—when Marcel drops anchor, the chains noisily clattering into the sea.

"Where are we?" I ask, looking around. We had been steadily moving back toward the many lights of land when we stopped. We aren't that far from shore; I can see the bleached, rocky edges of the land glowing under the moon and shrubs dancing in the light sea breeze, and I can hear the sound of the waves gently lapping over the rocks.

Olivier grins at me, his smile shadowed by the warm glow of the cockpit lights, and starts to undo his bow tie.

Meanwhile, Marcel heads down the stairs into the boat, throwing up a couple of fluffy towels.

"What's happening?" I ask, though I have an idea.

"Care to go for a swim?" Olivier asks, his tie now loose, his hands deftly unbuttoning his shirt.

Oh God.

"Um," I manage to say feebly, "I don't have a bathing suit."

"Go in your underwear."

"I'm not wearing a bra."

He smirks. "I've noticed." Then he shrugs off his jacket and shirt until he's topless.

Even in the dim light, he's a sight to behold. Wide, firm chest, rigid abs, those lickable Vs on the side of his hips—all wrapped up in a smooth golden package.

Speaking of package, now his fingers are undoing his belt, and I'm not sure I'm ready for what's next.

"I'm going in," he tells me. "You're free to join me. I highly advise a dip in the Mediterranean. The sea salt here is good for your soul."

I'll tell you what else is good for the soul: watching Olivier Dumont take off his clothes, that's what. The sound as he undoes his zipper is so loud it seems to bounce off the waves.

I quickly avert my eyes, even though the temptation to stare is overwhelming, and then he moves into my vision: his perfect shoulders, back, and, yes, one hell of an ass, all lit by the soft moonlight.

He stops just at the stern of the ship, climbs over the railing, and with one quick smile back at me over his shoulder, swan-dives naked into the sea with barely a splash.

I get up and scramble over as quickly as I can with my ankle and peer over the side.

He's swimming and grinning up at me, his wet hair pushed off his face. But that's not the only thing that's taking my breath away.

The water around him is lit up, like the moon's glow has saturated it. The light continues out from around him along the dark waves, like cool white trails snaking through the sea.

"It's called *une mer de lait*," he says. "The sea of milk. It's bioluminescence from a type of Mollusca."

"It's magical," I say breathlessly, trying to soak it all in. "We have something like this in the Pacific Northwest, but it's more blue and green. This is like . . . you're swimming in the Milky Way."

"Doesn't it make you want to jump in?"

It does. And so does the fact that he's so effortlessly bobbing in the waves.

"Is it safe?"

"Very much so."

"Warm?"

"Bien sûr."

I think about it for a minute. "What about my ankle?"

"You can use the steps and platform at the back, just there. Unwrap your ankle so the bandage doesn't get wet, and we'll put it back on you after."

"And my lack of bathing suit?"

"I just went in naked."

"I didn't see anything," I tell him quickly.

"No? That's a shame. It was the whole point."

I smile, feeling extremely giddy all of a sudden, like everything inside me is fired up and ready to go. Fuck yes, I'm going in.

"Okay," I tell him, walking around to the back, where there's a step leading down to a wide wooden swimming platform. I sit down on the step and start unwrapping my ankle. "But you have to turn around when this dress comes off."

"You do know by now that most women in France swim and sunbathe topless anyway?"

"And you know by now that I am not a Frenchwoman, nor am I most women," I tell him, pulling the rest of the bandage off and setting it aside before easing up to my feet. "Okay, turn around now."

He sighs but pivots in the water so he's facing the shore. I quickly reach down and slip off my underwear, not wanting to get them wet, then unzip my dress and pull it over my head. I toss it back on the deck and look to see if he's peeking.

To his credit, he's not, but he is letting out a sly whistle of sorts as if he might have been earlier.

"You better not have seen anything," I warn him as I hobble over to the edge.

"My imagination is pretty good at filling in the blanks," he says, and I can hear the grin on his face. "Though I have no doubt it won't do it justice for when I see the real thing."

"When?" I repeat with a dry laugh, but inside a million fireworks are going off.

Time to take the literal plunge.

There's nothing as nerve-racking as the moment before you're about to jump, when something goes from a concept that you've talked about and considered to a real, actual thing. It's scary. It doesn't matter if it's taking your first trip overseas or jumping into the Mediterranean Sea at night. The abstract becomes your reality, and it's happening.

So I close my eyes, take a deep breath, and jump.

CHAPTER SIX

SADIE

With a deep breath of the warm, scented night air, I jump into the bracing chill of the sea. I feel every inch of my naked skin dance as I drop deeper into the water, until I'm enveloped in the shimmering ocean like a mythical creature.

Then I'm rushing up to the surface and bursting through, gasping for air, tasting the salt on my lips, my legs kicking to stay afloat.

I push the wet hair off my face and wipe my eyes to see Olivier smiling at me as he swims over.

"You did it," he says, and I don't know how it's possible, but being in the water has transformed him into something larger than life as well, like he's some mythical merman.

"I did," I say, and my gaze is battling between staring at the shimmery, white stars in the water or the languid, sexual nature of his eyes.

I'm suddenly very, very conscious of how naked I am; the tops of my breasts are glistening from the moonlight, and he's drifting closer and closer to me as we tread water together.

My heart is really rocketing now, not only from the adrenaline push from the jump, but because I can feel myself being drawn to him like stars toward a black hole. If my body were to press against his, I would feel every single hard and wet inch of him, and I'm pretty sure I would combust, fire spreading out along the glowing water.

"You're beautiful, Sadie," he says to me, his chin dipping into the water as he stares up at me intently through his long eyelashes.

For once, I resist the urge to laugh it off or downplay it, like I usually do when someone gives me a compliment. I don't do anything like that, because it feels like Olivier is offering it up to me as a sign of reverence. Like it means something.

I swallow thickly, unable to say anything. I can only stare at him and the glowing water reflected in his eyes.

And then it happens.

His warm hand is at my back like a current, pulling me gently forward until my skin is brushing against his skin, and the water comes alive. One hand goes to my cheek, gripping me softly, while the other keeps us both afloat. He leans in, and it feels like whatever this is is meant to be, a cosmic dalliance, universes above and below us colliding in a sea of stars.

Another life becoming more real than the first one.

His lips press against mine, soft and slow and wet, tasting of salt and need and want. I gasp hungrily as I feel his erection press against my hip, sliding against me as my hand goes to his shoulders to hold on.

"You're too beautiful for words," he whispers to me, his lips brushing against mine. "None of the words in English will do. None of the words in French will do either. There is no language that can describe what I see before me."

And I'm melting. If I weren't holding on to his strong shoulders, I would be sinking like a stone.

But while I'm melting, I'm also firing up. Flames are building in my core, rising high, spurring a need in me like no other.

I kiss him hard, wanting so much of him at once, wanting to keep kissing him and drowning in his depths. My hands are roaming everywhere on his body as his hands do the same to mine, and we're barely staying afloat.

But if I drowned right here, I think I'd only need his kiss to keep me alive.

I don't know how long we make out like this, bathed in glowing water, indulging in the feel of each other for the first time, but eventually a noise brings us out of our fevered state.

We glance up to see Marcel at the side of the boat, averting his eyes. He says something to Olivier in French and then leaves to go back below deck.

Olivier nods and looks at me, giving me a lazy grin as he pushes the wet hair off my face. "We should go back now," he says to me. "Come on."

We swim to the back of the boat, and Olivier gets out first, and again he's not hiding anything, but this time I'm taking it all in like the secret pervert that I am.

The man is stunning.

And he's hung like a horse.

A French horse. Much more of an elegant-looking dick, not just large and in charge.

I can tell I'm already blushing, and I'm glad it's dark outside.

Once he's climbed on board, I do the same, ever so aware of my bare breasts, but, luckily, he throws me a towel so I can cover myself up before he helps me up onto the rest of the yacht.

"Let's get dressed," he says, grabbing our clothes, and I follow him down to the cockpit, where Marcel and the cook continue to pretend like we're not there.

I change back into my dress in one of the cabins, smiling to myself the whole time.

It happened.

He kissed me.

And the best is yet to come.

It's not going to end there in that moonlit water.

We're just starting.

The boat ride back to the dock goes by both quickly and slowly. Slowly, because I can't wait for us to be alone again in my room. Quickly, because I'm nervous. I'm afraid. Even though we were just naked in the sea with each other, this is Olivier, and this is the first person I will have slept with since Tom. Tom, who was familiar and safe and predictable.

With Olivier, I don't know what to expect. I don't know how it's going to make me feel. I don't know if I'll be rendered too vulnerable or if it will change things between us, making it harder for me to leave.

But who am I kidding? It's already going to be impossible.

We get off the boat, and Olivier is my crutch and guide as he leads me back to the room. My nerves are tap-dancing up and down my spine, and I feel like I'm so alive, so in tune with the air and the sky and the stars that anything is possible, and anything can happen.

"We should take a shower," he says, once we've stepped inside and he's closed the door behind us.

I raise my brows. I do need to rinse off that salty Mediterranean water before I go to bed tonight, but I'm not sure if this is an invitation or . . .

"Get naked and get in," he says, jerking his head to the bathroom. *"S'il vous plaît."*

I gulp. Okay. It's an invitation.

I walk past him to the bathroom, waiting until I'm inside to start stripping.

He follows, undoing his pants, his shirt—everything coming off until he's completely naked.

Again, I'm breathless. Speechless. The sight of him in all his nude glory with that perfect dick between his legs is scrambling my brain.

"Do you need help?" he asks, leaning past me to open the glass shower doors and get the water running.

"I can manage," I tell him, pulling off my dress, now completely naked.

Olivier's lustful eyes drink me in, from my lips all the way to my toes, and for once I don't feel so bashful anymore. I just feel powerful. Like I'm all woman. He makes me feel like I'm the most desired woman on earth.

"I still have no words," he murmurs as he kisses me, then takes my hand and pulls me into the shower, the hot stream of water running all over us.

He pours body wash into a sponge and then proceeds to soap me up all over, taking his time as he goes over my breasts, taking it between my legs.

I feel like a ticking time bomb, and the shower steam and heat are only making me feel hotter. I don't want just this soft teasing, I want him.

I want all of him.

I reach down and boldly grab his dick, making a fist over its firm, stiff length, and then moving my fist up and down.

He gasps, eyes rolling back as he drops the sponge.

I work him faster and faster, the suds creating a slick lube, and then when he sounds like he's about to lose it, he opens his eyes and grabs my face, kissing me deep and hard and desperately.

We're making out in a flurry of lips and teeth and tongue as we spin out of the shower and washroom, bumping into counters and walls, and I know it'll be a miracle if we even make it to the bed. Somehow, Olivier manages to lift me up in the air and then carry me over, practically throwing me on it, so I land on my back, my breasts bouncing freely.

I stare up at him, my lips throbbing from where he ravaged me, and then watch as he strides over to the bedside table and pulls out a condom. I'm not sure if there's always a stack of them in there as courtesy to guests or if he'd put them there, but, either way, I'm not complaining.

I am on the pill, but I like to be safe rather than sorry, and with him taking charge like this, it nips that talk in the bud.

I don't want to talk right now.

All I want is him inside me; I'm practically aching for him.

He can tell, too, because his eyes are focused on my pussy as he slides the condom on.

"Spread your legs wider," he says in a rough voice, the kind of tone that gives you goose bumps. "Let me see what your pretty little pussy looks like."

I gulp and then do as he asks.

His expression turns even more lustful, as if that's possible, his lids becoming heavy, his nostrils flaring.

He's going to devour me, I think to myself.

Good.

I spread my legs wider, and then before I know what I'm doing, I'm playing with myself, running my fingers over my swollen, slick clit in a teasing manner, watching what this is doing to him.

Then he growls like a beast unleashed, and he's grabbing my hips and slamming his cock into me.

My lungs empty, and I cry out in pain and pleasure and surprise.

"No more teasing," he says through a grunt, and then his grip grows tighter, and he starts to pound into me, relentless.

I can barely breathe; my heart feels like it's skipping its way out of my chest.

I manage to keep my fingers moving, the pleasure building up higher and higher as his cock sinks in deeper, and soon the pain and shock are pushed to the side.

Now all I feel is him and his desperate feral drive.

He pulls my hips up higher until my legs are around his back and then keeps up the pace.

My head rolls to the side, staring at the doors to the balcony. I can vaguely see our reflection: his tall, lean, and muscular body standing at the foot of the bed, my hips jerked up high as he thrusts into me, my breasts jostling with each quick pump of his hips.

It's so fucking erotic, I can barely believe it's happening.

It looks like a porno, just how wild and—

Wait a minute.

It almost looks like there's someone else in the room with us.

There's another face, staring back at me.

I look to the opposite side of the bed, but there's no one there.

Then I look back to the window.

I still see the reflection, I swear, a man out there watching us . . .

Olivier's pumping slows.

"Are you okay?" he asks.

I glance up at him with wide eyes. "Did you see . . . ?"

I look back to the window, but this time the reflection is gone.

He looks, too, and frowns, then lets go of one hip to wipe the sweat off his brow. "See what?" he asks, breathless.

I shake my head. I'm all over the place. "Nothing."

"How about we change things," he says, slowly pulling out. "Flip over."

I give a furtive glance to the window again, and then when I still see nothing, I turn over so that I'm on all fours, my back to him. At least this way I don't have to stare out the window and freak myself out for no reason.

Not that the idea of being watched while having sex is *that* freaky.

That's something the old Sadie would never admit to.

He places his hand on my shoulder blades and pushes me down gently into the mattress. I'm basically flattened against the bed, my ass high in the air. He starts to push inside me, and I grab hold of the sheets, holding on tight. Even though I'm wet as sin and greedy for his cock, the size of him takes my breath away, and I have to remind myself to breathe through it, letting him in farther and farther as my ass gets higher and higher.

He adjusts his angle behind me and then pushes himself in to the hilt, and I feel myself expand around his thickness, his dick dragging over every desperate nerve inside me.

An aching groan falls from my mouth.

"Ma chérie," he says hoarsely, "you will unravel me with your sounds."

God, please. I want him to unravel.

But, even as I think that, I know he wants me to unravel first.

He starts pounding me faster and faster, the bed slamming against the wall. I swear it might even be moving a few inches to the right.

I gasp, gripping the sheets harder, my hands sweaty. I can barely hold on, even with my cheek pressed into the mattress. I'm so full of him inside me, and he keeps hitting the right spot over and over again, so that nothing else matters to me now except coming fast and coming hard.

"You like this?" he whispers.

I can only nod and make needy little sounds.

I swear I can hear him grin.

He thrusts into me, his hips circling quickly, and the feeling inside me grows and builds and tightens until I feel like I might pass out. Our skin slaps loudly against each other, the sound echoing around the room, turning me on even more.

With one smooth movement, he pulls my hips up higher, angling himself down in a long, powerful thrust and he's hitting my G-spot at a hot, perfect pace.

Sweet Jesus.

I think I'm about to see stars.

Then all the tension snaps, a slingshot pulled back until there's nowhere else to go, and then—

I'm gone.

I cry out, flying through space at the speed of sound, my body quaking and quivering and shaking with a wild mind of its own. It's like I cease to exist, and the orgasm is the only thing left, the only thing that matters in this galaxy.

"Olivier," I manage to say, slowly remembering where I am and what blissful thing is happening.

Olivier moans as I pulse around him, and his pace quickens. He's driving himself inside me, so hard and thorough and punishing that I'm not sure if he's ever going to stop or if he's trying to break me in two. And I'm still riding my orgasm, each brutal thrust keeping me going on the wave, like I'll keep coming for as long as he's in deep. I'm up so high, high, high, and I can't come down, even if I tried.

Then he's coming, letting out hoarse grunts that fill me with both desire and a strange sense of pride, and I can feel the sweat dripping off him and onto my back, hear his ragged and frantic breath.

Finally, he pulls out and collapses beside me on the bed, just as I let my hips drop. My body is still shaking from the orgasm and the strain; my brain is still trying to make sense of this beautiful new world, and my heart has yet to return to my chest.

After a few moments, he reaches out and runs his hands over my body, smearing the sweat around. "We're dirty again," he murmurs, placing a hot, wet kiss on my lips. "I think we're going to need another shower. We might need a lot of showers tonight."

I watch as he pulls his condom off, and I smile. "I think we're going to need a lot of condoms too."

He grins. "Good thing you're dealing with a man who deals in excess," he says. "Also, good thing you're with a man who's only getting started."

My heart leaps at that, my body coming back to life even though the previous waves and buzz never quite left me.

He's only getting started. We're only getting started.

This man.

And me.

CHAPTER SEVEN

Olivier

I wake up before she does.

To be fair, I barely slept at all. Neither of us did, not when I was taking my time screwing her senseless throughout the midnight hours, but even when she finally dozed off, exhausted and satisfied, my eyes stayed open and my brain kept racing.

I have to say, it was the most peculiar feeling. For the first time in a long time, I stopped thinking about work as an asset. I started thinking about work as a hindrance in my life. If it wasn't for work, I wouldn't have to say goodbye to her.

But that was all assuming she wouldn't want to say goodbye. It's why I took my time with Sadie—I couldn't quite figure out the type of girl she is. One moment she's shy, the next she's bold, another minute she's an open book, the next she's clamped shut. She both eagerly takes in all the riches and experiences, and then shuns them with her next breath.

I still don't have a handle on her character. All I know is that I trust her for some reason, maybe just for this short while, maybe for something longer than that. I don't know. The most beguiling thing is that I want there to be more than what there is. Yet the chances of her feeling the same, feeling it enough to stay, are slim.

She groans, letting out a breathless little sigh before she rolls over.

Slowly, ever so slowly, she opens her eyes and glances at me through the long strands of hair across her face.

I can't help but smile at her like this. So innocent and wicked, naked and disheveled. I reach across and brush the hair off her face so I can stare into her endless blue eyes.

"Bon matin, mon lapin," I say, knowing I'm being cheesy as fuck, but hoping the fact that I'm speaking French will make up for it.

She bursts into giggles, and I know that she's called me out on it. "Really? First thing in the morning with the lines?"

I quickly run my hand down the smooth, soft skin of her back and pull her toward me. "I'll have you know, it's not so easy to rhyme first thing in the morning," I tell her, leaning down to place a kiss at the crook of her neck.

"Mmm," she murmurs, slipping her hand down the side of my waist and over my hip. "Maybe you should stick to things you're better at."

Well, well, well. I like this. I like that it's the morning after, and all formalities and awkwardness have dissolved, and we seem to know each other on another level.

Or maybe there are many levels yet to be discovered.

Maybe each level is right in our hands.

I nip at her skin, feeling her squirm beneath me, hearing her gasp and moan.

"You know I'll be dreaming of those sounds for years to come," I tell her, running my tongue up the side of her neck. "You've got the mouth of every wet, hot fantasy, unleashed."

"You flatter me," she says, acting every bit the minx.

"Just you wait," I warn her.

Last night was not enough.

I don't think it will ever be enough.

I straddle her, my thighs on either side of her hips, and reach down to ever so slowly leave soft kisses behind. She tastes sweeter than champagne, and I run my tongue over her skin, feeling it perk up under my touch.

I move back a few inches so I can kiss and lick all the way to her stomach, and her nipples harden, exposed to my hungry eyes. I immediately dip my head and lick them gently until she groans, arching her back. She is so perfect—the feel of her, the shape, the way her body responds to my every move.

Why can't I have this for more than a few days?

I clench my eyes shut and will it away. I can't think like this, not now. We *just* got together; it's too soon to think about how it could end.

Sadie runs her fingers through my hair teasingly, and I momentarily close my eyes at her touch, loving the way this feels.

The tenderness.

When was the last time I felt tenderness?

Such an underrated thing, such an important part of life.

And with a tenderness that I know will grow to fire and flames, I kiss her breasts from the soft outer swell to the nipple and back again, my tongue flicking them like I'm trying to lap up the rest of the richest cream.

But soon that tenderness from earlier starts to grow rough and impatient. Her nails are digging into my scalp, and she's getting restless, and I know she wants nothing more than my tongue or my cock between her legs, to have me inside her, bringing her relief.

She has to learn patience first.

I continue to work at her breasts, licking a warm path up the swollen corners toward the middle. I gently nip at her, bringing sharp bursts of pain with the soothing stroke of my tongue, alternating the two until she begins squirming beneath me, her face contorted with that anguished need for more.

"Olivier," Sadie groans softly, her fingers grasping my hair tighter and tighter, "come inside me. *S'il vous plaît.*"

I grin. I appreciate her attempt at French, but I'm in no hurry this morning.

"Relax, *mon lapin*," I tell her, my voice thick. "I will make it worth your while."

She sighs with a mix of pleasure and frustration and sinks farther back into the bed. I take my mouth and place it flush over the hard peaks of her nipples, sucking them gently and working them with my tongue. I lap and flick, my attention completely on her, trying to make her eyes roll back, her thighs shudder.

"Olivier, please," she gasps, licking her lips.

But I persist. Her breathing deepens, then sharpens, hot and heavy pants that inflame my own desire. I give and give until she's writhing beneath me and yanking my hair with all her strength. I squeeze her breasts, bite her nipples, and it's almost enough to make her come.

I quickly slip my hand between her legs, swiping along her slick clit. That one touch is enough to cause her to let go. Her body starts to quake uncontrollably, and breathless words come from her open, yearning mouth, wild and animalistic.

Such a perfect mouth.

Then her tremors slow, and her body relaxes into the mattress.

"Oh my God," she says, her head rolling back and forth, her wide eyes staring at the ceiling.

"Mon Dieu," I tell her, grinning, "if you're still trying to learn the language."

"Well, whatever you just did to me transcends any language, I'll tell you that much," she manages to say. "You have magic fingers, you know that? No, wait, you probably do."

"You're the one that's magic," I tell her as she reaches up and runs her fingers over my muscles. There's a hunger still in her eyes, like that was only the beginning, and she's just getting started.

She's not had her fill. I know what she wants; I know what she needs.

I kiss her, her lips sweet and rich, and pull back enough to stare into her eyes, my hands trailing up and down the soft slopes of her body, my fingers tracing her as if it will help me remember her years later, just like this.

Her eyes hold mine, and I know that she has to feel the same way, that we're going through this together, whatever this is.

All I know is that it's good.

It's very good.

Sadie murmurs something, then kisses me hard, wild and probing, and I move my body flush on top of hers. My fingers skip down her stomach and hips and settle in between her thighs. She is still wet and warm from her previous orgasm, and she feels like home to me, like this is a place I've been searching for, a place I've just found, a place I never want to leave.

I glide my fingers along her slickness and up inside her, thrusting deep and rubbing against her with even pressure.

I love the way her body gives in to my hands, like I can mold her into anything I want. Of course, all I want, all I need right now, is her.

Just like this.

She arches her back, knees coming up to give me better access, and I slip my fingers out and position my dick there instead.

I push in slowly, inch by inch, and let the sensation flood through me. Beautiful. Powerful. My eyes close, and when I go deep, as far as I can go inside of her, it feels like we are joined as one. We move as one, breathe as one. I'm sure our hearts might start to beat as one. There is energy here between us, crackling in the air, sizzling in waves between us.

"How does my cock feel?" I ask, my voice rough as I push in with each slow, wet thrust.

She gives me a lazy smile though her eyes are closed. "Like a god's."

The right thing to say.

"Your god?" I drive myself in deeper, and she lets out a moan.

"The only one." She opens her lustful eyes to stare up at me, and for a moment I think she's going to say something else. But then her head goes back into the pillow, and her eyes close, and she succumbs to the pleasure as I start to thrust in deeper, harder, like I can imprint myself on her this way.

Even as the pace of my hips quickens, I'm still in control, desperate to drive away the questions waiting for us on the other side. Beyond this hotel, beyond these sun-filled days with each other.

"Olivier," she whispers roughly, lips at my ear. "I'm coming."

A shudder rolls down my back, and I still myself, unable to keep going without losing it. Sweat pools between our overheated bodies, our hands gliding over each other, yearning to hold on. I am determined, but so is she.

I can't hold back any longer.

I'm brought to the edge in an instant, and before I can even moan, I'm letting loose. I come so hard into her that the bed shakes and I lose all control. My world both widens into a million galaxies and shrinks until it's only her. I'm calling her name, loud, grunting, letting loose powerful groans as this pleasure rips me apart. Her nails dig into my back, and she's crying out breathlessly, swearing over and over. She pulses around me, and we both keep coming, like we're unable or unwilling to stop.

But eventually our bodies can't handle it. I collapse on top of her and bury my face in her neck, holding on to her limbs and trying to breathe, trying to keep her here in this bed with me, holding on to this moment until it turns into another moment and another moment.

Our lives are made up of nothing but moments.

But I want to live in every moment with her.

◆ ◆ ◆

"Are you sure I can't bring you back something?" I ask Sadie as I slip into my suit that Marcel has dropped off for me.

"What would you get me? I have everything," she says lightly, gesturing to the room. She's sitting on the rumpled bed in the fluffy, Egyptian cotton Dumont house robe that we supply all the guests (worth about $2,000, if you're counting). Her foot is out in front of her on a pillow, though it's no longer bandaged, and the swelling is almost completely gone. Is it wrong to mourn the moment when she's fully healed, when she finds no reason to depend on me?

I'm being ridiculous, of course. Which, to be honest, is a new thing for me. I've gotten my dick sucked and come inside her more than enough times to consider her out of my system, but she's only gotten more inside, slipped under my skin like some form of silk that bonds to your bones.

"I'll be right back," I tell her. "I'll bring you a surprise."

She laughs, cocking a brow at me. "I don't even know what that could mean coming from you."

I leave her and head out of the villa toward the lobby to tell the front desk that I'll be in Saint-Tropez if anyone calls. I wasn't supposed to hang around in the area for more than a day, but, as luck has it, one of our investors is at his summer villa here and wants to meet. Saves him a trip up to Paris.

I'm striding through the tiled lobby, guests going to and fro and paying me no attention—probably because most of them are famous and don't have a moment to think about anyone else—when suddenly I feel the air change.

It sounds fucking crazy. It always sounds fucking crazy, even when I try to explain it to myself, but that's the truth.

The air becomes sharper, more acidic, as if an electrical storm is coming, the kind you know will ruin your bright and sunny day.

And there he is.

Without thinking I stop walking, pausing in the middle of the lobby, and my head swivels toward the corner near the elevators.

There he stands, in a rust red suit, white shirt unbuttoned, no tie, hair a mess, facial hair that could use a trim, especially above the lip.

My cousin Pascal Dumont.

His bright-blue eyes are fixed on me, like he'd been watching me for a while, maybe even as I left the villa—eyes that tell me they know everything, even the things about myself that I don't know.

Eyes that aren't kind.

They seem kind. They're photogenic in their intensity and lapis color; they crinkle at the corners when he gives an easy smile; they're often brimming with a million emotions, emotions you can take and make your own, turn into whatever makes you feel better about yourself.

But they aren't kind.

He's not kind.

And, of course, he's not here by accident.

My throat already feels thick, wondering what the hell he could want.

The thing with Pascal is that he could want anything.

And for most of my life, I've been willing to give him anything.

To make up for the things that I've done.

The terrible things that I've done.

He gives me his crooked smile, no teeth, and nods, coming over in such a way that lets me know he's been waiting a long time for this moment.

I can't remember the last time I saw him. Maybe at the start of the summer at his mother's birthday. I stopped by with Seraphine out of courtesy. Had some cake, and then we were gone.

We never stay long in that nest of vipers.

"Cousin," Pascal says to me, stopping just a foot away. He has a way of making his words sound the way oil looks traveling through water, something snaking and insidious that permeates the good parts of you.

Then again, everyone on that side of the family is like that.

"What are you doing here?" I ask curtly, unable to fake any formalities.

Pascal feigns being shocked. "Why do you think I'm here? You know, Olivier—you're not the only one who gets to jet off on vacations."

"I'm not on vacation," I tell him.

A small, knowing smile tugs at his lips, and he shakes his head. "No. No, of course not. You never take vacations. Still, I can't help but wonder, since you should have been back in Paris the other day."

I narrow my eyes at him. "You have nothing else to do but keep track of where I am?"

His mouth spreads into his easy, lopsided grin. "Oh, we have other people do those things for me, but sometimes I prefer to watch first-hand. Always more fun that way. Call it a hobby. But listen, now that I've seen you in the flesh, I can tell them to back off."

"What do you want?" I ask tersely.

"Nothing. Well, other than being concerned about your whereabouts."

"My whereabouts are none of your concern."

The corner of his lip twitches. "Hmm. Yes, but of course they are. You've been pretending for the last ten years, Olivier. Pretending that time isn't running out for you, that you don't have to make a decision. But you do. Very soon. And when you run off like this at the last minute, you can't blame me or my father for thinking you're trying to get out of it."

I give him a steady look, refusing to be intimidated, even though the mention of the contract and the deadline makes my heart do double beats. "I didn't run off anywhere. This is my hotel."

"So it is. A great excuse. You know, it made me think maybe I should take a break from the business too. There is a lot on our plates with the upcoming season. My father still thinks this should be the time, the year, we announce our emergence into e-commerce. Join the rest of the fucking world. You know."

"That's nice," I tell him. "Make sure to bring that up with him at the next Dumont meeting."

I move to go past him, but Pascal reaches out and pushes my shoulder back with the heel of his hand. "You're dismissing me so soon?"

I glance down at his hand and think about all the ways I could so easily break it. My eyes go across the room to the receptionist, who is both trying to check a couple in and glancing at me apologetically. She knows she is supposed to call me if anyone in my family ever shows up while I am here.

"Don't be mad at her," Pascal says softly, looking over at the same girl. "I told her to keep me a secret. I can be very persuasive, you know."

I don't even want to know what transpired there. All I know is that poor girl is now without a job. I can't employ staff who aren't loyal to me and would rather fuck or flirt with my cousin. Ever since my uncle made him the face of the Dumont "Red" cologne, and the ads were plastered all over the world, Pascal has become even more famous than he was before.

"I have a meeting to get to," I tell him.

"Oh, so you are doing business here," he says, removing his hand.

"Yes."

"I thought maybe you were busy fucking some sweet little American thing."

Everything inside me tenses like I've been shot with a dart.

American?

I breathe in sharply through my nose, trying to measure my next words. I can't give this man any extra ammunition. "And you thought I had a type?"

Pascal stares at me for a long moment and then lets out a laugh. "A type? You? Well, I suppose all this time here I thought you preferred them French, easy, and . . . married."

And there it is. Another passive reminder that Pascal knows.

That he has to know.

That ten years ago I had an affair with his then wife, Marine.

That ten years ago I made the biggest mistake of my life.

A mistake that will haunt me until the day I die.

Because of the promises I signed in my blood to my uncle.

Because of the promises I've had to live with and lie about and pretend don't bother me.

I manage a sour smile. "You obviously know I have no need to be picky."

"But that's where you're lying, cousin," he says, slapping his hand on my back. "You have a reputation, just as I do. Perhaps not as bad as mine, since you're the eternal bachelor, and I, well, I was married once. Remember that? Remember when I was married?"

Fuck.

I swallow thickly and meet his eyes, refusing to back down, refusing to let him see any shame in me. "I remember."

"Good," he says, smiling. "My father does too. So far, we're the only ones. I'm not sure how much longer that will last."

That's a loaded sentence.

I keep staring at him. "Is that all?"

His eyes narrow momentarily. He hates being dismissed, especially by me.

"Do you remember when we were young, just stupid little children, spending that one summer by the beach in Tarragona? Our fathers were still in Paris, doing business, working all the livelong day, so it was just us, just the children and our mothers, wandering about without a care in the world?"

I have no idea why he's bringing this up, and the memory itself is very vague. Every summer was pretty much as he described, albeit in different locations across Europe.

He goes on, though I see a flicker of anger in his eyes, like something just starting to simmer on low heat. "Remember one day, you and I were building sandcastles, trying to outdo each other. A contest. You would go higher; I would build mine higher. Up and up they went, until yours started to collapse. Your structure at the base wasn't sound. Mine was. I knew I had beaten you, so I called our mothers to come by and judge us. Do you remember what happened then?"

I shake my head, even though I do. It's all coming back to me, though I'm not sure why Pascal is talking about it now, of all times.

"I'm sure you do. It's fine. The truth is, I knew I won and mine was better. But your mother insisted that we both won. She gave you pity points—said you won for creativity, while I won for engineering. But then my mother had to give her verdict. She said that mine lacked vision and my father would be displeased. I don't know why it bothered me, since she was always like that, but it did. I guess it bothered me even more that your mother tried to make me feel better afterward. She insisted that I did a great job, that I was talented. Like your mother knew what my mother lacked. Compassion, I suppose. And it was then that I realized: you'll always think you're better than me."

I stare at him openly. This admission has caught me off guard. Pascal has always been surprising and slightly unhinged, but this is something else.

"I'm sorry," I say, even though I'm not, and I curse myself for saying it.

His gaze turns wicked; his posture stiffens. "There's nothing to apologize for, cousin. My whole point is that you come from a mother who loves and believes not only in her own children, but in others as well. You come from a line of the kind and selfless and good. And yet you're anything but. You pretend and pretend and pretend to be the good son, the one meant for greater things. But it's just pretending. It's all a lie. And, perhaps, the world will come to know the lie. Know who you really are and what you really did. And what it will cost your family."

He's not threatening me, is he?

Then he grins and slaps me on the shoulder.

"I'll let you get to your meeting. Just so you know, I might still be here when you get back. I'll be in the suite across from the villa."

The way he says "villa" tells me everything I need to know.

The villa where Sadie is.

I can hardly get air into my lungs, and yet I have to act like everything is normal. If I say anything at all, if I even react the way I want to react—protectively—that will tell Pascal everything he needs to know.

It will tell Pascal to go there while I'm gone.

Even if I get Marcel stationed outside of her door, I can't quite trust what might happen.

It sounds like my imagination is getting the best of me.

Who cares if my cousin knows I'm screwing Sadie?

But the thing is, he wouldn't care if she was just one of the run-of-the-mill models that I normally fuck for a night.

He would care if she were something more than that.

That was part of the deal.

That was the thing that I didn't even think about.

I have to play this so fucking right, or else I'm going to lose everything.

And until this moment, I hadn't realized how much that is.

"Okay," I tell him. "Maybe I'll see you then."

Then I turn and walk off.

Out of the lobby and down the steps.

To my car waiting below.

The entire time, my heart is crawling up my throat with every single beat, but I'm keeping up the facade until I've pulled out of the hotel driveway and am headed toward the motorway.

I quickly call the direct line to the villa and hold my breath for the first few rings, even though I know Sadie couldn't have gone anywhere.

"Bon . . . jour?" she answers, and I can't help but laugh.

"Very good, you're getting better all the time," I tell her.

"Yeah right. So, uh, you just left. Checking on me already?"

I clear my throat, trying to figure out the best way to put this. "Call me paranoid, I just want to make sure you're okay. Especially since the police haven't caught the man who attacked you yet."

A pause. "Gee, great, thanks for reminding me. Why did you leave again?"

"Duty calls," I say. "Isn't that what you say in America?"

"Mmm, in America we have a better saying. It goes, 'Don't leave a needy naked chick in your bed alone.'"

I laugh. "I like that saying. Pity you didn't teach it to me earlier."

"Oh no, this isn't my fault."

"Well, anyway. I'd feel better if you made sure that your doors are locked, the front and the deck. And don't ever answer the door unless you look through the peephole first, even if you just called room service."

Silence fills the air. "Are you okay?"

"I'm fine. I just care about my guests, and one in particular."

"Do you normally get break-ins here?"

"Just be careful, that's all. I'll be back in a few hours."

"Okay, okay," she says, and I can hear her grunt, as if she's getting out of bed. "You know, after what happened to me the other night, you don't have to tell me twice. I guess all the sex distracted me from everything ugly and cruel out there in the world."

The very obvious thing is that the same goes for me.

But now, after seeing Pascal, I'm hyperaware of everything. My meeting goes smoothly enough, but as soon as it's done, I race back to the hotel, hoping that Sadie listened to my instructions, hoping that I'm worrying for no reason.

I march right up to the front-desk girl from earlier. "Where is he? Is he gone? Pascal Dumont."

I know you know who he is.

She gives me a pleading look. "Yes, he got in a limo shortly after you left. Mr. Dumont, I am so sorry, I didn't know—"

I hold up my hand to silence her, grateful that someone else will be firing her for me. This is the kind of dirty work I try to avoid. "It doesn't matter. As long as he's gone."

"He's gone," she says quickly. "Everything's fine."

But I'm not sure that's true.

You can never be too careful with Pascal.

I'm starting to think you can never be too careful with anyone.

CHAPTER EIGHT

SADIE

"Mind if I join you?"

I twirl around in the shower to see Olivier outside the steamed-up glass of the shower. Even though his image is hazy, he's naked and completely breathtaking.

He opens the door and grins at me, his eyes raking over my body.

I can't help but smile, even though I automatically move to cover up my breasts. "Why is it that every time I'm in the shower, you end up coming in here?"

"I guess I just like to see you get clean after I get you very dirty."

Very dirty, indeed. This morning we've done nothing but have sex in pretty much every position imaginable, in every place possible. I never thought I would turn into one of those sexually adventurous girls, but there's something about Olivier that makes me put all my trust in him. Probably because the man makes me see freaking stars while I'm having an orgasm. I know whatever he wants to do to me is going to be worth it.

"Here, turn around," he says, stepping inside and grabbing a loofah and body wash.

"Think I'm not clean enough?"

"Actually, I like you a little bit dirty," he says, rubbing the soapy sponge down my back. I was pretty much done in the shower, but there's no way I'm heading out now.

"I don't know what I'm going to do back at home," I tell him, even though the word *home* puts a sour taste in my mouth. "I won't have anyone to give me a proper scrub. You've spoiled me."

The loofah stops midway down my back, and a thick tension fills the steamy air.

"So don't go," he says, his voice soft.

"I wish," I tell him, glancing at him over my shoulder. His eyes are on me, intense.

"I'm serious," he says. "Don't go."

I slowly turn around to face him. "I have to go."

He frowns at me, his hair already damp from the steam and sticking to his forehead. "Why?"

"You know why. I have school. I have my mother. I have a very empty bank account."

"You know I'll take care of you."

"Olivier, we barely know each other."

But even though it's the truth, he flinches slightly, almost as if I'd slapped him.

He swallows, licking his lips as he studies the shower walls. "Maybe we don't, but it feels like we do. I know you feel it too."

He's right. But it doesn't change the reality.

He continues, eyes back on my face, curious and hopeful and all the things I need from him. "Come with me to Paris."

It's like a net full of butterflies has been released inside me, his words setting them free.

"What?" I whisper, feeling every part of my body dance with promises.

He takes one of my hands and raises it to his lips, kissing my fingers. "I want you to come back to Paris with me. Stay with me. If you still need to go back in three weeks, then I'll make sure you get back home. But until then, I don't want to be apart from you. I don't want this to be our goodbye."

I give him a wan smile. I'm thrilled that he wants to be with me, that he wants me enough to invite me to stay with him in Paris, luxuriating in all the romantic words and gestures, yet I'm deeply saddened. Because I know that I have to use my head to see myself through this time. That my heart and body have to take the back seat if I want to do the right thing.

I slowly shake my head, and it's like the net comes back, taking all those butterflies away. "I'm so sorry. I wish I could. But I can't run away from my responsibilities, my problems. These last few days here have been some of the best of my entire life, if not the best, but I can't keep on pretending to be someone else."

"You don't have to. You just be Sadie. I'll be Olivier. And we'll be together."

"Until I have to leave again."

He closes his eyes, nostrils flaring as he takes a deep breath. "Until then." Then he opens them and nods. "At least I tried. Couldn't have lived with myself if I hadn't asked. But I respect your wishes, Sadie. I'll always respect you."

Little does he know that my actual wish would be for my brain and logic to take a hike.

He leans in and kisses me, softly at first; then his arms go behind my back, and he rubs the still-soapy loofah up and down, making me shiver. I ignore the pang in my stomach, as I'm sure he's ignoring his, and we fall into that easy, heady rhythm our bodies know so well.

All the regret and disappointment wash down my body, swirling into the drain until it disappears.

For now.

◆ ◆ ◆

It's been two days since Olivier asked me to come to Paris with him.

Two days since I turned him down.

Two days of spending almost every hour in each other's arms, within each other's touch. Other than the time he had to jet off to Saint-Tropez for a meeting, we haven't left each other's side.

It's like we've fused in some way I never thought possible.

That molecular level of connection that I was talking about before? Yeah, well that was *before* we even slept together.

Now that we've been having sex constantly, it's morphed into something else entirely. A symbiote? Who the fuck knows. All I know is that I have to leave him today, and every single part of my body, heart, and soul is *screaming* at me.

Telling me I've made the wrong decision—I should have agreed to stay.

Telling me that I'm harming myself if I go.

Telling me that my body actually belongs to his, like two magnets kept apart in separate drawers, inching up and up and up, trying to reach each other.

It's crazy.

I know.

It hurts my brain to know I even feel this way, because it goes against every logical cell in my body.

This is not something that Sadie Reynolds feels.

And this is definitely not the way that the sane Sadie Reynolds behaves.

I'm the girl who lost her virginity to her best guy friend to get it over with.

I'm the girl who went out with Tom because he seemed like the most boring guy on the planet and, therefore, the least likely to break my heart or give me any surprises.

And I'm the girl who tossed all that hard-earned cynicism aside in order to have a fling with the hot, rich French guy who saved her life.

But this has turned into more than a one-night stand, and it has the chance to turn into something even more than that. Don't get me wrong—I don't have any delusions that if I went with him to Paris we would turn into something more than a vacation romance. He has his business and his life there; I have my life in Seattle: school, my mother, my dwindling bank account.

It's just . . . I have a chance to keep this going. I have a chance to indulge myself in this man and everything he's offering me. This doesn't have to be goodbye.

And yet it will have to be goodbye at some point, so it might as well be now.

"Here you are," Olivier says from behind me.

I'm standing at the railing on the deck and staring at the sea, the salty breeze tangling my air and invigorating my senses, making me second-guess everything.

I slowly turn to look at him. "You have a way of sneaking inside," I tell him.

He walks through the door, his skin looking especially bronzed against the white curtains billowing behind him. With his reflective aviator sunglasses on—the Dumont brand, no doubt—he looks especially movie star-ish.

"Are you all packed?"

I nod and slowly walk toward him. I have one hell of a limp now, but at least I can put pressure on my foot. "It takes about two minutes to cram all my stuff in my backpack. At least it's all freshly laundered now."

He winces as he watches me walk and quickly rushes over, grabbing me. "Are you sure you don't want to take your crutches?"

"Have you ever tried to wrangle crutches on a train? I haven't. But it looks terribly awkward. I'll be fine."

His hand trails across my face. "But I won't be. I'll be unable to stop worrying about you. I'll be unable to stop thinking about you."

I manage a small smile, trying to mask this lump of wet sadness that's crawling up my throat. His fingers coast along my jaw, holding my chin with a warm grip. I close my eyes. "I won't be able to stop thinking about you either," I tell him.

"It doesn't have to be this way," he says gruffly, and then he places a soft kiss on my lips.

I'm almost powerless against him—the feel of his grip against my skin, his lips and tongue moving softly against mine. He knows what he's doing to me; he doesn't have to beg or ask. He can persuade me just with his body and the way it calls to mine. Intimately, honestly, hungrily.

I pull away, breathless, my face all flushed and my knees weak, and it has nothing to do with my ankle. "I wish things were different."

He sighs and runs his hand over his face before pulling at the back of his neck. "I do too. But we've spent nearly one week together here. Why go to Spain for another two? What's there for you? Why are you running from me?"

"I'm not running from you," I say, sounding more defensive than I mean to. I turn away and sit down on the lounge chair, the spotless fabric hot from the sun. "I'm just trying to do the right thing."

"I would go with you to Spain if I could, but I'm needed in Paris. Not just with the hotels—I could find someone to do my job for a while, but it's the autumn season. My family needs me. And I need you."

Fuck. I know that for all the romantic words that usually spill out of Olivier's mouth, I shouldn't be affected by this plea, but I am. I can feel the passion in it, the anguish that I myself am pretending not to feel, the same feelings I've been avoiding for the last few days.

You're being stubborn. A stupid, stubborn girl, I think.

And I'm probably right.

I glance up at him, wincing at the glare of the sun. In the reflection of his sunglasses, I look so small and tiny. I look like a liar. I look like someone who is about to run away. "The sooner I get on that train, the sooner I can go back to being a backpacker. That's who I really am. I'm poor. I'm a struggling student. I should be sleeping in dorm rooms again, and washing my underwear in the sink, and raiding happy-hour specials and tapas in order to eat. I should be just scraping by, because that's pretty much what my life is about. And I really should see Spain too. Then, after that, I fly home and return to my life. It's what I need to do. What I have to do."

He nods slowly, chewing on his lip. I wish I could see his eyes underneath the glasses. "I understand that, Sadie. I really do. As I said before, I respect your wishes, even if I wish they were different."

I expect him to say something else, to offer some other way of trying to convince me, but he doesn't.

It's like he's giving up.

I have to admit, it kind of sucks.

It means this really is the end.

Perhaps all this time I was waiting for something to convince me, when really I have every reason to be convinced already.

Olivier sits down beside me, resting his elbows on his thighs. "What time does your train leave again?"

He knows. We've been over this a few times, but I don't mind him asking.

"In an hour and a half."

He nods and pushes his sunglasses up over his head as he squints at me.

"That's plenty of time to make you come," he says smoothly. "More than once."

I slowly shake my head at him. We've already fucked a few times this morning—once in the bed, once in the shower—so I certainly wasn't expecting this proposition. But I'm not surprised. And I'm certainly not disappointed.

"You're always promising me the moon," I say, feeling my body flush at his words.

"I don't promise the moon, *mon lapin*," he says, leaning in. "I just promise that you'll come so hard you'll end up forgetting your own name."

"I certainly won't be forgetting your name."

He breaks into the cockiest grin. "Never." He then nods at me. "You better hurry and get naked."

I give him a look. "Me?"

"It's easier to make you come that way. But I do like a challenge."

"You're insatiable," I tease him, and, God, how I wouldn't have him any other way.

He sucks in his lower lip for a moment and then kisses me, his hands disappearing into my hair, pushing me back until I'm falling into the lounge chair.

Then he's grabbing me by the shoulders and twisting me around so that he's lying on his back, his hands deftly undoing his belt and fly. "Ride me," he whispers, his voice already thick with lust.

I blink at him for a moment, and in the back of my head I know this means my own pants have to come off, and that I have a train to catch, but the moment I see him bring his full, thick cock out of his pants, all those thoughts are deemed useless.

Though it's not very graceful, I quickly get my own pants and underwear off until I'm naked from the waist down, and he's staring at me with so much desire he's practically salivating.

Okay, well, that definitely helps put me in the mood too—to be looked at like that, to be wanted like that.

He holds his cock upright like a pike. It's so rigid and stiff and large, absolutely formidable. But I know I can take it. I know what it does to me.

I straddle him carefully, patiently waiting to position myself over him until he's got it wrapped in a condom. Once he does, I use the back of the chair for leverage and slowly, very slowly, lower myself down on top of his cock.

"Sadie," he moans and then says something else in French, his words coming out in grunts and groans as his eyes close and his head goes back.

I can barely breathe, let alone talk. With him holding his cock so hard, each push down feels like I'm losing all space in my lungs, and I'm being filled with every aching, hot inch of him. It's nearly painful, but it's a sweet pain, the kind that you could get addicted to.

Finally, I'm exhaling, and he's all the way in to the hilt, and I'm hit with the feeling that I'll be hollow and empty without him. It's almost silly to think that when you're in the middle of having sex, but it's true. This is more than sex now; this transcends that. I don't exactly know what it is, but right now . . . it's us.

"Ride me," he groans, grabbing my hips and moving me up and down. *"S'il vous plaît,"* he says.

"Talk some dirty French to me," I tell him, grinding out the words as he starts moving me faster and faster.

And so he does. He lets out a string of breathless expletives that sound effortless and dirty all at once. I have no idea what he's saying, of course, but the intention is all there, and he's letting his cock do all the communicating.

I keep riding him like this: me in charge of the depth with each roll of my hips, him in charge of the speed as he pumps himself up into me. It feels so good, too good, especially when his thumb rubs down my clit and my back arches and I'm staring up at the sun and the sky and it's blinding and beautiful.

Everything about us is blinding and beautiful.

"I need to come," he says hoarsely, and I look down to see him staring up at me with the most intense and passionate gaze that I've ever seen from him, the kind of look that holds your own eyes hostage and promises to never let go.

I don't want him to let go.

And I don't want to let go.

Not now, not ever.

But then he's about to go over the edge, and he always makes sure I'm coming along for the ride. I don't even have a choice in the matter. He strokes me expertly, his thrusts deepening, and I'm opening up wider and wider until I'm free-falling down, down, down.

The orgasm takes us both at once. It slithers up my spine and then explodes in a shower of fireworks and electricity, and I'm crying out his name, trying my best to keep my hips pumping even though my body doesn't know what direction it's heading in.

Neither does my mind.

Neither does my heart.

I'm ripped apart at the seams by this man, and after this, I'm not sure he'll be able to put me back together again, because he's not going to be there.

"Sadie, Sadie," he moans as the thrusting slows, his hands slick on my hips, "my beautiful girl."

But I barely hear him. I'm still somewhere in the universe, twirling around in strange galaxies, not wanting this feeling—the fact that he's inside me—to ever stop.

It does, though.

I collapse against him and roll over, just as he pulls out and makes room on the lounger beside me, holding me in his arms for a few seconds, his heart beating through his chest, as if wanting to join mine.

When I return to planet Earth and the blue sky above me stops spinning, I'm hit with a rush of emotions so intense, I have to pinch my eyes shut.

Fuck.

This was it.

That was the last time he'll ever be inside me, working my body with such skill and determination and lust that I can't imagine how I survived for so long without him. How was I able to go through life not knowing just what it was like to have someone be so in tune with every cell in your body, every drop of blood pouring through your veins? It's like before I met him, I thought just having food, water, and shelter was enough to keep you going. But it's not true at all. Sex is just as important, and sex with this man, this gorgeous, incredible man, is just as vital to my body and my needs as anything else.

I think I might decay without him.

"We should go," he whispers to me as he gets to his feet, disposes of the condom, and zips up his pants.

I nod and slowly sit up, pivoting away from him, afraid to look at him just in case he sees the tears in my eyes. I quickly pull down my shirt and adjust my bra, my nipples still hard and my skin covered in goose bumps.

"Hey," he says, and I look to see him holding out his hand to me. "Come on."

I put my hand in his, and he hauls me to my feet, then wraps his arms around me and pulls me into a hug. His embrace is warm and comforting and makes everything right again. It makes everything safe. To step away from his arms is to face a cruel and uncertain world. To stay here is bliss.

"I'm going to miss you very much," he says, whispering harshly into my neck.

"You're just going to miss the sex," I say, and I knew it was a mistake the moment I opened my mouth.

He pulls back and stares at me intently, a deep line formed between his brows. "Why would you say that?"

"I was just joking," I tell him, trying to look away.

He gives me a light shake. "No. It's not just the sex. I've had plenty of sex with plenty of women, and I know when it's just the sex. This isn't it. I care about you, Sadie. More than I ever thought possible. Yes, we've only known each other for a week, but in this week . . ." He looks away, licking his lips as he searches for his next words. "This week has been one of the best weeks I've ever had. In my whole fucking life."

I blink at him, wide-eyed.

Whoa.

How can that even be? I mean, he has to have one of the most blessed lives out there.

"I mean it," he says, his eyes coming back to meet mine. "Being with you . . . I could finally be myself. Or I could finally be someone else. Or maybe both those things are the same things. All I know is that I've felt wanted and happy and free, and I can't remember the last time I've had that."

I suck in my lower lip as my eyes roam all over his handsome face. I have such a hard time coming to terms with the idea that his life hasn't had all those things, that he hasn't had everything he's ever wanted.

"You have everything," I say softly. "How could this be . . . How can this mean so much to you?"

"I don't know. It just does. Tell me all of this meant something to you."

"Of course it did. It meant everything. I'm still trying to wrap my head around what happened here. With you and me. With everything. It's been a dream, a dream I've been so afraid to wake up from. A dream I will have to wake up from very soon, and when I do, it's going to hurt like a motherfucker."

That makes him smile. "Sometimes I forget how eloquent you can be," he says. "Perhaps I'll miss that part the most. Your dirty, dirty mouth."

"Oh, stop," I tell him, pushing back on his hard chest. "It's probably a good thing we part ways now, or else I'd turn you from a charming Frenchman into a foulmouthed sailor."

"You know I can have a foul mouth on me," he says, leaning in to take my earlobe between his teeth and tugging.

I let out a soft groan. I can't help it. Even though we just had sex five minutes ago, I'm ready to go again already.

"Sorry," he says with a wicked smile. "I know those ears of yours are one of your triggers."

"Like more than an emotional trigger?" I joke, not that I mind my bunny nickname anymore.

"More like a sexual trigger. It's too bad we didn't have enough time for me to discover all the rest of them. I bet if I licked the inside of your knee, it might do the same thing. A little hard to reach, but we could make it work."

I nearly shiver at the suggestion. "I think we should go before things get out of hand again."

"Always the voice of reason," he says. He leads me back into the room and then grabs my backpack just as I swing my cross-body purse over my shoulder. I'm almost out the door when something makes me pause and take a good look at this place. This room—this is where my other life began. This is where Sadie Reynolds was able to become someone else. Or maybe it's like Olivier said, and I both became someone else and myself at the same time. Maybe that's what it's really about when you let yourself be free from everything that's ever held you back.

I can feel heat tickling my nose, and I know I have to get out of here before I start crying.

Luckily, I don't cry when we say goodbye to the famous hotel or while Olivier drives me to the Cannes train station. I should be staring out the window at the craggy mountains and the deep blue of the sea, the sea that has become a friend and constant companion for a week. I should be soaking it all in.

But I choose to take in Olivier instead.

Sure, I know he'll live on in my memory, and anytime I want I can pull him up on the internet and ogle him, remembering the good times.

But it won't be like it is now, with him right beside me. As real and mortal and flesh and blood as anything can be. Not a picture, not a memory, but a moment that I'm currently living, a moment I'm trying to stretch into infinity. A moment that I know will eventually disappear.

So I soak in the details: the gleam of his Dumont watch on his wrist; the fine, dark hairs that tease it; the large spread of his hands on the steering wheel, fingernails in tiny half-moons. The man must get manicures sometimes, because there's no way anyone's nails can look that nice naturally.

Then my eyes are drifting over the cords of his neck, the hollow of his collarbone, the way his skin glows against his white shirt.

Then the sharp planes of his features, that mouth that can get me off in two seconds flat, either by sucking my clit into oblivion or by letting loose a thousand dirty obscenities into my ears. The height of his strong cheekbones and the sexy swoop of his dark brows over his eyes.

It's his eyes that I'll have a hard time recalling.

The pictures don't do them justice.

They don't capture the way he looks at me. They don't show the lust and the desire and the want and the need and the awe—the awe that I'm the most precious jewel on earth, found in a spot he never thought to look.

Even if they did, it wouldn't compare.

And then, before I know it, we're here, pulling up to the train station.

I didn't have enough time, a voice screams inside me. *That was over too fast, there wasn't enough time.*

Like a crazy person, I frantically try to stare at him one last time, as if that will finally cement his image into my head, as if that will keep him there forever.

But it's too late.

"Are you okay?" he asks me, frowning as he looks me over.

I shake my head. "No. No, I mean, yeah. I'm fine, but . . ."

He swallows, looking pained. "I know. I know."

And even though he doesn't say it, I can still hear it in my head. Maybe it's not his voice at all, maybe it's mine.

It doesn't have to be this way.

It takes a lot of effort to get out of the car, like my waterlogged heart is pulling me down to the ground and my legs and arms are filled with lead. The same goes for when we go inside the train station. I can't even blame my ankle; it's hard to just put one leg in front of the other and go.

Finally, we stop right beside the train. People are lining up, getting on board. It looks chaotic.

I turn to look at him. "I guess this is it."

He nods at the compartment. "I'll help you with your bag."

"I'm fine, really," I tell him, reaching for it.

He sighs and lifts it up, and I turn around so he can slip the straps over my arms.

It feels heavier than before. It's funny, when you're backpacking—and especially when you've been doing a stretch by yourself—your pack becomes a part of who you are. It's a friend; it's a pillow; it's something to hug at night when you're lonely.

But now, the pack feels different. Like it belonged to someone else other than me. Maybe it did.

One of the train conductors blows the whistle, and people start piling into the train faster.

This is it.

Time to go.

"Tell me we'll see each other again," Olivier says, placing his hands on my shoulders and leaning in, his forehead resting on mine. "Promise me that."

I don't like making promises, especially when I know the chances of seeing him again are slim. So I say, "I'll do everything I can."

He swallows, nods once, and then kisses me quickly. "Goodbye, *mon lapin*."

"Goodbye, Olivier," I whisper.

Then the train dude blows the whistle right in my ear, yelling something in French.

Even Olivier looks startled.

We break apart, and I step onto the train.

Look back at him.

Give a little wave.

He gives a little wave right back.

Then I go and find my seat.

The train pulls away, and I strain to see Olivier through the people settling in, but I can't.

He's gone.

I'm going.

I let out a long sigh, feeling the sadness come for me, and rest my head against the window. I don't even notice the way it rattles as the train goes over the tracks.

Next stop: Barcelona.

Next stop: same old Sadie.

A loud beep from my phone goes off, interrupting the gloom in my head and the tightness in my chest, and I start to think that maybe it's him. We exchanged phone numbers the other day—maybe he's texted me to say something, anything at all that will make this better.

But it's not him.

It's an email from my mother.

Since it's the middle of the night at home, I'm instantly worried that something is wrong.

But when I open my email, it's a few paragraphs.

They say:

> Dearest girl,
>
> I had a dream about you just now. You were a baby bird, and I was a mother bird. Maybe a seagull. I'm not sure, but I had to watch you from afar, and you were learning to fly. You didn't want to leave the

nest. You kept looking at me, and I kept telling you to do it. That you needed to, or you would die. Then eventually you spread your wings, and you leaped off the nest.

You fell! At first you didn't flap your wings, and I was terrified you would fall forever. But then you started to fly. You rose up on the wind, and then you were gone, and as sad as I was that I was alone, I was happier knowing that you were finally on your own. You were finally free to be you.

I don't know why I'm telling you this, but I feel like maybe you should know.

I know you're coming home in two weeks, and I know you feel like you have to because of school and because of me, but I just want you to know: if you want to keep flying, keep flying. You deserve it. You deserve everything, my baby girl.

Go, and be free!

Love,
Your crazy mother

I'm stunned. Not that my mother wrote me this—she often writes me about dreams and other things that come to her suddenly. She's often random and impulsive.

It's just that this is what I was waiting to hear. To not go back home is ridiculous—I don't have the money for that, and I wouldn't be able to get a job in Europe unless it was under the table. I need to go back for her, and I need to go back to school, and, despite what she says, those things are nonnegotiable.

But I can keep flying.

I should keep flying.

My heart starts racing even before the thoughts are forming in my head.

I glance up at the electronic schedule in front of the cabin doors.

Next stop is Cannes-La Bocca, by the water.

When the train starts to slow, I get up, grab my backpack, and exit, probably to the bewilderment of the people behind me.

Once I'm on the train platform, it starts to pull away, and I curse myself for possibly making the biggest mistake of my life. After all, if this doesn't work out, I have absolutely no way of getting to Spain now.

But I wouldn't know if I didn't make the leap.

I take out my phone and text Olivier:

Want to come get me at Cannes-La Bocca station?

I'm grinning as I press "Send." Nervous as hell and giddy, all at the same time.

He texts back immediately:

Are you serious?

My grin spreads across my face until I fear it may break it in half.

Absolutely. I'm not done with you yet.

CHAPTER NINE

OLIVIER

Paris, France

Contrary to popular belief, the Dumont company headquarters isn't actually located in Paris. Any tourist (and even some Parisians) would say it's still in the city, but the actual address is in Neuilly-sur-Seine, in between the iconic Arc de Triomphe and the ugly Grande Arche de la Défense. My father fought for years to keep it at our old location in Montparnasse. It wasn't the Right Bank, but at least it was in Paris.

But then Chanel moved locations, and Gautier thought it would make sense for us to do the same—to the extent that the Dumont global headquarters is now located across from the Chanel one.

Secretly, I think the only reason my uncle even goes to the office is so he can spy on Chanel's designers from across the street.

The office is a place I try my best to stay away from. First of all, I don't actually work there; I'm always just popping in to see either Seraphine or my father, and yet somehow I always get roped into something the minute I step in. That's the price for having Dumont as my last name—and the fact that most people believe I should be serving as president of fashion instead of Seraphine, even though she's the one who has fought hard for it and deserves it more than anyone.

Second of all, traffic is a bitch to get there from my apartment in Le Marais, and I'm not about to take the Métro.

Third of all . . . Sadie.

Mon lapin.

The other day I was in for the surprise of my life.

After I said goodbye to Sadie and put her on the train, I was resigned to the idea that I might not see her again. It was a feeling I had been fighting for a week, heightened when Pascal showed up at the hotel making vague threats and, thankfully, left right after without a fuss.

Then she texted me about ten minutes later, and that was it.

I drove like a madman along the waterfront until I pulled into the train station and saw her standing there, backpack slumped at her feet and the biggest, purest smile on her face.

It made something in my heart twist and fizz, as if a champagne cork had finally come dislodged.

I grabbed her, kissed her, and told her she'd be the death of me.

I wonder just how true that might turn out to be.

Regardless, she's back at my apartment, in bed, waiting for me, and I've just battled through traffic like a fucking warrior, selfishly hoping the meeting with my sister and father goes quickly so I can go back to her.

Now that I have her for two more weeks, every single second we have together is precious.

Naturally, I can't tell them that. I've always been notoriously tight-lipped about the women I see, even when it comes to my family. I've been there for Seraphine for every agonizing moment of her recent divorce, but it doesn't go the other way.

I park the car around the corner. I drive a Mercedes when I'm down in the south of the country, but here in Paris I have a small Audi. I have a thing for German cars, preferably as fast and nondescript as possible.

As I walk around the corner to the building, I can see my cousin Blaise's car in Gautier's parking spot. It's a red Ferrari, the complete opposite of my car. Whereas my side of the family believes in discretion and hiding your wealth—to an extent—that side of the family believes in being as flagrant and vulgar as possible.

But I should be glad that it's just Blaise in the office today. I don't like him, but he's not Pascal, and he's not his father, which means I can at least ignore him. I can't really do that with the other two, especially when they zero in on me like they do.

I step inside the building, the front-desk clerk and concierge nodding to me as I go. I climb the stairs to the third floor.

"Mr. Dumont," Nadia, the receptionist, says to me, getting to her feet, "I wasn't aware you were coming."

"I'm not surprised," I say to her, glancing around the office. For all its quiet elegance with glass and white walls and black details, it's absolutely chaotic, with harried-looking employees running all over the place. With autumn releases hitting the stores, Paris Fashion Week around the corner, and the annual Dumont Masquerade Ball next week, everyone is losing their minds.

Ah, the world of fashion. Makes being a hotelier look like a walk in the park.

"Should I let them know?" Nadia asks me.

I lift my hand. "It's fine. They do know I'm coming; they probably forgot to tell you. Are they in my father's office?"

She nods. "They've been going back and forth a lot. Blaise is in there too."

Ah, fuck. I had hoped he would have stuck to his large corner office on the opposite side of the building.

I stride down the hall, take a deep breath, and knock on the door that says "Ludovic Dumont, CEO" on it.

Someone shouts a frantic "Come in," and I open it.

My father's office is chaos. He's normally fairly neat and organized, but it was really my mother who kept him in line. Ever since she died . . . well, a few threads in his life have come loose, so to speak, and it's always most apparent when he's under deadline as we near launches.

Right now, he's on his feet, leaning against his desk and staring at a stack of papers, fiddling with his eyeglasses as if they're the problem. More papers are piled in corners around the room, some being blown at by a fan by the open window. Crookedly hung certificates and awards hang from the walls, and his shelves are stacked with books upon books upon books, with the occasional handbag on display.

In the corner, Blaise is firing up the Nespresso machine, giving me a tepid glance, while Seraphine is standing by the desk with her arms crossed, obviously in the middle of lecturing my father about something.

"We made nine point six billion dollars in revenue last year," I announce as I step in, closing the door behind me. "Father, I think you can afford to get air-conditioning for your office."

"Nonsense," my father says, briefly glancing at me. He waves his arm toward the fan. "That fan works fine."

"The office in Montparnasse had air-conditioning," Seraphine says, glaring at Blaise.

He just shrugs and takes a casual sip of his espresso. "It also couldn't handle all the new growth, especially the growth to come our way once we start an online department."

Oh God, they're arguing about this still? Again? Already?

Seraphine scoffs, her eyes narrowing into slits. "Are you stupid or just naive?"

"Well, I'm glad you guys invited me here for a meeting," I say quickly, before things get out of hand. Seraphine is a tough cookie, but she still gets along with everyone. She even tolerates Pascal and Gautier. But for whatever reason, Blaise really gets her blood boiling, and he can be just as sharp-tongued with her. I've never understood their feuding, but then again, I don't understand a lot about these people I have to call family.

"I didn't invite you," Blaise says as he finishes his coffee and saunters past me. "And I've told your father and sister that you usually only complicate matters. You chose to work with hotels; there's no need for you to be here."

"Blaise," my father scolds him, "you're sounding like Gautier now."

"Apple doesn't fall far from the tree," Seraphine snipes.

Blaise shrugs, one hand on the door. "Just being honest. Someone here has to be."

Then he leaves, shutting us in the room.

I jerk my thumb at the door. "Why is he even in here? Drinking your coffee?"

"His machine is broken," my father says tiredly, flipping through papers. "And, like it or not, we do have to work together."

"How are you, brother?" Seraphine asks, shaking the animosity away from her bright face. She comes over to me and gives me a kiss on the cheek. "You look like you've gotten a lot of sun."

"So much for working," my father says under his breath.

"I was working," I tell him, which isn't a complete lie. "Believe me, there's a world outside of the office."

"Mm-hmm, so who is she?" Seraphine says with a cheeky grin.

"She?"

"You don't take vacations, Olivier, so I have to assume that there was someone else in the picture. Someone who might convince you to relax by the sea for a week and get some sun."

"There's no one," I tell her, and she looks disappointed. She's always harping on me to find someone and settle down—if only she knew the truth about that—but I'm certainly not going to tell her about Sadie.

Which reminds me.

"By the way, have you seen Pascal lately?" I ask.

She frowns. "He was here yesterday for a minute. You know he's always in and out."

"I saw him at Cap-Eden-Roc," I tell them. "Just randomly. Like he was spying on me."

"You're always so suspicious," my father says, straightening up and putting his hands on his lower back with a groan.

"Everyone should be a little more suspicious," I tell him. "Is your back okay?"

"Oh, yes, yes," he says, waving me away and walking to the fan to adjust it. "You'd be in pain, too, if you had to deal with all of this."

"And if you stood hunched over the desk like some raving reporter," Seraphine says, walking over to him and giving his arm a gentle squeeze. "We know you're in charge, but I do think while I'm in the office, you owe your daughter some respect, which means listening to what she says. Sit down."

She tugs on his arm, and, reluctantly, he's led over to his chair, where he sits down.

"And you're right, Olivier," Seraphine says to me as she wrestles with the window for a moment until she's able to pop it open an extra inch. "We always should be more suspicious."

"That's not how your mother and I raised you," my father says grumpily, taking his time to glare at both Seraphine and me.

"No, you raised us to be perfect angels," she says, giving his shoulders a squeeze and kissing him on the top of his balding head. "But, unfortunately, your brother raised a bunch of devils, and we have to work alongside each other. In this business, it's kill or be killed."

"You're family."

"And it's family that I'm *very* grateful for," she says. My parents adopted Seraphine when she was nine years old. She was in the public system for some time before that, jumping from family to family. She says we're the first real one she's ever had.

She goes on, "It's just that there really was no reason for Pascal to show up at Olivier's hotel."

"How did he even know I was there?" I ask.

She gnaws on her lip for a moment, but somehow it doesn't mess up her perfect red lipstick. It must be the cosmetic brand's new long-wear kind, the one she insisted be named after her. "He asked where you were, and I told him," she says. "Sorry, I obviously didn't know he'd take the next plane out."

"So his cousin wanted to check on the hotel, nothing wrong with that," my father says. "Can we get back to the real issues at hand?"

"Which ones?" Seraphine asks dryly.

"Yes," I say, conscious of the time. "What exactly did you want from me?"

My father balks. "That's a little brusque of you, son."

"Sorry," I say with a sigh, sliding my hands into my pockets. I'm rarely rude with my parents, another trait that they passed down to me, even though there's been a time or two when my temper has gotten the best of me. "I've got plans."

"Again, who is she?" Seraphine asks.

I ignore her.

So does my father. "Well, as you know, we've got the ball and the show coming up, and we're a little shorthanded."

"Then hire more staff. We can afford it, can't we?"

He nods, pinching the bridge of his nose. "We can. But I need someone to help keep them in line."

"I assume you mean our family, whose praises you were just singing."

"There's a difference between singing someone's praises and not being suspicious and contemptuous of them at every turn. It's some-where in the middle, Olivier, and you should learn to live there." He sighs and sits back in his chair. "Same goes for you, Seraphine. Now, Gautier, Pascal, and Blaise were really pushing for the autumn releases to coincide with our first online store. That's not going to happen now; it's not going to happen ever. Suffice to say, I have the final word, even over my brother, and that's the way it's going to stay. Until, of course, you take over my job."

This again. I immediately stiffen, my hands growing clammy, my pulse skipping against my wrist. Soon my father will find out I'm forfeiting all my shares to Gautier, and he won't understand why. He's already deeply disappointed that I've distanced myself from the company, and yet I can tell he thinks I'll come around soon, maybe when I've lost interest in the hotels. It's going to kill him when I have to hand it all over.

Seraphine clears her throat loudly and gives my father a pointed look.

"What?" he says. "Oh, you know Olivier has been groomed for this from the very start. It's written into the contracts; it always has been. Gautier even signed off on it. Once I'm out of the picture, Olivier takes my place."

"Even though he doesn't know a thing about how to run a company," my sister says snidely.

"Hey," I tell her, pointing my finger at her, "I run my own damn company. I don't need this one."

"Fine," she says, rolling her eyes. "But this is the Dumont brand, and we have done things our way for as long as I can remember. You have no idea what it's like to run this place."

"We're not having this argument again," Father says. "I'm not going down this path, and we all know that I'm not going anywhere. I just had my annual checkup. Mentally and physically, I'm as fit as a fiddle and sharp as a razor."

"Good," I tell him. "Because I have no plans to take over. Especially when my sister here would shoot me in the face if she had to."

"You're so dramatic," she says.

"Back to the point . . . is this heat driving everyone insane? There's a reason why everyone in this city leaves in August. We're the only poor souls stuck here, slaving away for fashion," my father drones on.

"You're slaving away for money, don't forget that," I remind him. "And yet another reason why I'm happy running my hotels: I don't have any fashion weeks or launches to worry about."

My father glances over his shoulder at the fan on the window. "Maybe I should get another fan and start a cross breeze."

"Father," Seraphine reminds him, "stay focused. Olivier obviously has places to be."

"Right, right. And here I was talking about how sharp I was. Anyway, there's a lot of fighting in-house right now, dear boy, and it would be nice to have another hand on deck. If you could check in here every other day and see what Seraphine needs you to do, that would be fantastic."

Seraphine exhales sharply. "Right. Well, for starters, I could use some help with the masquerade ball. I have my assistant going through the guest list, but I know you're more in tune with high society than I am. Perhaps you could go through it and see if there are any potential problems. Actresses who don't get along, models who are out for revenge. That sort of thing." She pauses. "You're obviously bringing a guest."

I shake my head. "No."

She frowns. "That's very unlike you. Are you sure you're well?"

"And there you were so certain that there was someone in the picture."

"No date, Olivier?" my father muses, back to reading his papers and scribbling something in a leather diary. "Are you planning to turn into Blaise?"

Blaise is always getting needled over his lack of love life. The tabloids have speculated that he's gay and afraid to come out of the closet, but I don't think that's it. I've seen the way he looks at women, and, at any rate, half the male workforce here is gay. No one really cares.

But just because I won't publicly have a date doesn't mean I'll be going alone.

If I'm in charge of the guest list, I can easily place Sadie's name on it.

And since it's a masquerade ball, no one will be the wiser.

Fueled by this new revelation, I excuse myself from the meeting and tell my father and sister that I'll be here for them whenever they need me, even if it means stopping by the office every few days. Lord knows the last thing I want to do is spend any more time away from Sadie, especially as I have my own work to attend to, but I don't have much choice.

I will make it up to her, though.

On the drive back to the apartment, I stop by a charcuterie and wine shop, picking up bread, wine, cheese, meats, and a picnic basket.

Since we've been in Paris these last two days, I haven't been seen with Sadie out in public. It's too risky. So while I'm gone, she's been exploring Paris by herself. This morning before I left, she lamented that she wanted to have a picnic with me beneath the Eiffel Tower, like she'd seen all the tourists do.

I had to tell her I couldn't be seen with her in public. I felt awful. I've explained to her that the paparazzi watch me like a hawk here, and I want to protect her from that, but it's not even close to the truth. Sometimes the paparazzi will take my picture, but it's usually at an event—and I go to a lot of events. But walking down the street, eating at a restaurant on a date? No. The media here is far more respectful than they are in England and the States.

So I decided having a picnic inside is one way of making up for it. I hope she'll at least find it charming.

After I park, I head into the building, nodding hello to the concierge, then take the elevator up to the fourth floor, which is entirely my apartment.

The building is about one hundred years old, and I like to think it was being built at the same time that my grandfather, Alex Dumont, was coming up with the idea about a handbag. I appreciate the history of it all, the understated elegance, the old-world ideas that seem to meld seamlessly with the present.

Sadie, of course, was beyond impressed. Not just by the size of the place, but by the way I've turned the apartment into a gallery of sorts. As I was getting started in the hotelier business, I spent some time learning about art. I traveled and studied, really getting into the idea of having galleries in my hotels. That didn't quite happen, though most of my hotels do have an artistic slant to things.

But my apartment is where everything I admire comes to life.

Some may call it cluttered. My brother, Renaud, often says it's a sight for sore eyes, and Seraphine jokes that I've got a hoarding issue for expensive art. My father understands it, though. I guess I like to collect beautiful things as much as he likes to create them.

I quickly unlock the door and step inside while carrying the bag of groceries, looking for the most beautiful thing of all.

There she is, sitting on the velvet couch, sipping from a mug of tea.

"Honey, I'm home," I tell her in my best Ricky Ricardo impression. She grins at me. "And you brought things!"

"I did, fresh from the streets of Paris," I tell her as she sets her tea down and comes over to me, throwing her arms around my neck and pulling me in for a kiss.

God, she tastes so fucking good. I hadn't realized how needy and starved I was for her all day until this very moment.

"I missed you," she whispers against my lips, and I have to adjust myself before I drop the groceries.

"I missed you too," I say, kissing the corner of her mouth. "Remind me to never leave you again."

"That would be nice."

I pull away and put the bag on the kitchen counter before everything falls. "So what did you do all day?"

"Not much," she says with a shrug, doing a tiny pirouette on the tile floor. "Well, I attempted to learn the piano." She points to the white grand piano in the middle of the sitting area. It was once owned by Liberace. "But the ghost of Liberace did me no favors. Then I attempted to read up on all the art in your apartment."

She eyes a stack of art books on the coffee table. "Unfortunately, I fell asleep once I got to Monet. I don't know what it is about him, but he bores me to tears."

"Apparently," I comment. But secretly I am thrilled that she's taken an interest in it.

"So what's all this?" she asks, peering at the bags.

"I figured you'd be hungry," I tell her, starting to sort through them. "I also know how much you wanted that picnic under the Eiffel Tower. So I thought the best thing for me to do was to bring the Eiffel Tower here."

I take out a foot-high replica of the tower, the kind you find on every street corner, and place it in the living area by the window. Then I grab a thick red blanket from the linen closet and spread it out on the floor. I gesture to it. "Voilà. Have a seat."

She gives me a disbelieving look. "We're having a picnic inside?"

"Don't act like you're not impressed, *lapin*. Now sit, and I will do the rest."

She takes a tentative seat on the floor, crossing her legs, and then watches me with interest as I start laying the items out in front of her. I start with a bottle of Dumont red wine because I know that's the key to her heart. After she has her glass, I lay out the cheeses, meats, and baguettes.

"You really shouldn't have," she says, eyeing it all in awe.

"Actually, this is the least I can do," I admit, sitting down beside her. "I feel terrible that I've been leaving you alone like this."

"Olivier, please," she says as she sips her wine. "I knew what coming to Paris would mean. I knew you'd be working. Okay, so maybe I didn't know about the whole hiding me thing, but hey, I'm nothing if not adaptable."

126

"I'm not hiding you," I tell her, wishing I could just tell her the truth. But then what would she think of me? *Sadie, I don't want my cousin or uncle to know I have someone like you in my life, or they'll make it their mission to break us apart. Because Pascal and my uncle have it out for me, because of something I've done, because my side and their side have always been at odds.*

"It's okay," she says. "I'm just happy you're here now. I mean, don't you have friends you need to see too?"

I shrug. "I have friends, sure. Some from university, most from the hotel business. But they're just as busy as I am."

And to be honest, I've kept myself guarded over these last ten years. It's hard to be open with people and make true friends and lay your soul bare when you know you're hiding something from them, from the world. Sometimes I feel it's all or nothing with me.

That's how I feel with Sadie. I want to give her my all, but I don't know how I can, and I don't know what future we can have, even if I tell her my truth.

"And anyway," I point out, "I haven't heard you talk much about your friends back home."

She gives me a small smile, and I feel like I may have touched a nerve. She starts tearing off pieces of the baguette, taking her time. "I have friends. I just don't have a lot of friends. I've always been a bit of a loner, to be honest. When my father left and it was just me and my mom, especially for that first while, I wanted to be there for her as much as I could. You don't understand . . . she was a mess. Way more than she is today. If I couldn't hold her together, she'd fall apart on her own. Plus, the fact that I was studying like crazy to get a scholarship to college and working when I could . . . I just didn't have time for anyone else. I mean, in school I met Chantal in my communications class, but she's the only one I'd consider close to me."

"And your ex," I say.

"Yeah, Tom. But he didn't turn out to be a very good friend, did he?"

"You dated for a long time," I mention, and I know it's in poor form for me to bring up her ex, but I can't help it. "You must have been close."

"We were," she says slowly as she pops a chunk of baguette in her mouth. "But not as close as you'd think. At the time I thought he was my best friend, you know? But I don't think I let him in like I thought I did, and he didn't let me in either. The more I think about it, the end was probably a long time coming for us."

"He was still an asshole to break it off with you in the middle of your vacation."

She laughs dryly. "Well, technically I broke it off because I found out he was cheating, but, yes. He is an asshole. But had I really gotten to know him, I would have seen that coming. Instead, I was blindsided. I'm starting to think that my pride took the biggest hit of all."

I shouldn't feel good about that, but I do. The fact that whatever she had with Tom wasn't real—and certainly wasn't strong—means she's still not in love with him, or at least not pining for him.

"But, honestly," she continues, "I don't think about it anymore. And in some ways, I'm glad he did what he did. I wouldn't have had the adventures and independence I've gained from having to travel on my own. And I wouldn't have met you."

The way she meets my eyes, vulnerable and almost shy, makes my heart beat faster, my dick hard in seconds.

"Uh-oh," she says, putting down her bread.

"What?"

"You have that look about you," she says.

I get on my knees and start prowling toward her, pushing aside the food. "What look is that?" I murmur, stopping so that my face is just inches from hers.

"The one that tells me that you're about to devour me instead of the food."

I grin. "You know me so well." I lean in and kiss her softly. "Let's just eat it all later and call it dessert," I murmur against her mouth before she sinks back onto the floor, giggling as I start to feast on her.

CHAPTER TEN

SADIE

"Bonjour, madame," the waiter says to me. I glance up from the menu I've been trying to decipher and give him a big smile.

"Bonjour."

"Would you like the English menu?" he asks, quickly switching to English after hearing my accent.

"Oui, merci," I tell him, stubbornly trying to stay in the language. Though Lord knows that the last few times I've tried to order in French, things have gone horribly wrong.

"Anything to drink? Coffee, water? Still or sparkling?"

"Sparkling, please, and a double espresso. No, make it a triple."

He gives me the once-over when I say triple espresso, as if gauging how much I need the caffeine, and then scuttles off.

I sigh and stare out the window across the Seine, at the Île de la Cité and the back end of Notre Dame, and try to summon some excitement that I'm in Paris.

Don't get me wrong—I'm excited to be here. I love Paris, probably more this time than when I was here earlier with Tom. I feel like I'm reunited with the city after saying goodbye, much the same way I was with Olivier after I hopped off that train.

But part of the problem is just that: I was here first with Tom, so a lot of my first memories are with him. A lot of firsts are tainted. As I said to Olivier the other night, I don't really think about Tom often, and I'm not hurting over him, but it's hard not to compare the recent memories. You'd think that being here now, as the lover of an actual Parisian, those memories would be quickly buried.

Except . . . they aren't.

Because I've been here five days now, and I've barely seen Olivier at all.

He's always working.

And I know this shouldn't be a surprise, and I shouldn't complain. I knew all this going into it. It was one of the reasons why I was going to keep going on to Spain, knowing that he had a life he needed to get back to.

It's just hard.

We only have so much time together.

Just over a week before I have to fly back home.

And I knew the days would go quickly, I just thought I would see more of Olivier in them.

So now I wander the streets of Paris, alone, trying to be charmed by this beguiling city, trying to keep the romance alive in my heart.

Because, believe me, it's there.

More than it should be.

Despite Olivier's absence, I'm craving him more than anything else. My body aches for his touch; my heart beats for his words. When we were in the South of France, I was swept away by how romantic he was, addicted to the sex, to the way he set my skin and soul on fire.

Now we've become something else. The next level, even though something inside me was warning me to never let it get to that. Now I've become addicted to him in general. The way he makes me feel, the way he makes my heart trip over itself every time he steps into his apartment.

The way my heart sinks every time he leaves.

I have it bad.

There's no other way to put it.

For all my cynicism and heartache and impulse to roll my eyes at everything romantic and lovey-dovey, something has changed inside me. A switch has been flipped. Maybe it's all just a trick; maybe it's because, for what it's worth, I am still living another life, a life with an expiration date.

But the way I feel about him, the way that he makes me feel . . .

It's like every cheesy song I've heard on the radio has suddenly become true, and the space in my chest that I never thought would belong to anyone again—he's filled every hollow crevice of it. When I walk through the streets of Paris, I'm practically floating, even when I'm doing nothing but missing him.

The waiter comes back and gives me the espresso and the sparkling water. I don't know if it's because I'm attempting to speak French or if I'm just more open, but the Parisians are so much nicer this time around. Maybe I'm just seeing them in a different light.

I have to say, I like the fact that Olivier is so old school. He's talked a lot about the company and the way the Dumont family has done things, and I admire how he sticks to his guns. It speaks to the way that he values his family and tradition. It takes guts to stand for something when everyone else in the world wants you to change.

Granted, I mean, he's a slick, rich thirty-year-old with the world at his feet. But there's something inherently sexy to me about someone who is strong in their convictions.

I just wish . . . well.

Even when he isn't at his father's office or doing his own hotelier thing, I wish that we could go out into the streets of Paris together. Have dinner at a nice restaurant. Or, hell, a dodgy dive bar. See the sights. Walk hand in hand or at least near each other. But he's so insistent that we aren't to be seen together.

I know he's said that it's because he doesn't want the media to make a big deal out of it, but I'm not sure that's the case. I've been doing a lot of online stalking of Olivier Dumont since the moment I met him, and while the press have definitely photographed him, it's usually in a very public setting, like a fashion show or the opening of a hotel or restaurant. And, yes, the babes on his arms are always changing, but there doesn't seem to be any fuss made over him. It just is who he is.

Is he afraid that if he's seen with me more than once, it will look like we're an item? Maybe that's what he's afraid of: the fact that we aren't an item, that I'm supposed to fly back home in eight days.

Or maybe it is worse.

Is it that he's ashamed of me?

That he doesn't want to be seen with me at all? That he's slumming it with some American student? After all, compared to the beauties he's always with—some of them even famous actresses—I'm . . . nobody. I can't hold a candle to them.

I swallow hard, feeling doubt mingling with the sadness. This is why I hate being alone these days; it gives me too much time to think and obsess. I take a sip of my espresso, and I can practically feel my hair standing on end. I was hoping the caffeine would lift my spirits, but in the end I think it's just going to give me a panic attack.

When I'm done and pay the bill—my bank account is crying every second, even though Olivier insists on subsidizing me—I head back out onto the streets.

It's busy and chaotic and just before noon. I had a late start today, and now the sun is out in full force, beating down on all the tourists who cram the narrow streets of the Marais.

"Well, you're in Paris," I tell myself out loud, trying to be cheerful. "Go somewhere, do something."

I haven't even scratched the surface when it comes to the museums and sights, and I have to resist the urge to be swallowed up by the waves of people and have them lead me back to the apartment. As glorious as his place is, once I'm there I know all I'll do is mope and wait for him.

I decide to go check out the Picasso museum. All the art that Olivier collects has renewed my interest in it, and I know he gets a kick out of the fact that I can converse with him about some things. Maybe after the museum I can teach him a thing or two about moody Picasso.

I'm waiting at the light to cross the street when I feel an odd chill run over my shoulders, which is doubly odd since it's boiling outside.

I slowly turn around, expecting to see something, though I don't know what, but only see smiling tourists instead.

Then a man passes, quickly ducking into a mobile phone store. I only see him in profile and only for a second, but there's something familiar about him. I have a feeling he's handsome, even though I didn't see enough of him to draw that conclusion.

My heart skips a beat—maybe because for a split second I'm imagining that it's Olivier. There was something about the man that reminded me of him, perhaps his jaw and his sleek movements.

But the guy wasn't quite as tall, and there's no good reason why Olivier would be following me down the street. He'd want me to see him, wouldn't he?

The lights change, and I'm ushered across the street by the crowd.

I take out my phone and look at the directions, trying to read the streets on the map and figure out where I'm walking in real life. I bump into numerous people and almost step in dog shit before I decide to put my phone away and pull up the mental map in my head instead.

It's then that I get the feeling again.

I stop and turn around, the hairs standing on my arms, my body buzzing with electricity.

There's a man a few yards away, his back to me as he leans against a wall. He's got a newsboy cap on his head, covering the thick, dark hair that curls at the nape of his neck. His shoulders are very broad, like a swimmer's, and I'd put his height at about just under six feet.

I can't help but stare at him, almost willing him to turn around.

And then, as if he feels my will, he looks up from whatever he's doing and moves his head just an inch, just enough so that I can see the edge of his sunglasses. Just enough so that he's glancing at me out of his peripheral vision.

The shoulders under his gray T-shirt are tense.

Waiting.

This spurs something dark inside me, like he's activated an internal panic button.

I need to get to the museum.

I need to get out of here.

I start walking, faster now, hoping that I'm not about to get myself lost. I make it about a block before I have to stop at the next light.

I glance over my shoulder.

The man is walking toward me, his hands shoved in his jeans pockets, head down and cap pulled forward so that I can only see the bottom of his chin.

It's a distinctive chin.

That's why it feels so familiar.

Like I've seen it before.

For some reason an image flashes across my mind, a memory.

Having sex with Olivier for the first time.

Thinking I see a man on the balcony watching us.

The chin.

But that can't be it.

No one had been there.

And with him walking toward me at the rate he is, I don't want to hang around to see how I know him.

I turn the corner, not wanting to wait for the light anymore, and hurry down another street, walking so fast I'm almost at a jog, my poor ankle screaming at me for the extra impact.

I do this for three blocks, essentially taking two left turns and going around in a circle back toward where I started.

I don't look back, not until I get to the end, because I know if I do and he's still there, it means he's there for me.

But eventually I have to know.

I stop beside an oak tree just outside of a little café with a few tables on the street, people packed in shoulder to shoulder, smoking and watching the day go by. At least I feel safe.

I look back, and for a moment, I think I see him. At the back of a row of Japanese tourists, just the hint of a newsboy cap.

BEEP.

My phone lights up, scaring the shit out of me, and I quickly glance down to see it's a text from Olivier. I breathe a sigh of relief just seeing his name and look back up, expecting to see that man again, closer.

But there's no one there at all now, just a pigeon walking back and forth, cooing, following the tourists.

"You're being paranoid," I scold myself, wishing that I hadn't put so much pressure on my ankle. It's throbbing again. Or maybe it's the memory of being attacked on the streets of Nice.

I calm my heart rate and take a better look at Olivier's text:

Meet me tonight at Hôtel Rouge Royale. Seven pm. Room 508.
Wear something nice . . . or nothing at all.

Though I'm smiling, I'm a little hurt that this means I won't see Olivier until this evening. But a quick Google search brings up the hotel. It's swanky as fuck—and, of course, one of Olivier's.

Well, at least this gives me something to do now.

Screw the Picasso museum. I'm going lingerie shopping.

At six forty-five I enter the opulent lobby of the Hôtel Rouge Royale and stride inside like I know where I'm going. I turn a few heads, but, thankfully, it's not because I look like I don't belong there.

Olivier made sure of that.

After getting his text, I did go shopping for tonight.

Of course, on my budget all the shopping was to be done at H&M. I couldn't even afford Zara.

And I could only get a black lace bra and nothing else.

But when I went back to his apartment to get ready, I was in for a major shock.

He'd gone shopping for me.

Laid out on his massive bed was a burgundy balconette bra, all intricate lace and boning, coupled with a matching thong and stockings with garters. Naturally, they were all in my size, as was the pair of black patent kitten-heel Louboutins next to them.

As was the Dumont label black trench coat, folded neatly at the end of the bed with the note on it: *Pour ce soir.*

For this evening.

He wants me to wear the trench coat and nothing else underneath except for the lingerie.

At least, I hope that's what he wants, because that's what I'm wearing right now as I stride as confidently as possible toward the elevators. I feel like everyone can tell I'm practically naked underneath and am going up to have a wild tryst with someone.

But if they can tell, they certainly don't care. That's the French for you—they're pretty good at minding their own business, especially when it comes to sex, and I have no doubt that this hotel, with its use of red satin curtains and velvet sofas and black marble floors, is a total fuckfest location.

The thought of that sends a thrill through me as I step inside the tiny elevator and ride it to the fifth floor. The old Sadie thought blow jobs were the ultimate in dirty sex. The new Sadie thinks nothing of wearing lingerie under a trench coat to meet her secret French lover for a forbidden tryst.

Okay, I don't think nothing of it.

Actually, I'm kind of nervous.

As intimate as we have been every night, this is still all so new to me, and Olivier is always full of surprises. It speaks volumes about how I've changed that I'm willing to go along with whatever he has planned.

When I get to the fifth floor, I walk slowly down the velvet-lined hallways, marveling at how lucky I am to be here, that the man I'm meeting for hot sex is the same man who owns this hotel. The same man who picked out my lingerie.

The same man who put me in these horrible shoes.

Ouch. Even though they're kitten heels, and I'm sure he thought he was being sensible not putting me in high heels, thinking about my ankle and all, the truth is Christian Louboutins may look pretty, but they hurt like hell.

No pain, no gain, I remind myself as I step to the door of his hotel room and take a deep breath before I knock.

A few seconds go by before the door opens.

I gasp.

For one, the hotel room is huge, with big glass windows and candles lit up absolutely everywhere.

For two, Olivier is holding a bottle of champagne in one hand and a rose in the other.

For three, he's wearing a suit.

And a mask.

Like a theatrical mask you'd find in Venice.

"Wow," I say. Even with the mask covering his eyes, he is disarmingly beautiful. "Are you auditioning for *Phantom of the Opera*?"

He grins at me. "Why, yes. Do you think I'll get the part?"

"I think you'll get every part you go for," I tell him as I step inside and look around. "Do you own any shitty hotels, or are they all fit for kings and queens?"

He laughs and hands me the rose. "This is for you."

"Thank you," I tell him and bring the flower to my nose. For some reason I don't expect it to smell, but it does. "I don't think I've ever smelled a rose like this."

"That's because most roses are bred to be long lasting, in order to be shipped around the world like they are. It comes at the cost of scent. But these roses are from my mother's garden."

"Your mother's?" I ask him as he opens the bottle of champagne.

"My mother used to grow them. She was obsessed with her garden, and her roses especially." He pauses before he pops the cork. "Now it's kept up by the gardener. I'm sure if my mother were still here, she'd complain about what a disarray they're in, but I think they look and smell just as good as they did before."

He gives me a quick smile before he pours the champagne into the flutes, but even with the mask I can see the hint of sadness in his eyes. "Must be nice, in a way, to have her legacy keep growing on like that, even after she's gone."

He nods, chewing on his lip for a moment before he brings the glass over. "Memories aren't erased easily, no matter what people say. Here." He raises his glass to me. "Here's to making new memories."

I clink my glass against his and keep eye contact as I take a sip. I'm not about to risk seven years of bad sex, or whatever the superstition is. I have too much at stake right now.

"So, about the mask," I say. "Not that I'm judging, I mean, I'm wearing pretty much nothing underneath this, so you know I'm game for whatever."

He slips it off, and I see his wonderful face again. "I was trying it on when I answered the door. I have one for you too. And, no, I didn't get them for tonight, unless you want to try it out."

He disappears around the corner into the bedroom and comes out holding a white-and-gold mask with plumes of pastel feathers coming off the eyes.

"This is for you," he says.

I take it and stroke the feathers admiringly. "This is beautiful."

"I was hoping you'd wear it this weekend, at the ball."

"I'm sorry, what?"

Ball? He really does think he's the Phantom.

"I told you. The Dumont Masquerade Ball that happens this time every year."

"Well, to be fair, I've been hearing a lot of Dumont this and Dumont that—it's hard to keep up. And anyway, if I did hear you mention a party, I would have assumed I wasn't invited. Because of the whole you-being-ashamed-to-be-seen-with-me thing."

I expect him to roll his eyes, but instead he grips my face in his hands, his eyes intensely searching my face. "I am not ashamed to be seen with you. I just . . . this is a very complicated matter. You have to understand. But, please, I wish I could show you off to the world. I wish everyone could see you, see how happy you make me."

A lump forms in my throat. "I make you happy?"

"Oh, *mon lapin*," he whispers, kissing me softly, "you are the only thing that's good and pure and real in my whole life."

Damn. He means it. I can taste his intentions, feel how raw and open he's being.

"You mean everything to me," he says, his lips leaving little kisses and nibbles from my mouth to all along my jaw and down to my neck. Meanwhile, his hand reaches toward the sash around my trench coat and undoes it.

He steps back and then opens the coat wider to get a look at me. In that moment I wish I actually had high heels on instead of these mini ones, but I can tell from the heated look in his eyes that he doesn't even notice.

He drinks me in like a dying man's last breath.

"You're too beautiful for this world to contain," he tells me.

Damn.

I feel that one right in my core, causing an explosion of fireworks down my spine.

But those fireworks are quickly replaced with even bigger ones as he takes me in his arms and kisses me passionately. I'm gasping for breath in seconds, my body on fire in this desperate, primal way. My hands run up and down his suit, wanting it off him, while he devours my lips, ears, neck, making his way down.

He pulls aside the lace of my bra and brings out my breast, his lips sucking my nipple with a long, hard pull. I feel it travel through me in hot pulses, and I'm already panting, wanting more.

The trench coat drops to the ground, and then his hands take a meaty hold of my ass, and then he's lifting me up as if I weigh nothing at all. Instinctively, I wrap my legs around his waist, the tiny kitten heels pressing against the small of his back.

"You need to take off your clothes," I tell him, trying to undo his shirt and hold on tight at the same time, but he just gives me a heated grin and spins me around until I'm pressed up against the glass windows.

I turn my head and try to look down. We're only four floors up, but, even so, it's a bit unnerving to be pressed up against the glass like this, like we could go crashing to our deaths at any moment.

Not to mention the fact that anyone can see us.

"Uh, I know the French are pretty relaxed with sex and nudity, but are you sure about this?" I ask him as he continues to devour me. His hands are slipping down to his pants, and he's undoing his zipper.

"I'm sure the neighbors out there are used to this," he murmurs from my neck, where he sucks and licks and makes my skin feel like a live wire. "And they can't see your face. Can't see mine either."

He's got a point. He doesn't live here; this is just a hotel. A hotel he owns, but a hotel nonetheless. We're completely anonymous.

And even the idea of someone watching us have sex is a bit of a turn-on. Maybe it wouldn't have been in my previous life, but here and now, with my lingerie-clad ass pressed up against the window, it is.

And I don't have to be ashamed to admit it, even if just to myself.

He pulls his cock out and holds me harder against the glass for balance as he digs out a condom from his pants pocket.

"If I were staying longer, I would suggest we both get tested," I tell him. "I'm already on the pill."

He glances up at me through his mask, and I feel like apologizing for the very unsexy safe-sex talk at a moment like this, but he says, "If only you were staying longer."

I swallow hard, not wanting to think about that right now.

"If only."

He rolls the condom on, and I dig my heels into him, holding on tightly as he slowly pushes deeper and deeper inside.

I gasp, and then my gasp turns into a moan, and then I'm trying to catch my breath as all the air leaves me and all I can feel is him. My hands grab the back of his neck tightly as he licks up the length of my throat. He sucks and moans just below my ear as his hands cup my breasts, pinching at my nipples, and his cock thrusts in again and again.

"You're so hot, so tight," he whispers hoarsely. "So perfect for me. How are you so perfect for me?" He draws out slightly and drives back inside, pushing me harder against the glass. Every cell in my body is dancing with excitement and pleasure, and my heart is beating so fast I'm afraid it might run away and never come back.

He pumps into me again, arching his hips up, his cock so thick and stiff, filling every inch of me. I can feel his ass flex against my legs as he thrusts deeper and harder, intense and primal. His mouth is wet and hungry as it ravishes my neck, and I feel so strangely powerful right now, like he would do anything for me, like he's a slave for my pleasure.

Our rhythm picks up the pace, and even though I'm concerned about the glass, I don't care if anyone is watching. All I care about is him, this man in the mask who is pumping into me, wild in his lust and lost to his desire.

He grunts with another long, hard thrust, and I'm calling out his name.

"My name has never sounded so good," he says hoarsely as he continues to rut into me, the sweat from his brow dripping onto my tits. "Don't stop."

"*You* don't stop," I warn him just as his hand slips to my clit and he presses his thumb there, rubbing with each thrust. "Oh God, especially not now."

Even though I'm closer to coming now than ever, and when I come, it'll all be over.

I grab him tighter, my nails digging in, and in the glimpse of his eyes behind the mask, I see something change. It scares me in the most delicious way. It's like something inside him flipped, and he's now in another place, one where he's a wild animal and I'm his prey. His pace quickens, his hips firing like pistons, again and again, until I think either he's going to break me in two or we're going through the window.

What a sweet death that would be.

And then the orgasm is upon me, slinking up slowly from behind until I'm totally blindsided. It fires out from my core, spreading out in a wave of hedonistic lust until it obliterates me. I yell garbled words, holding him so tight I might be hurting him, but I don't care. All I can feel is him, and my body responds in kind, jerking and quaking around him, barely hanging on.

He comes with rough grunts and a few final, powerful thrusts, like he's actually trying to impale me, and even though the window holds, it still feels like we're falling.

Falling, falling.

Into each other.

I collapse into his arms, not even able to keep my head up, my legs falling to the side like I'm a rag doll.

He grabs my waist and pulls me off the glass, turning me around and placing me on the immaculately made-up bed, then lies down beside me.

I open my eyes, trying to focus as he takes his mask off.

"Turns out, it was me all along," he says by way of a joke.

But there's some truth to what he says.

It was him all along.

All this time, all these years, I've been looking for someone who would set my world on fire and make me new again.

It was him all along.

CHAPTER ELEVEN

OLIVIER

"Going for the *Phantom of the Opera* look, are we?"

I glance at Blaise as I pass by him in the hallway. He's been taking the invitations from the guests, and I'm surprised he didn't badger me for one.

"You know, the Phantom doesn't have a monopoly on white masks," I point out and then gesture to Blaise's own face, which is covered by a red velvet mask with golden sequins at the edges. "It looks like you stole that mask off a showgirl from the Moulin Rouge."

"Very funny," he says. "You know, the Phantom knew a thing about branding himself. Perhaps you should take some of that inspiration."

"What does that even mean?"

"It means the Olivier Dumont brand is nonexistent," he says with a calm shrug, a look of disdain in his eyes as they rake over me. "Always the same, the typical billionaire hotelier playboy."

"Better that than the guy who drives a fucking red Ferrari with a matching showgirl mask."

"At least I'm known for something," he says, and then his attention is torn away to a masked couple coming across the moat bridge with their invitations out.

Right. The moat.

You see, the ball is almost always held at one of the vineyards we own. We've had it at one of my hotels once or twice—actually, the Hôtel Rouge Royale where I met Sadie the other night—but my father has always insisted that it's more of a special event when it's somewhere outside the city.

In this case, it's far outside the city.

We're at the Château la Tour Carnet winery, one of those that Renaud operates from afar, which is not only located all the way in Bordeaux but is in an actual castle. It's a small castle, but a castle all the same, complete with a moat, a drawbridge, and groomed grounds filled with peacocks and swans. The peacocks are beautifully cared for, and there's even a rare white one. The swans are evil creatures who love to terrorize any guests who wander from the back terrace.

On the first floor of the castle, there's a medieval room filled with old knights' armor, weapons, and rare books and tapestries, as well as a few other little rooms that have been transformed into coatrooms and champagne stations for the party. Upstairs, the long dining hall and music room have been transformed into the dance floor and main party areas, while the study and bedrooms are off-limits. Then there's the kitchen, where numerous chefs and waiters are creating amuse-bouches and drinks, and a long spiral staircase to the very top, where guests love to lean out the windows and listen to the band assembled on the terrace below.

It's extravagant, with every single inch of the castle transformed to celebrate the upcoming fashion week and the autumn launch—but, of course, everything is gaudy and luxurious in the fashion world. People have come from all over—from New York, London, and Dubai—all fighting to get an invite to this very famous, very exclusive event.

But there's one guest who didn't have to try at all.

Sadie Reynolds.

She's not here, but I've been watching out for her like a hawk—one of the reasons I'm hanging around Blaise like I am. He doesn't seem to be suspicious that I'm without a date, but he doesn't exactly like having me around either.

"Olivier, can I have a word with you?" my father asks, appearing beside me.

He looks good: black suit, black mask. Very simple and traditional.

"Of course," I tell him.

He starts to lead me away and says to Blaise over his shoulder, "Be extra vigilant tonight, Blaise. There were rumors of invites being sold on the black market."

"Is that true?" I ask my father as we head out through the armor room and back doors to the terrace. The band is playing, and a few people are already dancing. It's seven at night, but the sun is still out, and it's hot, though cooler out here than it is inside. Being my father, he never once thought to add air-conditioning for the event. He'd think doing such a thing to a castle would be sacrilegious.

"Is what true?" he says.

"That invites are being sold on the black market." The thought of it makes my stomach sink. I know that I added Sadie to the list myself, having sent it to the room at the Hôtel Rouge Royale, and that it would have come straight from Seraphine's assistant. But even then, I don't want Blaise questioning her. I don't want anyone questioning her.

"Oh, no, I made that up," he says. "Gives Blaise something to do, makes him feel important."

I should feel more relieved than I do. I guess the whole idea of Sadie showing up here is messing me up more than I thought. I just want her to be here with me, to see my family—even if from afar—to know this part of my life. Even if it's a part I don't always like.

At least, I used to like it more. But ever since meeting her, the whole life in the fast lane with the glitz and the glamor, it doesn't have the same weight anymore, doesn't have the same value. Now that she's in my life, the real value is in her.

And she's leaving you in a week, I remind myself. *Back to her real life, and you'll have to go back to yours.*

I've been trying not to dwell on it, and it's certainly helped that I've been so busy with work and with this party. But now that the night is here, the truth is starting to sink in.

The clock is ticking.

"Are you all right?" my father asks me as we pause by the willow tree, out of earshot of the party. We've been walking across the back lawn, which was carefully scoured for goose poop earlier, but that doesn't stop me from watching every patch of grass in front of us.

"Yes, I'm fine," I tell him.

He squints at me from beneath his mask. "I'm not sure about that," he says. "I know you, my son. I know when there's something on your mind, and your mind has been elsewhere this last week. I'm not sure it's been anywhere good."

I try to smile. "I'm fine. Really."

"I don't like it when you keep secrets from me."

I raise my hands in innocence. "There are no secrets."

"Women make terrible secrets," he says in a low voice, and for one terrible moment I fear he might know. I fear he might be talking about Marine. About my betrayal and failure all those years ago.

But then I think he might be talking about Sadie, which isn't good either.

"Look, Olivier," he says after I haven't said anything. I pretty much just incriminated myself. "All I've ever wanted for you is to be happy. Actually, that's not true. I've wanted you to take over my position. But perhaps you wouldn't be happy doing my job."

I swallow, wishing I could just confess. Wishing I could tell him the truth about his own brother, wishing I could warn him.

But my father has always seen the best in people, and that includes family and that includes the wrong people. He's seen the best in me when he has no idea what I've done. How I don't deserve it. And he sees the best in his brother, my uncle, who has no good in him at all.

And yet I can't tell him that. I can't shake his belief in me like that, especially after so long. It might even be that my father has a good idea of just how rotten Gautier can be, and yet he stubbornly loves him anyway.

He's good like that. Such a better man than I will ever be.

"I think Seraphine would be much better at your job," I tell him, the same old thing I always say.

"You always say that," he points out. "And Seraphine always says that too. But—and this might be the old traditionalist in me—but . . . you're my son, Olivier. And from such a young age, you were always the one interested in taking over the brand. In continuing the name. You were always learning from me; you'd spend all your days in my office. Do you remember that? You wanted to be me so badly. It was touching, truly. And it was right. You were meant for this job, always were, and you knew it. And then one day, one day you just . . . poof. You went away for a few months, traveled the world, and you changed."

"People always change when they travel," I say under my breath, watching the breeze whip the willow branches around.

"No," he says, shaking his head, hands behind his back as he paces around me. "No, that was not the case with you. You went traveling because you were running away from something. That much I know. When you came back, whatever you ran away from, it was still there. It's still here, Olivier." He presses his finger into my chest. "I can see it in your eyes. It's always there, this ghost, this guilt. This fear. You live in fear, never getting close to anyone except your own family. Why is that?"

I have a hard time swallowing, wanting to look away. Even through the narrow slits of the mask, I can see my father's honest and loving eyes, and, God, I just want to be a good son to him. I know how badly he wants me to take over, and he'll never know why I can't.

I hate having to live with the fact that I'm disappointing him.

That's what's in my eyes, along with the guilt and the fear.

Because of my mistakes, I'll never truly be the man he needs me to be.

I'm a failure.

"Hey," he says to me, placing his hand on my shoulder and giving it a firm squeeze. "I am your father, and I love you. I will always accept you and always forgive you, no matter what you've done, no matter what you do. Your mother always used to say that you were the child with the most potential, not just for greatness in success but greatness of the heart. You have a good one. I wish one day you'd stop pretending you don't. I wish you'd own your golden heart and wear it with pride. Do good, be good, be proud of who you are. I am. I am so proud of you."

Fuck. Now that lump in my throat is growing wider. I have no words except "Thank you." The words come out garbled and hushed, but I can only hope he knows how much it means to me. He has faith in someone he shouldn't, but it's his faith all the same. And I'll hold on to it as tight as I can, for as long as I can, even if I don't believe it.

He leans in and embraces me in a tight hug, patting me on the back.

"Whoever she is, she's a lucky woman," he says to me.

I pull back and laugh. "She? I told you—there's no one."

He smiles at me. "Oh, Olivier." Then he turns and heads back to the party, with me following.

Of course, now I'm extra paranoid that something is going to go wrong tonight. If my father has deduced that I've fallen for someone, what about everyone else? I know my father and even Seraphine wouldn't really care all that much—they'd just be happy for me—but it's the others that I have to worry about. And I know that when my uncle makes a threat, it's a threat that sticks for life. It's never forgotten about. It's never wiped away.

We go back inside, and the party slowly starts to fill with more and more guests. The costumes this time seem even more elaborate. The actual dress code for the party is just to wear a mask, but because this is in a castle, a lot of people have gone full-on Renaissance, medieval, and every other time period. I've seen a few ladies already who could pass for Marie Antoinette.

It isn't until another hour has passed and I'm starting to get worried that I see Sadie coming over the drawbridge. I'm looking out the upstairs window, the sun having already gone down, and there she is, lit up like an angel.

I didn't tell her what to wear. I'd only given her the mask, but she'd played up the feathers by wearing a simple white summer dress and a pair of flat sandals, her hair spread across her shoulders in shimmering waves.

I hold my breath as she gets to Blaise and hands him the invitation. He scrutinizes it like he's been doing to all of them, looking her over and then holding it up to the light. But then after a moment, he lets her pass, not giving her a second glance.

At least that went smoothly. Because she had to take the train from Paris, which, thankfully, is only two hours, and then get in the hired car from Bordeaux to the estate, there's a lot that could have gone wrong. I texted her once or twice but can't be sure if she got them or not. Her phone's service has been rather weak—maybe because her phone itself is a relic.

For a split second I tell myself I should buy her a brand-new one, but then I realize how silly that is. It's not like she's staying here forever.

I try to push my heavy heart to the side and stride through the crowd of partygoers. I grab a glass of champagne from one of the waiter's trays and head down the stairs, hoping to grab her without anyone noticing.

I see her in the corner of the armor room, peering into the caged mouth of one of the helmets. My eyes do a quick sweep, and I wonder if there's anyone who would take notice of me. Blaise is still outside, though he'll probably come in soon since most guests are here. I haven't seen Pascal yet—I haven't seen him all week, in fact—but that doesn't mean he won't show up. I last saw my father talking to Seraphine upstairs, and I caught a glimpse of Gautier, but he pretended not to see me and vice versa.

I take my chances.

I approach her, holding out the glass of champagne. *"Madame,"* I say, and her eyes widen underneath her mask. "Allow me to welcome you to the masked ball. Champagne?"

"Is it the Dumont label?" she says stiffly, raising her nose. "Because that's the only brand I drink. The only brand I wear."

"Oh, is that so," I say, enjoying our acting. I lean in and reach behind her, pulling the back of her dress away from her skin, glancing at the tag. "Is that why this is from H&M?"

"Mmm," she says, stepping away, eyes darting, catching my paranoia. "I know better than to flaunt my wealth."

I'm getting hard just looking at her. "You know, you do this roleplaying so well," I murmur, taking a step toward her until she's against the wall.

"Careful," she says, placing her glass between us. "We don't know each other. We've never met."

"That's true. You arrived here all right?"

She clears her throat, looking sheepish. "I may have missed the first train, but yes."

"Fashionably late. Good thing the crowd here feels the same way."

She smiles at me, and then her eyes go over my shoulder to the front door, where Pascal steps in. My heart thuds in my ears like a drum. We're enough in the shadows that we're mostly out of sight, and he doesn't even glance this way, only toward the back doors, where two giggling girls in mounds of tulle and lace come out clutching their petticoats.

I watch him carefully, holding my breath. Pascal loses interest in the girls, even though they certainly know who he is. His mask might disguise his eyes—even his nose, in this case, since his is elaborately Venetian—but they recognize his chin. He gives them just a smug smile and heads up the staircase with them trailing behind, like ducks picking up bread crumbs.

I exhale slowly and glance at Sadie. She is also watching Pascal and has the most puzzled look on her face.

"What?" I ask her.

"Who was that?" she asks.

I groan. Why does everyone want to know Pascal? "That was my cousin. Pascal Dumont."

"Oh," she says, and I can tell she's frowning underneath the mask. "I thought maybe I knew him from somewhere."

"Well, you did say you had been stalking my family online. He's definitely one of the so-called bad boys the press likes to cover."

She gives me a sharp look. "So-called? Isn't he the one your father and sister are always battling against?"

"Yes," I say reluctantly. "He and my uncle. And the man who examined your ticket, that was my cousin Blaise."

"The bad side of the family," she muses softly.

Normally I would correct her, but I've pretty much been talking shit about them this whole time. And to be honest, it's a little dicey with her not knowing the whole truth.

I want to tell her.

I just don't know if I should do so here and now.

I've already been talking to her for too long.

"Can you make me a promise tonight?" I ask her, searching her eyes.

She nods and stares at me in such a way that I know she'll keep any promise to me.

"Can you stay away from them? They aren't good people, and I don't trust them around you."

"But they don't know who I am," she says. "Right?" Her words come out harsh, fearful.

"They don't," I assure her. "I just want to keep it that way. I've already been talking to you for too long as it is, and I need to get back to my father and the guests. Just promise me that you'll stay away, and if for some reason they talk to you, give them nothing, and if you have to give them something, make it a lie. Okay? Make it a lie."

"What's going on, Olivier?" Her voice is quiet, almost trembling.

"I'll explain later. That's my promise to you. *D'accord?*"

She nods. *"D'accord,"* she whispers.

It takes everything in me to not kiss her on the cheek. "Enjoy the party, *mon lapin.* I'll talk to you soon."

Then I turn.

And I leave her.

The angel in the room of armor.

I wish I could encase her in all of it.

CHAPTER TWELVE

SADIE

I've never been to a masquerade ball before.

Or any ball, actually.

I went to my homecoming and my prom, but that doesn't really count.

This is the type of ball you read about in historical novels and watch in sexy movies. It always looks so opulent and cool and fun.

And, well, it's certainly the first two.

I mean, this is held in an actual legit castle.

And seeing all the costumes and everyone mingling with their masks on and the waiters coming around with drinks and tasty little weird things on silver trays, it's definitely cool.

But fun? Well. This isn't so much.

It probably has a lot to do with the fact that I don't know anyone here except for Olivier, and he has to pretend to not know me. When I first accepted the chance to come here, I knew that was going to be part of the deal. That I would have to pretend to not know him, that I would remain an anonymous person. I thought I wouldn't mind.

But I do. It sucks. I can't help but watch his every move; my eyes are drawn to his movements like a moth to a flame. I watch as he talks to every guest, always charming, always smiling, always laughing as if the person he's talking to said something hilarious, and I'm quite certain they didn't.

He's mine. That's all I can think. He's mine and no one else's, and yet I'm kept in the shadows, a girl behind a mask, wishing she could remove it, wishing she could remove his. Wishing we could just be together. No secrets, no shame.

But he has secrets, if not shame.

And they all come down to his cousins and uncle.

I know that's the cause.

I know that's why he doesn't want to be seen with me.

I've seen his father; he's even come and said hello to me. It was brief but very kind. I've seen his sister too. Absolutely the most fucking gorgeous woman I've ever encountered. I was nearly drooling on myself. They both seem like the good people I've been told about. They exude it.

And then there's Blaise and Pascal and Gautier.

Gautier has to be the worst of them.

He's younger than his brother and yet somehow looks older. Thankfully, I haven't made eye contact with him, even when I felt him staring at me for a really long time. But from the glimpses I've seen of his eyes when looking around the room or talking to other people, they seem to glow with malice. I'm not even exaggerating. There's a coolness to him, a confidence that doesn't come from knowing who you are, but rather from knowing that you'll do anything to stay at the top. He's a snake on two legs, and even if Olivier hadn't warned me to stay away from him, I would have naturally.

Oh, and here's another reason why masquerade balls aren't all they're cracked up to be.

They're creepy as fuck.

I'm going downstairs to head to the back terrace to get some fresh air since it's still so damn hot inside, when I literally run into some man with a mask that has three sets of eyes.

He giggles maniacally at our encounter, reaches over to pinch my ass, and then runs up the stairs. I don't even have time to yell at him or react, and, for all I know, he could go and switch into another mask, and I'll never know who he is.

Yup. Having people stare at you without your even knowing is one thing; overt sexual harassment is another.

"Ugh," I say to myself, smoothing down the back of my dress and feeling dirty. I'll be sure to tell Olivier when I get a moment to talk to him, because I don't stand for that shit, and I don't care if it's going to be a problem. That's probably the vibe I'm picking up on at this party. Like a Marie Antoinette version of *The Purge*, where everyone is free to flirt and giggle and grab and leer and get stupidly drunk, all while remaining coy and supposedly anonymous.

Outside it's only a little bit cooler, and while the band is playing and people are dancing on the terrace and on the grass, there's a swan that seems to take an interest in me, and not in a good way. With my feather mask and white dress, I might look like one of his relatives.

I start going back inside, but before I reach the doors, I see Ludovic, Gautier, and Pascal all step out of a room that Ludovic locks behind them. I hang back and wait, and Gautier and Ludovic then move past the row of armored knights toward the stairs, but Pascal turns toward the doors.

Toward the outside.

Toward me.

I gasp internally and then quickly spin around so that he doesn't see me.

Which, unfortunately, leaves me nearly face-to-face with that swan.

It opens its mouth and hisses.

I open my mouth and hiss right back.

For a moment the swan seems stunned, and I think perhaps it actually worked. If he thinks I'm a swan, maybe he thinks I've said *fuck you* right back in swan language.

Then he waddles toward me and honks lightly.

"Don't worry—his honk is worse than his bite," a smooth voice says from behind me, and suddenly Pascal comes and stands right between me and the swan, his back to me. He mutters something to the swan in French and makes a sudden movement. That sends the swan pivoting around, flapping his wings, and waddling away.

I'm staring at just Pascal's back, and already it's familiar to me.

Do I know you? I want to say. *How could I?*

I don't say anything at all.

Pascal turns around and grins at me. "But, of course, his bite is pretty fucking bad."

I blink at him, trying to remember what to say and do. It's all on me.

"You speak English, don't you?" he asks me.

I nod slowly. "I do. How did you know that?"

"I heard you talking to some of the guests. Your accent stands out, like a siren call among a sea of sharks."

Odd analogy. And yet it reminds me so much of Olivier.

"You must be Pascal Dumont," I tell him, straightening my shoulders and raising my head, forcing myself to be someone else.

He tilts his head and runs his hand slowly over his chin.

That chin.

If I let myself think too much about it, I could swear it was Pascal following me on the streets the other day. But I don't want to think about it because then I'm going to fucking panic.

"You know who I am," he muses, and even beneath the mask I can feel this cold intensity in his eyes, like I matter to him a lot more than he lets on, but only in the way a mouse matters to a cat.

"Of course. I wouldn't be here if I didn't."

His eyes narrow beneath the mask, just a bit. I can't tell what color they are—it's too dark—and the result is a bit unnerving. "But if you know who I am, I can't say I know who you are."

"Sadie Reynolds," I tell him, giving a faux bow. I know better than to make up a name for myself—besides, it says Sadie on the envelope. If he or anyone else wants to look me up online, they won't find much on me.

"And what brings you to my party, Sadie Reynolds from Seattle?"

I freeze. What did he just say?

I try to smile, to act breezy. "How did you know I was from Seattle?"

"I can tell. I'm very good at accents. Comes with the business," he says. "You know, we have an account with Nordstrom. It was the first American store to carry Dumont handbags."

"I didn't know that."

Okay. I want to get out of this conversation now. I look around, trying to see if maybe there's a waiter with a drink I could get or someone I know. I'll even settle for the guy with three eyes.

"Planning your escape?" Pascal says, his voice strangely soft. He takes a step toward me. The corner of his mouth quirks into a crooked smile. "Am I making you nervous?"

I laugh. Nervously. "Nervous? No. I was looking for something to drink. It's so hot outside."

"It is," he says with a sigh, rocking back on his heels slightly. "Though I do have that effect on women."

"Making them nervous?" I eye him quickly before looking again for something, anything.

"Making them hot."

Now I'm turning to face him, brows raised. "Only a small man would take credit for the weather."

I know I'm playing with fire here, and after everything Olivier said to me, everything he made me promise, I know I need to head inside, find some excuse. The last thing I should be doing is firing insults at Pascal.

But Pascal seems to like it. He's laughing. A genuine laugh too.

"I like you, Sadie," he says. "I really do. Here I was thinking that maybe you were some stupid American tourist who decided to crash the party uninvited, but now I'm not so sure."

His words strike fear back into me. I swallow. "I'm not stupid. And I'm not crashing this party. I was invited."

"By whom?"

I had prepared for this. "By Seraphine. Your cousin."

"Hmm, and how do you know Seraphine?"

"Dance class." This lie is a gamble. Not so much that Seraphine could be asked who I am, because she apparently has a bad memory and knows way too many people and would just say she knows me anyway. But that I'm not a dancer. I mean, I had dreams of it when I was young, and I took lessons before my dad left, but if Pascal is about to ask me to do some sort of move, I'm going to fail miserably and probably be thrown out of the party.

His eyes rake over me, up and down, pausing at my legs, my crotch, my chest, then my lips. "I would have pegged you as more of a gymnast. I am sure you are very, very . . . flexible."

Holy shit. That was definitely innuendo, but it also came from some place of *knowing*.

Then I'm staring at his mouth, the way he's licking his lips. The smattering of a mustache, the goatee along his chin. That very familiar chin.

And once again a memory jabs into my head in a red-hot haze.

Sex with Olivier.

A face at the window, eyes in the shadows.

The very same face I'm looking at now.

I can't even hide the fear, and there's no question that he can see it.

But I have to pretend. For Olivier's sake, I have to pretend.

And then I have to get out of here.

No matter what, I have to get Pascal to believe my lie.

"A little too flexible for the likes of you," I tell him, reaching out and patting him on the chest. "Sorry, pal, I know you get a lot of girls because of your little perfume campaign, but I'm not interested."

It works. His mouth turns sour, into a pout. "I'm not hitting on you," he says.

I shrug and wave my hand at him. "Whatever you say."

Then I walk away.

I even do a little sashay, swinging my hips, like I'm proud to have just turned him down, and I can only hope it's enough for him to buy it, enough for him to forget his objective. I hope that his injured pride and bruised ego, something he never even put on the line, is enough of a distraction that he'll forget everything else he thinks he knows about me.

I walk inside the doors, back into the armor room, toward the stairs.

Start going up them.

And the hair on my arms starts to rise.

I glance over my shoulder to see Pascal following me, his mouth set in a grim line. He doesn't look so easygoing anymore. The cat doesn't like to lose the mouse.

I get to the top of the stairs and look around as subtly as I can, trying not to look like I'm searching for Olivier.

But I am.

And I spot him, standing by the doors to the music room, talking to his father and some other man I'm pretty sure is Tom Ford. I don't know my fashion designers, but this man is as recognizable as the pope and handsome as fuck.

Even though the three of them are in conversation, there's a small crowd around them, giving them space, but also staring at them in adoration. And why not? This is the fashion world, and these men are some of the gods. No wonder everyone is hanging on to their every word and nodding along as if they're part of the conversation too.

I pause, watching them, hoping I'll be passed over the same as everyone else.

And yet I feel Pascal stop right behind my shoulder.

He doesn't say anything, but he's there. My skin feels like I've gotten an electric shock that I can't quite shake.

I should move, should go somewhere. But I feel powerless from fear. Like I'm waiting for him to do something.

And he's waiting too. Maybe for me to do something.

Then something does happen.

Something across the room.

There's a shout and a cry, and for a moment I think that maybe someone got a surprise or dropped something.

But when my eyes travel over, I see Ludovic clutching his chest, face red and strained as he rips off his mask. Another man is leaning over in concern, and then Ludovic's legs are buckling and Olivier is right behind him, trying to hold him up.

Olivier starts yelling something in French, and people are taking out their phones, and, oh my God, I think his father is having a heart attack.

Another man is behind Ludovic, helping Olivier, but then he slips to the floor, unresponsive now. The crowd is gathering, and I can't see a thing, but I hear Olivier crying out for his father.

I have to be there for him.

I run toward Olivier, glancing back once at Pascal, thinking he must be following me, going to help his uncle.

But Pascal remains behind.

Standing there, completely still.

His mouth and face are unreadable.

His eyes are dark.

All I know is that they're following my every move.

I get to the crowd, trying to break through, to get to Olivier, but there are too many people, and they're panicking. Blaise is in front of them, keeping everyone back, yelling in French. I wish I could understand what the hell was going on, but I know it's not good.

Not good at all.

I can't even breathe.

This can't be happening. His father was doing fine earlier, at least he looked like he was.

Now Gautier is in the picture, barking at people and pointing. Seraphine comes running through the crowd, crying. It's a mess, and I do my best to stay out of the way to let people help. Someone in the crowd seems to be a doctor and is doing CPR. It doesn't look good; it doesn't sound good.

Then sirens fill the air, and a fire truck shows up, followed shortly by paramedics, who take Ludovic away on a stretcher. Then the police, who order everyone to go.

I have to go too. We all do. I want to stay with Olivier, but he doesn't even look for me. He doesn't need to. His father is the only thing on his mind right now, and when Olivier rips off his mask and throws it to the ground, his eyes are wet and red with tears, and I know that his father is probably dead.

I break for him. I want to be there for him. I want to shoulder his grief and his burdens and be his shoulder to cry on.

But he has his sister, who is sobbing into his shoulder, beautiful even when she's crying. And they follow the paramedics out, as do the rest of us, gathered at the front of the castle on this hot summer night, the air filled with cicadas and the sweet smells of the vineyards.

I don't even know where to go. Everyone here seems to know each other, and they're all staying at nearby hotels and wineries and Airbnbs. All I know is that I was supposed to stay with Olivier when all this was over, in one of the castle's many bedrooms.

That won't be happening.

For the first time in a while, I feel absolutely lost and unmoored, and I know that my feelings matter so little right now.

But that hurts too. Knowing they matter so little.

That I matter so little right now.

I'm alone, anonymous, a hidden girl, about to be abandoned in the countryside. I don't know the language, and I don't have much money to my name, and I've been depending on Olivier for everything so far, and I've only been kept in the dark.

And now his father is gone.

Now his world has completely turned over.

I have no idea where it will place me.

I sigh and try to recover some resilience. I do have my clutch purse with train tickets and a credit card, and I have my phone. I won't bother Olivier, and for now I can at least figure something out.

I'm trying to Google what the local taxis are, since the car that took me here from the Bordeaux train station certainly won't be arranged for me now, when I feel a presence beside me.

I glance up to see Pascal, mask off, smoking a cigarette. The fact that I'm just so brazenly staring at his face is momentarily jarring, like I'm seeing something I'm not supposed to see.

But just like he was with the mask, his expression now is unreadable.

"I'm sorry about your uncle," I say softly, trying to find the words. I might think Pascal is a total creep, but I'm not heartless. "He was . . . that was horrible."

Pascal nods slowly, taking a deliberate drag of his cigarette. "It was."

"Is he going to be okay?"

Pascal looks around him, the moonlight bouncing off his dark eyes. Then he shrugs. *"Je ne sais pas."* He glances at me. "Where are you going?"

I can't tell him the truth. "I was going to find a way back into town. To Bordeaux. Stay at a hotel."

"You don't have a ride," he says.

I wave my phone at him. "My phone isn't pulling up the driver I had earlier."

He frowns. "You can have a ride with me."

"No," I say quickly. "Please. That's okay."

I'd rather walk.

He gives me a terse smile. "I meant a ride from me. I'll call you one of my drivers. I'm staying here tonight." He pauses. "Unless you want to stay here too? Don't worry . . . I'm not hitting on you. You would know it if I were."

I swear to God, sometimes he sounds so much like Olivier it's uncanny. And yet the two of them couldn't be further apart.

I remember his uncle, and I resist the urge to say something witty. "I would really appreciate it if you could call your driver for me."

He nods and blows out smoke away from my face, and as he turns, he faces the lights from the castle, and I see his eyes. They aren't dark at all, but the palest, iciest blue. He texts something on his phone and then puts it back in his pocket. "He's just at the end of the driveway. He'll be here in a minute. Black Mercedes."

Then Pascal turns and slowly walks off back toward the castle, and it's this view of his back again, the way he moves, that makes me think it really was him I saw on the street the other day.

He'd been following me.

Why?

How did he know about me or who I was?

Why is it his business who Olivier is with?

I can't let him know that I know, but I can't be complacent either.

"Wait," I call out after him. "How do I know this driver isn't going to murder me and dump my body on the side of the road somewhere?"

But the moment I say it, I realize it's not exactly the best thing to say after we all pretty much witnessed someone dying.

He doesn't even glance at me, just waves his hand, his cigarette making light trails. "There are a bunch of people heading to Bordeaux over there. I'm sure a few of them wouldn't mind getting a ride with you."

Then he walks off, back over the drawbridge and into the castle.

For the first time all evening, the air loses its heat, and the breeze turns cold.

And I realize I still have my mask on.

I take it off, glad for what little anonymity I had, and then head toward the group of bewildered and displaced guests, finding someone to come with me on the drive back to Bordeaux.

CHAPTER THIRTEEN

Olivier

Grief.

I'm no stranger to grief.

When my mother died in the car accident, grief settled down into my life and became a constant companion. It was a friend of sorts, the type of friend you knew only meant well, even though they flattened everything around you. There was no escaping from grief; it was natural, it was something that had to be felt. My mother was a kind, wonderful, caring person, and she deserved the grief that we all felt because that's how much her loss hurt us.

The grief never left, it just got easier to manage. My sister, my brother, my father—we all depended on each other to get through it. We were the crutches that allowed each other to keep going. Without our family, none of us could put one foot in front of the other.

But now . . . now my father is dead.

He's gone.

It's just me and Seraphine now, and Renaud, whom I have to call in a few hours and tell the horrible news to. It's just us, and without our father, how can we go on? We're his children, now orphans. We're alone, marooned, helpless, breaking apart from the inside out.

I can't even think. I wish I couldn't feel, but I can, all too well.

The confusion.

The anger.

One minute my father was fine.

The next he had collapsed on the floor.

He was pronounced dead when he arrived at the hospital, and even now as Seraphine and I talk to the doctors, I don't understand how any of it can be real.

A heart attack, they say.

It happens, they say.

But it doesn't happen to someone like my father. Not in his good health and his good shape. It doesn't happen to someone who literally just had a clean bill of health at his checkup. It doesn't happen to us . . . it can't happen again like this.

"It's late," Seraphine says in a dull voice, her hand on my shoulder. "You should go to the castle. Get some sleep."

I stare at her red-rimmed eyes, only now realizing the depth of my exhaustion. "I'm going to Bordeaux," I tell her. Because that's where Sadie is. I've been in contact with her. I haven't forgotten her. I need her more than ever, and she feels so weightless and translucent, like maybe she never existed, and she was just a dream, or perhaps I lost her, too, when I lost everything else.

Seraphine nods. She doesn't ask. Perhaps she thinks I need to be alone. Perhaps she doesn't blame me for not wanting to go back to the castle.

"Are you going to be okay?" I ask her.

She nods, but in her eyes I see it all. She's not going to be okay, and neither am I. My father was my idol. I think he was her best friend. This loss is going to weigh on us more than either of us could have imagined.

I get to my feet, not wanting to leave her. "Come to Bordeaux with me. I'll get you a room."

She shakes her head, wiping away a tear that had fallen a long time ago. "No, I want to stay here."

I look around. There's no one else here. Gautier was here for a second when the ambulance brought our father in. Neither Pascal nor Blaise showed up. Some friends of my father did try to hang around, but they were shown the door.

It's a cold feeling to know that we are the end of the line. That we are all that's left on this side of the legacy.

"There's nothing left for us here," I tell her. "He's gone."

She shakes her head, and I know she's going into shock, that she can't quite understand what has happened, that he's not going to get up and walk back to us.

"Are you going to have an autopsy?" she asks.

"No," I tell her. "I brought it up to the doctor, but he said there's no need. He had a heart attack."

She gives me a sharp look. "You don't seriously believe that."

I sigh, running my hand down my face, wishing I could sink into the floor and never get up again. "I have to. Look, it doesn't make sense, but I'm going to have to trust the doctors on this one. We can't keep this going, delaying the inevitable. We need to be able to mourn him, and an autopsy is only going to delay it. Besides, what are you hoping to find?"

"I'm not hoping to find anything," she says softly.

"Want me to call Cyril?" I ask.

She stiffens at the mention of her ex-husband. "Don't you dare. You know he'd only pay lip service."

I nod. Cyril was a charmer (hence, how he was able to woo someone as fiery as Seraphine), but his charm wasn't enough when Seraphine realized he married her for her money.

"Just go to Bordeaux," she says with a tired wave. "I'll be fine."

"Did you want me to call Renaud?"

She shakes her head. "No, I'll do it. I need to talk to him."

I'm grateful for that. I would have done it, but Renaud isn't an emotional man. He's closed up in many ways, and I think his sister would be better at breaking the news.

I hug Seraphine goodbye and head out to my driver, who has been waiting for me all night.

The drive to Bordeaux feels long in the dark, such a contrast to the bright lights of the hospital. My driver doesn't talk except to offer a few words of condolence, leaving me alone in my thoughts. But the longer I'm in the car, the more I feel anonymous and removed. Like whatever happened at the ball, at the hospital, it happened to someone else.

I should revel in the numbness. I should wrap it around me like a shroud and put another mask on, one that says that the show must go on. But I don't want to. It feels like an affront to my father.

I keep seeing the image of him in my head as he fell to the floor, and I make myself drown in it because I don't want to forget, I don't want to pretend it didn't happen.

There was such horror in his eyes. He stared right at me as he clutched his chest. Afraid and in disbelief and in pain, and yet there was something else. Something I can't quite describe, perhaps because it's something you only feel when you're about to die. But whatever it is, it will haunt me. It's like he felt betrayed, and I guess he was, by his own body.

By the time the car pulls up to the hotel across from the opera house in Bordeaux, I feel like I'm on autopilot, reliving his death again and again.

I make my mind switch to Sadie.

Sadie, who I left at the ball because I could only think of my father at the time.

Sadie, who is independent and intrepid enough to find her way here.

Sadie, who I told to check in, and I would come find her.

My phone died on the ride over, so I go to the front desk for the extra key and make my way to the room. The grandest rooms weren't available on such short notice, but it doesn't matter. No one is trying to impress anyone anymore.

I knock on the door, and when I don't hear an answer, I swipe my key and step inside, the door closing behind me. For some reason I fear the worst, as if death has come for her, too, but then I see her lying on the bed in her white dress, her eyes slowly opening as she takes me in.

"Olivier?" she whispers as she pushes herself up on her elbows.

Her hair is falling across her face, and in her dress she looks like an angel.

I thought I could make it across the room, but I can't.

The sight of her brings me to my knees.

It makes all the loss and grief swell up like a balloon before it bursts, and then it's pulling me down, and I'm drowning.

"Olivier," she cries out softly, and then she's at my side, arms around me as the tears fall. The shock has worn off, or maybe it's come on stronger, but I can't keep it together anymore. I can't even stand.

I cry into her arms and tell her I'm sorry for leaving her like I did at the party, and I'm sorry she had to see everything, and I'm sorry I've been hiding her, because it turns out I need her most of all.

She's everything to me, and without her, I don't think I could get to my feet again.

She just holds me and tells me she's here for me and tells me that she's not leaving and tells me that I'm hers. She doesn't try to make me feel better, doesn't try to stop my tears, doesn't try to get me to my feet.

She just lets me feel it all, feel everything, and keeps holding me together in her arms, holding me in such a way that I know I can keep cracking, but I'll never truly fall apart.

◆ ◆ ◆

I don't know how I survived the next few days. All I do know is I couldn't have done it without Sadie by my side, supporting me in every way she knows how. Even just looking at her face gives me a wave of strength, knowing she's there for me.

Unfortunately, she can't be with me every step of the way. There is so much paperwork and so many phone calls and affairs to sort out that have me pulled in every direction. I'm not the oldest or next of kin—that would be Renaud—but even though he's now in Paris with us, he's in over his head. Renaud has been living in California and running the wineries for the last eight years, and I don't think he's stepped foot in Europe more than a couple of times since then. He has no idea what's happening or what to do, but neither do any of us.

It's now the morning of the funeral. Sadie and I arrived separately. I know she's out there in the crowd of mourners who showed up early, and, like usual, I'll have to pretend to not know her, especially on a day like today. I don't want anything taking away from my father.

I'm in the funeral home waiting for Seraphine and Renaud to arrive. The priest should be here soon too. I hate the smell in here. I hate the weight to the air. I hate knowing the sorrow and grief that has lived in this place, some of it so sharp it can never leave, like cigarette smoke that lingers long after the flame is out.

I'm sitting on a chair in one of the Dumont label's finest suits, and I can't help but stare at the buttons on the cuffs—black obsidian—my heart crying because I remember my father talking about these very buttons once. About how he wanted something understated and classy, that the gray swirls in the obsidian would give the wearer a sense of elegance every time he looked at them.

But I don't feel elegance, I just feel loss. The loss of such a thoughtful, smart man. A good man, one of the few good men left.

"Olivier." Gautier's voice comes from the doorway behind me, and it's like someone pulling shades across the sun, the grief inside me turning into something insidious.

I turn my head and see Gautier, his wife, Camille, Pascal, and Blaise, like a troop of nightmares waiting at the door.

"I didn't know if you needed some more time alone," Gautier says carefully. It sounds like he's being concerned, but I swear there's something mocking in his voice. Or perhaps I'm hearing what I want to hear. You couldn't blame me at this point.

"It's fine," I tell them, my voice gruff, and go back to leaning forward in my seat, elbows on my thighs. I'm not getting up.

"We're so sorry, Olivier," Camille says, coming over. She drops to her knees beside me, hand on my arm, and peers up at me. I try not to shudder. Camille is a beautiful woman, a good twenty years younger than Gautier, and always plays each part perfectly. Right now, she's being the sympathetic aunt, even though I know she doesn't have a sympathetic bone in her lithe body.

But I play along. I don't have the strength to do otherwise.

Besides, I know why they're all here. It's not because of my father. It's not because they all wanted to be early to his funeral.

It's because of business.

I raise my head and take the rest of them in. My uncle with his arched brows and sour smile, Pascal and his blank expression, except for his eyes, which have a strange gleam to them. Blaise at least has the respect to appear subdued. And Camille, of course, is just an act.

Seeing them all here like this, my family by blood, them against me, has me mourning again in a different way. What went wrong with us? What family secrets originally drove our parents apart? I know that it couldn't have just been old-fashioned sibling rivalry or a difference in egos and temperaments. There had to be something else that caused the rift between them, which then created a rift between all of us.

But I won't get any answers today.

"Will you give Olivier and me a minute alone?" Gautier asks them, and they all file out the door, more than willing to leave.

I should be nervous. I can't remember the last time I was alone with my uncle. I've done all I can to avoid exactly that, in case he wanted to add something else to our bargain. But I don't fear anymore. There's nothing left to lose.

Gautier pulls up a chair across from me, comfortable and elegant, and I'm reminded of that fateful day ten years ago.

"We need to have a talk, Olivier," he says smoothly, putting on a wince that I guess is supposed to be shame. "I know this isn't the right time, but it's never the right time, is it? And you're a hard man to get ahold of."

"I've been busy," I mumble, avoiding his eyes, not wanting him to glean any information from me, information he can use to his advantage.

"I understand," he says, folding his hands. "But the truth of the matter is that we had an agreement. You signed a contract. In one week, you have to make a choice."

"Have?" Now he has my attention.

"Yes. Because, well, my brother is dead, and you currently hold his shares, shares that were willed to you, along with your own. You do realize you have complete control of the company, don't you?"

I do realize. I've met with the lawyers. I know that with my shares combined with my father's, I hold all the cards.

Except that I don't.

My uncle does.

Just that one card, signed in blood, but it's enough to steal the entire deck.

"I know you don't want control of the company, Olivier," Gautier says. "I know that you'd rather concentrate on your hotels. That's something that's all you. That's something you built from the ground up, and in just ten years. You should be proud of yourself. I know your father never acted like he was, because all he wanted was for you to do exactly as he did, but I'm proud of you, Olivier."

My gaze fixes on him, hard and cold. "My father was proud of me."

Gautier smiles and shrugs. "Of course, he was. Of course. But he also knew you didn't want the Dumont brand. Never did figure out why. But we all hope to keep it that way, even after his death."

"What are you saying?"

"I'm saying that the contract has been modified. I need you to give up your shares—and your father's shares—now. Not next week. Now."

"And if I don't?"

"You know what will happen."

"My father is dead," I grind out, my jaw so tense it feels like my teeth may shatter.

He nods. "He is. I'm not sure if I'll ever get used to the idea. We were closer than you think, you know. And I loved him dearly. There wasn't a better man out there, that much I know is true. We all know it."

He pauses, taking a deep breath in through his nose, his eyes pinched shut. In this moment I can only sense the conflict inside of him. He might even be sincere.

When he opens his eyes, they're wet and full of anguish. "He is dead. He is gone. But his legacy remains. Your legacy remains. Do you want to throw that all away? Do you want to tarnish his memory?"

"It was my mistake, not his," I growl.

"You're wrong. The sins of the father pass on to the son, and the sins of the son pass up to the father. If it were to come out what you did, that you had an affair with your cousin's wife, it would ruin the Dumont name. Not just for your father's sake, but for all of us. You would bring all of us down, including your brother and sister. Including me."

"So then don't tell the world."

He sighs and runs his hand over his hair. "Sometimes I think you don't understand business at all, my nephew." He gets up and stares down at me.

I look away, trying to think, but the grief has muddled my brain, making it harder to see the clear picture. I was always so afraid of upsetting my father, and I let that fuel me in keeping secrets. But the truth is, it's more than that. It's my own pride. It's my family's pride. If it were something I could admit to Seraphine or Renaud and keep it between ourselves, I would. I would own up to it, and I know they wouldn't shun me.

But that's not how my uncle works. If this truth comes out, it's going to be bigger and worse than I could have ever imagined. He would make sure of it.

That's what he does.

"Come on," he says to me, holding out his hand to help me up, and it takes everything in me not to break his arm instead. I would if I didn't know he'd have someone doing the exact same thing to me after. "Let's go tell your family what's happening. That you're forfeiting your shares and your father's shares to me."

"What about Seraphine?"

"She'll have her job. Don't worry. You can have a job with us, too, you know, if you ever get bored."

I ignore his hand and get up on my own.

I feel like I'm betraying my family all over again.

"You're doing the right thing, Olivier," my uncle says, his voice silky smooth. "I assure you, by doing this you'll be happier in the long run. Distance yourself from us, that's what you've always wanted anyway. Concentrate on your own legacy. Build a family. Fall in love." At that, I look at him sharply. He smiles. It's all cold. "But I promise you, if you don't do this, you won't ever find love again."

I know from the way he's looking at me, like a dog that's caught a scent, that he knows about Sadie. That whatever I've tried to do to protect her, to hide her, has been a waste of my time. He knows about her and will use her as leverage if he has to.

Another reason why I have to do this.

I'll give all power to the devil if it saves Sadie from his grasp.

CHAPTER FOURTEEN

SADIE

You'd think that going to the funeral of someone you didn't know would be a somewhat easy thing to do, but in some ways I think it's harder. You're not quite sure how to act, what to say. You feel so removed from the person and the situation and all the people mourning around you that you want to apologize for it.

That's how I felt at Ludovic's funeral.

Granted, it wasn't a small affair at all, and not a single soul there was looking at me wondering what I was doing there or caring if I was crying or seemed distraught or not.

Everyone was focused on Ludovic Dumont and his legacy.

There were celebrities, models, actors, chefs, fashion designers, socialites, and billionaires. So many rich and influential people that you couldn't swing a cat without hitting one of them.

The flowers were beautiful, the procession was beautiful.

The speeches were endless and heartfelt and heartbreaking.

Especially Olivier's.

His speech is the one that made the tears spring to my eyes and fall freely down my cheeks. It looked like I was mourning Ludovic, but instead I was mourning Olivier.

I was mourning the fact that now he, along with Seraphine and Renaud, were orphans. That he lost a man who meant so much to him so soon after losing his mother. I knew family meant absolutely everything to Olivier and that he talked about his father often and with a great sense of pride. He was so proud to be his son.

And that was especially apparent in his eulogy, one that he had to stop a few times to compose himself because the heartache was too much.

But even after all that, I still feel like I shouldn't be here. I mean, I'm not even with him. He didn't talk about "hiding" us anymore, but he said he didn't want the tabloids to focus on the mystery woman he brought to the funeral, so it would be best that I sit with the general public.

So that's where I am now, watching as the casket is lowered into the ground, feeling like I got off the hook when everyone else is so affected.

Watching Olivier as he grapples with saying goodbye, his sister leaning on him on one side, his older brother, Renaud, leaning on the other.

So much is going to change now. The company and wills. I can already tell that things are going to get really ugly with his uncle and everyone else. They were at each other's throats before this happened, and now . . .

It's really the perfect excuse to leave.

If I was someone else, I would.

In fact, I think if I were the Sadie Reynolds I had been pretending to be all this time, the one who threw caution to the wind and chose to stay in the French Riviera with a stranger and follow him to Paris to have hot sex, I think that Sadie would say *au revoir*.

After all, Olivier is going to be extra busy now.

He's not going to have any time for me.

He's going to be dealing with all this change and grief and loss and stress, and I'm the last thing he needs to worry about.

I need to go.

I need to get to Madrid and get on that plane the day after tomorrow and go.

It would be better for him to deal with all this on his own.

But that's not me.

I'm not that person who leaves. At least, I don't want to be that person.

I want to stay.

I want to make sure Olivier is okay.

I want to be that shoulder for him to lean on, the same way he lets me lean on him.

I don't want to be the person who turns around because a situation gets difficult.

That's not what he would do for me.

If this situation were reversed, he would give it all up to make sure I was okay, that I was taken care of.

It's one thing for him to tell me to go.

But even if he did, I won't.

It's scary to decide this, right here, right now.

But I'm deciding it.

I'll have to defer my studies for another year, but at least they'll still be there when I get back (an added bonus is that Tom won't be in my classes anymore, but who gives a fuck about Tom).

And I won't be with my mom.

That's the worst thing. That's the only real thing that keeps me tied to Seattle. I don't want to let go of her. But the more I've been talking to my mom lately, the more I've realized that her dream wasn't just about me spreading my wings and learning to fly—it was about her. She's relied on me, and it was that reliance that made me rely on her. Now she's better. Slowly, but surely, she's becoming a better, more independent person.

I'll still have to call her and explain the truth and hope to God that she understands. If there's any tremor at all in her voice, the kind that tells me that her life will collapse without me there, then I'm getting on the first plane back.

But if that doesn't happen, if she's convinced she'll be fine on her own, and if she can bring herself not to worry too much about me, then I'll stay.

I have to say, my decision scares me.

But it's not just about our relationship—yes, I'm afraid of whether Olivier even wants me around (it wasn't what we agreed upon)—and about what it means to take it to the next level, to turn this from a vacation fling into a full-blown relationship.

But it scares me because . . .

His family scares me.

And Ludovic was the kind, smart, gentle soul holding everything that they are together.

Now he's gone, and the threads are going to start unraveling.

And like it or not, now I know that, somehow, I'm going to be tangled up in those very same threads.

It might not be pretty.

I'm slowly walking away from the gravesite with the crowd, lingering by the trees at the cemetery, when I feel a rush of a cold breeze pass over my arms and then hear, "There you are again." The voice comes from behind me, but I'm not even surprised.

A little scared but not surprised.

I stop and turn to face Pascal.

His face is stoic, no charming crooked smile, no coldness or heat in his eyes. It gives me nothing and prepares me for nothing.

"How did you recognize me without the mask?" I ask, and I'm grateful that my voice isn't shaking. I'm immediately taking on the power pose with him—chin up, shoulders squared, and just a hint of contempt in my eyes.

His lips twitch. "Who says you aren't wearing a mask right now?"

I can only stare at him, wanting him to lay out his cards, the reason for this conversation. His interest in me.

"I trust my driver got you to Bordeaux safely?" Pascal asks. "You are here in one piece, not in a body bag on the side of the road."

I purse my mouth briefly. "Yes, thank you for that. I don't know what I would have done otherwise."

"You could have spent a night in a castle. Wasn't that always the plan?"

My heart starts to climb up my throat. "Plan? I never knew the ball was also a sleepover."

"Sleepover. Oh, you Americans do have funny words for things. So what are you doing at the funeral?"

"Ludovic was a great man."

"You didn't know him."

"Did anyone here really know him?"

"Yes. I did. He was my uncle."

An uncle you didn't see eye to eye with, an uncle you seem so unmoved over.

"I just wanted to pay my respects," I say. "I should get going."

I turn, but he reaches out and grabs my wrist, his grip strong and hot.

"No. Don't. I think we have a lot to talk about."

"What?" I ask, subtly trying to get my wrist out of his grip but failing. His fingers only tighten, and I don't want to cause a scene.

"For one, I know you know who I am."

"Of course I do."

"No," he says softly and gives my hand a squeeze. "No, not like that. More than that. You've seen me around. Don't pretend."

"I'm not pretending," I say haughtily. "I've seen your face in the ads. I told you—that doesn't impress me, and the perfume smells like ass."

Another twitch of his lips. "You're trying to be funny again. Worked on me the first time, but I don't think it'll work the second time. Sadie Reynolds, the American. A student doing her communications degree at the University of Washington who is backpacking around Europe."

Holy. Shit.

Shit.

I breathe in deeply through my nose, trying to hide the fear that must be swimming in my eyes. "May I say, you seem very obsessed with me."

"I am," he says simply. "You're a very beautiful woman, and I love beautiful things. I like to collect them and possess them and have them. And I don't like to share. I'm just like my cousin. Just like Olivier."

He knows. But of course he knows. He wasn't stalking me for any other reason.

"It sounds like you might have some issues with your cousin," I tell him, and finally rip my hand out of his grasp. "I don't think your issues are with me."

I turn and try to get out of there, to get swallowed up by the crowd of mourners, but Pascal calls out after me so softly it's nearly carried away by the breeze. "That's what you don't understand. You are my issue now. The moment you decided to be with him was the biggest mistake you ever could have made."

I stop. I freeze. I can't move.

Is that some sort of threat?

I close my eyes and take a deep breath, but it goes in shakily and comes out in a tremor. I need to keep it together; I need to figure out what this all means.

A hand goes to my shoulder, and I jump, gasping, expecting to see Pascal.

But an older woman dressed in black is beside me and whispers something sympathetic in French and keeps walking.

I whip around to face Pascal.

But he's no longer there.

In fact, I don't see him at all.

Okay, it's over, you're safe, I tell myself. *Remember what Olivier said, and go meet him.*

I take another breath, gathering some courage, and head out to the big oak tree at the corner of the cemetery near the gates. Farther down the street, people have gathered on the road, getting into limos and town cars, and there are rows of cameras and film crews trying to pick up every moment of the funeral.

With shaking hands, I check my phone and see a text from Olivier.

Be right there, it says.

I find I can breathe a little easier, and it's not long before everyone in the family is filing out, along with the more important guests, and then Olivier steals away from the crowd and comes over to me.

Instinctively, I duck behind the tree.

"It doesn't matter," he says to me, his voice rough and broken. "Who cares what they record?"

The words are on the tip of my tongue, almost spilling out into the air:

I'm hiding from Pascal.

But I take one look at Olivier, and I know that Pascal is the least of his problems right now. In front of me is a broken man—eyes red, hair mussed, lips raw from chewing on them.

I put my arms around him and pull him into a hug. He's reluctant at first, and I know it's not because it's me, but because he wants to keep being strong, especially here.

But then he relents and collapses into me, and I think he might break down entirely if not for the fact that a hired car pulls up beside us and gives a light honk.

Olivier pauses and pulls back, then ushers me into the back seat of the car. Once there, he leans back, undoing his tie, holding both hands to his face.

"You did good," I tell him, knowing my words are feeble and mean nothing right now.

He shakes his head. "I should have said more." He breathes in and out, his chest rising with ragged breaths, and then his hands fall away from his face. His lost and pained eyes seek me out. "I could have done more."

"You did all you could. He would have been so proud. He is still so proud."

He stares out the window. "I can't even process this. I can't. I don't know what to do, you know?" Then he lapses into a string of mumbled French that I don't understand, but that I certainly feel.

"I know," I tell him, rubbing my hand on his leg, trying to comfort him. "It's okay. Everything you're feeling, it's okay."

"It's not okay. I don't want to feel it. I don't want to feel any of this. I just want to . . . turn it off. Like a tap. Make it stop. I want to be numb. I don't want to feel anything."

"You don't want that either," I tell him. "Trust me. That's the void. At first the void seems like the easiest place to be because you don't have to feel anything. No sadness. No pain. No grief. Sometimes anger, but it's not even real anger. It's weak. And then you no longer feel happiness or joy or creativity. Nothing."

"I wouldn't mind. I need that."

"You would mind. After a while there, you would mind. You feel nothing in the void, but because you stop feeling, you stop processing, and you stop . . . being. You know? We all need to feel, even the bad things. It's what makes us human. If you stay in the void for too long, you'll start questioning your humanity. If you're even a person. If you're even real. If you're even here. And when you start with those questions . . . then you're in too deep."

He stares at me, biting his lip for a moment before saying. "You talk as if you've been to this place."

"I have. And I got out. I just know it's not a place you want to be. But believe me, I'm going to do whatever I can to help you. To be here for you. You won't face any of this alone."

He grimaces and lets out a sharp sigh. "But I will. You won't be here. You're leaving in a day."

I shake my head, smiling just a little. "No, I'm not. I'm not going anywhere."

"What are you talking about?"

"I'm staying, Olivier. In Paris. With you. Even if you think it's too much and too soon, I can stay at a hostel for a while, maybe get work under the table. I mean, I think I'd have to."

"No," he says, flinching as if I'd slapped him.

Not exactly the reaction I'd hoped to get.

I swallow my burning pride and try to make him understand. "I don't want to leave you. Not now. And really, not ever. I can defer my studies to next year, it's not a big deal."

His eyes pinch shut, and now my cheeks are flaming with embarrassment.

"I know you're going through a lot, and I don't want to add to your problems," I say quickly. "I just want to stay with you."

He leans back in his seat, eyes focused on the ceiling. They're so wild and raw, and yet I can't read any of the millions of emotions that are rushing through them.

Eventually the words croak out, "You can't be here."

"Is it because of the whole Schengen visa? Because I can figure something out." But I know he's not talking about overstaying the visa.

"Please, you have to trust me on this."

I open my mouth to say okay and give him a free pass because he's grieving, but on the other hand . . . no. I'm tired of being hidden and being kept in the dark. He never even told me what his deal was on the night of the ball. So many secrets are being kept from me, all the time, from him, from Pascal.

"I can't trust you on it," I tell him. "Because I don't want to be lied to anymore. I want the truth. Why can't I stay? Why have you kept me hidden? What do your cousins want with me?"

He takes in a sharp inhale through his nose, eyes darting to the driver who is paying us no attention; then he leans in close to me. His eyes are dancing with hope and pain and fear, latching on to mine, and I can't look away.

"Sadie," he says, in a very deep, low voice, the kind that gives me goose bumps, "I want you to stay here with me." He takes my hand in both of his and squeezes it. "I do need you. More than you know. That isn't the issue at all. The issue is . . . something I've never told anyone. Something I'm deeply, deeply ashamed of."

This is a surprise. I squeeze his hand back. "You can tell me anything."

His expression becomes strained. "You'll think less of me."

"I won't. I wouldn't. Please, Olivier, I want to trust you, and I want you to trust me, but I can't, it can't happen until we're both honest. I'm being honest with you. I want to be with you because . . . I'm falling for you. In a bad way. And I can't handle the idea of just leaving you, leaving us and all that we have a chance of becoming."

He manages a small, sad smile and swallows. "I want to give us that chance too."

"Then tell me your truth, please."

He nods, his focus now on our intertwined hands. "When I was twenty years old, I made a foolish mistake."

"We all make mistakes when we're young. I think we'll make them when we're old too."

"Yes, well. This was . . . bad. I fell in love." I stiffen, not expecting that. "I fell in love with a woman who didn't belong to me. We had an affair. I . . . I wasn't thinking. She was older by five years, and she came on to me. She showed interest in me, and she made me feel special. And, of course, she was beautiful."

I should be jealous about the way he's talking about her, but there's no love in his words, just bitterness, like he has a bad taste in his mouth that he can't get rid of.

"But she wasn't mine. She was someone else's. She was Pascal's wife."

Oh. My. God.

This explains everything.

He glances at me anxiously, then looks away again. "Maybe I already hated Pascal, and I did it out of revenge. Our families had always been so at odds with each other growing up. Maybe I was just so taken with Marine and the way she came after me, doted on me, that it didn't matter that she was his wife. They'd only been together for a short time, and she seemed so lonely that I figured . . . maybe I was doing her a favor. I was a fucking fool."

"And Pascal knows," I say.

"What makes you say that?" He frowns.

Because of everything that's been happening.

"Because he must." I give a little shrug, not wanting to get into it right now.

He studies me for a moment, then sighs. "I think so. Yes, he must. We've never discussed it. It was his father who caught us. He promised he'd never tell Pascal, that was all part of the deal, but who knows. So much time has passed."

"What deal? You made a deal with your uncle?"

He closes his eyes. "Yes," he whispers, "I made a deal. Signed with blood."

"What was the deal? What did you agree to do? Isn't that blackmail?"

"Yes, it's blackmail. He's been blackmailing me for ten years, and he'll do it until the end of my life. Or, fuck, who knows now. I did it so that he'd never tell my father, and as far as I knew, he kept that end of the bargain. And now . . . my father is dead. Guess it doesn't matter."

"What was the deal, Olivier? What did you agree to?"

187

"I agreed to step aside from any company matters. I signed a contract that said in ten years I would have to relinquish all my shares of the company and give them to Gautier."

"But you just said all of this happened ten years ago."

He nods. "And so the deadline was just around the corner. And now . . ."

"Is that why you didn't want to have anything to do with the Dumont brand?"

"Ten years ago, I had to make a decision that I would go in a different direction. I was never going to go into hotels originally. I was going to have Seraphine's job, then my father's. It's what I wanted, it's what my father had wanted for me. It was expected, it was needed . . . and I had to step aside. It's been so long that I'm okay with it—I like being a hotelier, I like what I do, and I'm good at it. But I've never been able to tell my father, or anyone, that I didn't step aside because I didn't want it. I did it because I had to."

This is blowing my damn mind. "You've had to live this lie all this time?"

"All this time."

"And your fucking uncle. How dare he? How dare he blackmail his twenty-year-old nephew into doing that!" Suddenly I'm so full of rage I think I'm going to blow steam from my ears. That horrible man with the horrible eyes. "He could have lectured you, not threatened you, not extorted you."

"I went along with it. I would have done anything for him not to tell Pascal or my father. I was so ashamed. I know it would break this family, shattering it more than it already was. And . . . Gautier . . . he doesn't leave you a lot of choice. You understand? He's not like us."

"You've said that many times. Obviously, I see why."

"No, I mean," he says quickly, licking his lips as he positions himself closer to me, holding my hand tighter, "he's a dangerous man. Okay? He was then, and he's even more so now. He has friends in high places and low places. The mafia. Cartels. Russia. Who knows? You don't get to his level of success by playing it nice."

"But your father did."

"He did by working hard and sticking to his guns. Gautier has done nothing. He's only where he is because of who he was when he was born. My father was the oldest, the one primed for it. Gautier only took interest and was made cochairman because my father was too nice. Too loyal. Too trusting. And now . . ."

"Now?"

"Now Gautier will take over the company."

"What about Seraphine?" I ask.

He shakes his head slowly. "The deal was that I step aside. I was the final obstacle, and I was removed. There are wills and documents that will say that I am the next boss, that I am taking over my father's role. And I will have to publicly stand up and say that I am handing the keys to Gautier. There is no doubt that Pascal will then take over Gautier's role, and Blaise will take over Pascal's. Seraphine will stay where she is . . . if she's lucky."

"This is crazy. Olivier, you can't let them do this. You can't let them win."

"We all know what will happen if I don't."

"No one will care? You think Pascal doesn't know you slept with his ex-wife? He knows. You can tell. And as for Seraphine? Renaud? They're family. Your real family. The good ones. They won't care."

"It's not that easy."

"It is."

"You don't understand, it's not just about keeping all of this a secret in order to spare myself from shame. It's about power. I gave them power, and now it's too late. If I don't do this, there will be consequences. Dangerous ones. I told you who my uncle is connected to. Don't for a second think he won't retaliate. He knows about you, and

I know that he's going to go out of his way to make sure we're driven apart." He grows quiet. "Or worse."

My mouth drops open. "What?"

"That's what I couldn't tell you. You have a mark on your back, a target, and they're the ones holding the arrows."

"You can't be serious," I say but then trail off because again it's making sense. What Pascal said. It's not just that he's out for revenge, it's that he wants what Olivier supposedly took from him. If Olivier slept with Pascal's wife, then his uncle probably thinks he has a right to ruin our relationship the way that Olivier did his son's.

"I wish I wasn't, but that's what my uncle told me, and I have no reason not to believe him. Why do you think I've never settled down?"

"Uh, because you're young and hot and filthy rich. Why wouldn't you have a different model for a different day?"

"Because that's a stereotype that I play into. Because no one questions it. Because people expect it, even want it. But that's not me. Sadie, that isn't me at all."

"He can try to fuck with your relationship all he wants, but if it's a good one, it won't crumble just because he's gotten involved. What's he going to tell me? You're cheating on me? Is he going to set it up to have someone seduce you? Seduce me? Will there be staged photos leaked to the press? It doesn't matter. I'm yours, Olivier. They can't take that away from me."

"And I'm yours, Sadie. More than you know." He kisses me softly at the corner of my mouth, and suddenly I'm aching for this man, this broken and bruised man who not only lost his father but lost ten years of his life due to a lie he can't shake. "But they will try to break us apart. And when it doesn't work . . . I shudder to think what they might try next."

I refuse to even entertain that thought. "You say they. So you think Pascal knows."

"I'd never known for sure but . . . Okay, I'm sorry I didn't tell you this earlier, but I saw Pascal at the hotel in Cannes."

I blink at him, my heart sinking deeper. "He was there?"

"I ran into him in the lobby. He wouldn't tell me why he was there or how long he'd been there. I knew he just wanted to fuck with me. I didn't know why, since he's not someone I run into that often. I make fucking sure of that. But he was there, and . . . I had a feeling it may have had something to do with you."

"I never saw him," I say.

But that's not quite true, is it?

The man at the window.

That hadn't been an illusion. That had been him.

Tell him, my words cut across my head. *Tell him about Pascal. At the ball, now at the funeral. Tell him.*

But I can't. I will, but not right now. He's already dealing with too much. The fact that I know the truth is enough. Now I know what I'm facing, what and who I am up against.

It doesn't scare me, as long as I'm with him.

CHAPTER FIFTEEN

SADIE

Guilt is a tricky thing. Even when you have no reason to feel it, even when it has no purpose in your life, it finds a way to burrow into your heart, like a lost but determined worm. It just wants you to feel it, and once it's lodged in there, it's nearly impossible to get out.

Case in point: I've been warming up to calling my mother about the fact that I'm not getting on a plane out of Madrid today like I had planned. All this time, whatever guilt I felt about deferring my studies and not coming home was pushed to the side. I had more important and pressing things to focus on—basically, everything to do with Olivier. I felt good about the decision, strong on my feet.

But now that I've dialed her number and the phone is ringing, it's like guilt is punching me in the stomach with every single ring.

You're abandoning her.

She needs you.

You're selfish.

She's your mother.

I'm just about to hang up in panic when my mother finally answers.

"Hello?"

"Hey, it's me."

"Sadie? What's wrong? You never call me."

"Nothing is wrong," I say quickly, not wanting her mind to run away with her. "I'm good. Really. Did I catch you at a bad time?" It's so hard to know with her wonky work schedule and the time difference. It's the early evening here, which means it's the morning over there. Olivier stepped out to one of his hotels, so I figured this was a good time to call.

"No, I woke up a few hours ago. Been getting up with the sunrise. Always getting those extra hours before everything turns dark here in the Pacific Northwest. I really do think sunshine is medicine for the soul."

Well, at least my mother sounds far more positive than I expected.

"So why are you calling, darling? What's really going on?"

I take a deep breath through my nose and steady myself. Why is it that mothers are so strangely terrifying sometimes?

"I have some news."

"You decided to stay."

"What? How did you know that?"

She sighs. "Oh, a mother knows. She has feelings. She has a connection. She has dreams. And you were supposed to be on your flight a few hours ago, so . . ."

"Right. Well then, yeah. That's the news. I've decided to stay in France."

"You're not even in Spain?"

"I never made it to Spain," I say quietly.

"Okay. Who is he?"

"Wow, you are on a roll today."

"I'm telling you, the sunshine sharpens my brain. So tell me who he is. I know you're not skipping school on account of just wanting more time to lie around in the sun. That's not like you. That's not my daughter. You wouldn't even think about staying if there wasn't someone else involved, and I'm going to just assume it's a man—though if it's not, no judgment here."

I laugh and look around Olivier's apartment, so happy that I can finally share the truth of where I am and who I'm with.

Who has my heart.

"It's definitely a man. His name is Olivier. He's French."

"Is he nice?"

"He is very nice. An old-school gentleman. You would really like him."

"And so you're with him where?"

"In Paris. In his apartment."

"I see. And what does this Olivier do?"

"He owns hotels."

A long pause over the line. My mother is obviously in shock. "Come again?"

"I said he owns hotels."

"And he's not lying to you?"

I chuckle. "No, he's not lying. I've been in them. He's the real deal."

"Olivier what? What's his last name?"

I hesitate to give it because of all the news around him lately, and there's no doubt that she's going to immediately Google him. "It's Dumont."

"Dumont . . . Dumont," she muses. "Wait, I know that name. It's like Chanel but for French people."

"Mom, Chanel is French."

"Yeah, but I mean, Chanel is everywhere, and Dumont, that's just in France."

"Well, they're everywhere too," I say. At least they will be after Gautier is done with them. "But, yeah, it's mainly known here in Europe, and also the Middle East, Singapore, Japan, China . . ."

"You sound like you work for them now . . . Is he going to get you a job?"

"Uh . . ." I mean, it had crossed my mind, until I realized I would be working for his evil uncle, the very person I'm supposed to avoid, but I don't feel right telling my mom that Olivier is my sugar daddy either. "Maybe. I might just get a job at a bookstore or something. Under the table, but I think Olivier can pull some strings."

"Bookstore? Darling, he's a hotelier. Work at one of his hotels."

"I'm sure something will work out," I reassure her. "So you're not mad that I'm staying?"

"Mad? Not at all."

"But I'm still throwing away a year of school for a guy I've only known three weeks. And I'm abandoning you."

"Listen," she says rather sharply, "we both know what it's like to be abandoned, and this isn't it. This is just you being a twenty-three-year-old student. Some do all their years in one go. Others quit. Others go back to it. What can you expect? You're young and you're discovering who you are and you've fallen in love."

"I didn't say I love him," I tell her quietly.

"Oh, come on. You do. I can tell. You wouldn't be doing this if you didn't."

"I barely know him."

"You know him far more than you think you do. Sadie, dear, embrace it. Don't worry about school, and certainly don't worry about me. I'll be fine. In fact, I've been doing great. I started going to that free counseling again, and I've made some friends at work. I think you going to Europe was the push I needed, and I think you needed it too."

Tears spring to my eyes, teasing at the corners. "I miss you."

"I miss you, too, and I'll always miss you, but you need to do this. You're a good kid, Sadie, and you're smart, and you just have to trust yourself. I trust you."

I'm about to turn into a blubbering mess when suddenly there's a knock at the door.

"Uh, hold on, Mom, there's someone at the door," I tell her, and my heart is starting to race, the hair on my arms standing straight up.

"I better let you go then—"

"No," I say sharply. "No, no, it's okay. It might be Olivier. Maybe he forgot his key."

Please let it be Olivier, please let it be Olivier.

I go to the door and look through the peephole, fully expecting to see Pascal standing there. If I let my imagination run away any further, he'll be holding a gun.

But it's not Pascal.

It's not Olivier either.

It's Seraphine.

Oh shit.

"Uh, Mom," I say into the phone, "I've got to go. I love you, and I'll call you tomorrow."

"I love you too."

I hang up and then try to come up with some sort of story as I'm opening the door.

But the moment Seraphine looks me up and down, the story goes out the window.

I wasn't kidding when I said Seraphine was gorgeous.

She's tall, like nearly six feet, with long limbs and thick, lush hair and the biggest, most beguiling eyes. If I hadn't known she'd been adopted by the Dumonts, I would now, since they're all very white and French, and she's of Indian or Pakistani descent, her accent a mix of Parisian and posh British.

"Who are you?" she says to me, brushing her heavy bangs out of her eyes.

Again, someone addressing me in English.

"How did you know I speak English?" I ask her.

She eyes me up and down. "Well, you certainly don't look French. Is Olivier here?"

I shake my head. "He went out to the office."

She sighs. "I was just there."

"Not . . . that office. A hotel." It's then that I notice underneath her thick eyelashes and the bright-red lipstick, she looks ashen and worn. The poor girl. "I'm so sorry about your father."

Her lip quivers, and she nods. "Thank you." She tilts her head. "You were at the funeral. I saw you."

"Just wanted to pay my respects." I step back and gesture to the apartment. "He might be back soon. Do you want to come in? I know how to use the espresso machine now and wouldn't mind the extra practice."

She stares at me for a moment, looking lost, then she manages a smile. "Okay. *Merci.*"

She steps inside and closes the door behind her, and I go over to the espresso machine to try to tame the beast. It's a bit awkward and nerve-racking to have her here, especially when I don't know what to say about myself, but at least she's got a rather gentle, calming way about her.

"What's your name?" she asks me, walking slowly around the room and poking at Olivier's stuff.

"It's Sadie," I tell her.

"Sadie what?"

"Sadie Nobody Important." She stops and stares at me, and I fiddle with the machine. "Sadie Reynolds."

"I saw your name on the invites for the ball."

"Yeah."

And then she stops at the feathered white mask hanging off one of the shelves. "And you were there. Wearing this."

"That was me," I say brightly.

"I see," she muses and then comes over to the kitchen island, leaning against it, her bright-gold bracelets jingling against the marble. "You're the girl."

"The girl?"

"Yes. The girl I've been badgering Olivier about. The secret one, the one he's been denying exists. You're that girl."

"Well, I hope you're right, or else I need to have a talk with him."

She lets out a weak laugh. "Yes, well. I have to say, it's a relief to know that I'm right. I just don't understand why he would hide you."

I freeze, and she quickly goes on. "Not to say there is anything to hide. I'm just not used to his denial, which is why I was suspicious anyway. Normally, if I ask about a girl, he'll tell me. They never last long. Oh shit, I am making things worse, aren't I?"

"You're not," I assure her as I get the machine going with a noisy clang. "Olivier had his reasons."

"What?" she yells over the noise.

I motion for her to wait a moment, and then I finally get the espresso pouring out perfectly, with a light coating of crema on top, just like Olivier taught me.

"Here you go," I tell her, placing the cup in front of her.

She picks it up daintily. "Impressive. So what were you saying about reasons?"

"Just that Olivier had his." I wonder how much to tell her and then realize it's not my place to tell her any of it. She can't know, or else she'll see how it all started in the first place. "I think he just wanted to know if we had a sure thing before the paparazzi got wind of us."

"And are you a sure thing?"

I shrug. "I'm not going anywhere. In fact, I just missed my flight back home a few hours ago."

"So that sounds serious," she says, taking a sip. "This is very good. I have a feeling you'll be a bona fide Parisian in no time."

I laugh. "I have to learn French first. You know, we weren't properly introduced."

She sighs. "I know, how dreadful are my manners, just assuming everyone knows who I am? I'm Seraphine."

"It's nice to finally meet you. I've only heard nice things from Olivier."

"Olivier says nice things about everyone, I wouldn't read too much into it."

"He's a lot like your father."

Her eyes grow noticeably teary, and she swallows loudly. "Yes, he is. I just . . . I don't understand why Olivier is doing this."

"Doing what?" I ask cautiously.

"You've seen the papers. It's everywhere," she cries out softly, looking both confused and disgusted. "He's stepped aside. I mean, all this time he wanted as little to do with the company as possible, but we still thought—we still assumed that if it came to it, if father ever . . . died, that Olivier would take over. Out of love for our father, out of duty. But he's just . . . he's giving it up. Right into their fucking hands. It's going to ruin everything."

"It's not his fault," I tell her. I'm so automatically defensive over him that it takes me a moment to correct myself. "I'm sure he thinks your uncle would do a better job."

Her nostrils flare. "My uncle. Oh, Olivier knows he won't. He knows it. We all do. This is what my uncle wanted from the start. Now with everyone taking over . . . I don't even know if I'll have a job left. But that's not even the point . . . this was all planned."

"Planned?"

She finishes her espresso and pushes her bangs out of her face. "I don't know. I'm upset. I'm not thinking right, I know this. And I'm so angry, I want someone to blame. I want to blame Olivier because it would be so easy for him to save us all, but he won't, and that's not like him at all." She pauses and glances up at me, brows knit together. "Has he said anything to you?"

I try to keep my face blank. "About what?"

"About . . . Oh, this will sound ridiculous, keep that in mind, everything is so fucking ridiculous right now." She taps her red nails along the table. "My father was in perfect health. He'd never had any health issues, let alone heart issues. He'd just had an annual checkup. And yet he had a heart attack, just like that, in front of everyone, and he just . . . I saw him, he was dead. So fast, it happened so fast, he was . . . gone. It didn't seem right."

"Death never seems right," I offer feebly.

"It's not that," she says with a shake of her head. "I don't know, maybe it is that. They ruled it as a heart attack right away, they didn't question it. No one did. But I guess I do, and I wonder if Olivier does too."

"But . . . ," I say slowly, not wanting to overturn this rock, knowing what could be crawling underneath, "if it wasn't a heart attack . . . what was it? Aneurysm?"

"No. If it wasn't a heart attack . . . then I think maybe someone murdered him."

I stare at her, dumbfounded. "M-murder?" I repeat.

And yet the moment the word awkwardly leaves my mouth, there feels like truth to it.

Of course, murder.

How very fucking obvious who would have done it and why.

"I know it sounds . . . dumb," she says with a nervous laugh. "Oh, it sounds so dumb just to say it, and I'm saying it to you, and I don't even know you. But . . . I can't help but feel that, deep inside me, that this whole thing was planned to get my father out of the picture, to make Gautier the head of the company, to give them all the control. To run our traditions and everything we've bled over into the ground."

"So you think your uncle murdered his own brother?"

She shrugs. "I don't know. Gautier is a horrible person, but I can't really imagine him murdering his own brother. It seems too ghastly."

"What about your aunt? His wife?"

"Camille? Oh, she's a witch. But as nasty as she is, she's not ambitious or conniving enough. To be honest, she lacks the brains."

"So then it would be someone who would benefit . . . your cousins."

Her lips press hard against each other, and she seems to wrestle with what she's about to say. "That's the only thing I can think of. And I don't want to."

"Would it be Pascal or Blaise?"

"You know so much about them."

"I know a lot by now."

She sighs. "You know what? I shouldn't even talk about it at all. I mean, it's ghoulish. It's fucked-up. I'm essentially accusing a family member of murder, and that's not a thing that's taken lightly. Forget I said anything." She gets out of her seat.

"You're leaving?" I ask her. "You can't just come here and bring up murder and then leave. Jesus."

She gives me a tight smile. "I've said too much, and I've burdened you with problems that aren't yours."

"But they're your problems. Therefore, they're Olivier's problems. Therefore, they're my problems."

She raises a brow at me as she heads to the door. "You're very sweet, you know that? I think you might be a little too sweet for this family."

"But you're from the good side," I say to her as she opens the door.

She steps out into the hall and glances at me. "Good side, bad side. Sooner or later we're all going to bleed into each other. And who knows what side will remain." She gives me a short wave. "Tell Olivier I stopped by. Please tell him to call me. I need him now more than he knows."

I nod. "I promise."

And then she's out the door, and I'm left alone again in Olivier's apartment with an even bigger bombshell in my hands. I feel like if I put it down for one minute, it might just blow the whole apartment away.

Murder.

Is that really what happened?

When I saw Pascal, Gautier, and Ludovic leaving the study the night of the ball, right before Pascal came to talk to me, had Ludovic been given something by one of them? By both of them?

Did I witness a murder?

Or is everyone so desperate to find someone and something to blame, they'll go for the easiest scapegoat?

A shiver runs through me, and I head right over to the door, sliding the chain across and locking the dead bolt.

◆ ◆ ◆

I'm already in bed when Olivier gets home. It's not even that late. It's just that after Seraphine left, I felt that bed was the safest and most comforting place to be.

And let's be honest—I'm exhausted.

Even ignoring all the talk of murder, which left me extremely on edge, my brain is finally processing what is really going on.

I missed my flight.

I'm officially staying here.

This is it.

I'm in it for the long run.

In a foreign country, where I don't know the language, where my bank account is quickly approaching the negatives, I am here to stay.

Completely relying on Olivier, when in fact he's the one who needs to rely on me. He needs someone to help shoulder the burden, so I'm shouldering his while dealing with my own shit.

So yeah, exhausted enough to curl up beneath the covers and sleep.

Olivier seems just as exhausted as I feel, probably even more so.

He stops at the foot of the bed, the light from the hall illuminating him from behind as he starts to undress. *"Désolé,"* he whispers, his voice sounding gruff. "I didn't mean to wake you. I thought you would still be up."

"I'm tired."

"You aren't alone," he says, pulling back the covers and sliding in beside me. Naked, as he usually is at bedtime.

I don't read much into it. We haven't had sex since before the ball. It hasn't been on my mind, and I can guarantee it hasn't been on his.

He sighs and sinks back into the pillow, his eyes closed.

"How was work?" I ask softly.

He shakes his head slightly. "I don't know."

"You don't know? Isn't that what you went to do?"

"Yes, I was there, and things were said, but I don't remember any of it. I probably should have stayed here with you."

"You would have seen your sister."

He opens his eyes and fixes them on me, his hair mussed, forehead creased. "What do you mean? My sister was here?"

"You seem as surprised as I was. She dropped by looking for you. She needs to talk to you in a bad way."

"What about?"

Really?

"What about?" I repeat. "How about everything? She's your sister, Olivier, and you've just thrown her under the bus."

His eyes flash at me. "Thrown her under the bus."

"It's a saying—"

"Yes, I know what it means," he snaps. "I haven't . . . You know why I had to do what I've done."

"I know, but she doesn't. She doesn't understand. Says it's not like you."

"I'm doing what I need to do. I have no choice," he grinds out. "You're supposed to support me in this, I don't have anyone else who knows the truth."

"I do support you, but I just want you to know how the rest of the family is taking it. She's afraid she's going to lose her job."

"She won't," he says. "Gautier doesn't hate her the way that he hates me. She's useful, more so than his sons. He'll keep her around. Is that all you talked about? Didn't she wonder who you were?"

"She said that I was *the* girl."

He grunts in response.

"And," I go on, "she has a theory, and it's why you need to talk to her, because even I have a hard time telling you."

"Tell me what? What's the theory? Theory about what?"

He looks so pained already that I think telling him will only hurt.

"You'd better ask her yourself. She needs to talk with you, not through me."

He sighs and settles back into the bed. "Okay, I will go see her tomorrow."

"Promise me," I tell him, holding out my pinkie finger.

He stares at it. "What are you doing?"

"Tell me you have pinkie swears here in France."

"Children do . . ."

"Just touch your pinkie with mine."

Finally, a smile cracks on his face, and for a moment I see the old Olivier. "Touching pinkies. I don't know if I'm ready for that."

I laugh and reach over, wrapping my pinkie around his. "I'm serious. Now it's official. Promise me you'll talk to your sister."

"Don't mention my sister when I'm thinking about the dirty things I want to do to you."

I blush. "Dirty things! You got that from a pinkie swear?"

He shrugs lazily. "You must admit, there is something sexual about it."

I shake my head. "I'm admitting nothing." But I'm still giggling.

He brings my pinkie to his mouth and slowly sucks on it, his tongue warm and wet, immediately sending shivers down my back. I manage to swallow. Okay, so I'm never looking at a pinkie swear the same way again.

Olivier slowly pulls my finger out of his mouth, and all the thoughts leave my brain. He grips it tightly in his hand, another hand cupping my chin.

"I never told you how grateful I am that you stayed," he says to me, his tone soft and rough all at once. "Never told you how much it means to me that you're here. That you're really here."

"I'm here," I whisper, kissing him softly on the tip of his nose. "I'm here."

"I was so scared when I came back, I thought maybe for a moment you would be gone. I imagined what that would be like, to come in and see your backpack missing and the bed empty, like you decided to catch your plane after all. And I was paralyzed from the fear. I couldn't breathe, I couldn't move. It was like my heart stopped, and that's when I knew that my heart no longer belonged to me. My heart belongs to you."

Oh, damn. There's a nest of hummingbirds inside my chest, just taking flight for the very first time. I'm almost afraid of what he may say next, afraid because to say it is to feel it, and what if the feeling is too big for my soul to contain?

"Sadie, *mon lapin, je t'aime,* I love you," he says. "I love you so very much that I don't even know if you can feel it from these words, because there are no words really to explain it."

He loves me.

I love him.

"I love you," I whisper. "You don't have to explain it. I know it. I know it like I know your heartbeat. I know it like I know the breath you take, the world you see. Since the beginning, I thought I was crazy to feel the way I felt about you."

"And how did you feel about me, *ma chérie?*" he whispers, his hands disappearing into my hair.

"Like . . . there was something deep inside me that saw something familiar deep inside you. Like my very being recognized yours, and like your cells and my cells were almost the same." I look away, grateful for my hair falling over my face. "It sounds so stupid to say it out loud, but it made sense before."

"It makes sense," he says roughly, pulling my chin up to meet his gaze. His eyes are so deep and rich and burning, I can't look away. "You've always made sense to me."

He kisses me with more passion than I've ever felt before, the kind that steals your breath, ignites your heart, makes your body and soul burst into flames.

He kisses me and kisses me, and all I feel are his lips and tongue and heart. I feel his heart, I feel his love.

I feel how fucking hard he is.

I grin as he moves back down the bed, and his head goes lower, licking down the center of my stomach until he gets between my legs. He loves to take his time there, and usually I have no complaints, but now, with my heart brimming with my love for him, our love for each other, I want him inside me.

He kisses and nibbles down the V of my hip bones; then he slides his long, wet tongue along where my legs and pelvis meet. The skin there is so sensitive I nearly cry out as he gently laps at it, teasing up the sides, coming close to my clit and then backing away.

"Please," I can't help but moan, "come inside me, Olivier."

He ignores me. His tongue snakes along my clit, and I suck in a sharp breath, trying to compose myself. I'm seconds from coming, and he knows this. He just wants me to come any way possible, and I suppose since we haven't been with each other like this in a while, I might as well take everything he's offering.

He works me fast, his tongue flicking rapidly and so hard as I swell beneath him, the pressure in my core building and building, hotter and hotter.

Then he withdraws, and I'm left gasping for him.

Bereft.

Desperate.

"You better get your cock inside me or your tongue back down there, or there will be hell to pay," I tell him.

He grins at me, cocky as all get-out. He knows he's got me panting for him.

"Have I told you how much I love it when you beg?"

"Yes, you have," I say pointedly, full of impatience.

He straddles me with his heavy thighs, and I feel himself position the hard tip of his dick onto me. With slow ease, he pushes himself inside as I widen around him, my body needing him, craving him. In seconds he's in to the hilt; he's a part of me, and I don't think I've ever felt so beautifully stretched before.

"Sadie," he groans as he pulls himself out and thrusts in again, his rigid length dragging along all the right spots. "You feel so good. So beautiful. You save me, you know? All the time. You make everything around me easier to bear."

My heart skips three beats at once at this admission.

That's all I want.

I just want to make him happy.

Loved.

Then I gasp as he drives in harder and then pulls out, achingly slow for a few beats before he starts pumping into me faster, and I reach up for his ass, digging my nails in and shoving him in deeper.

The moan that comes out of his lips is the most erotic sound I've ever heard.

Sweat drips from his body onto mine, and I'm surprised I'm not sizzling from the heat. He slips his hand down, making a fist over the base of his cock as it slides into me, and in his breathless, low voice, he tells me how good I feel, how he doesn't want this to ever end.

He tells me how much he loves me.

My heart responds in kind, swelling over his words while the rest of me burns for his body.

His fingers then slide over my clit, in rhythm with his merciless thrusts.

And that's it.

I come, moaning loudly, calling out his name as starbursts form behind my eyes and my body explodes in a hot wash of nerves, like bubbling champagne. I'm writhing, bucking, floating into pure bliss, out of this bed and into the stars.

He's coming too, groaning my name as the bed shakes, and he comes inside me. I'm so glad we decided to get tested because having him fill me up like this, feeling his come hot inside me, is more intimate than anything else.

Eventually we regain our breath, and the room stops spinning.

But my heart won't stop spinning for him.

It's his now.

CHAPTER SIXTEEN

Olivier

It's taken ten years to actually know what it's like to fall in love.

Perhaps that's normal.

Perhaps it's not.

All I know is that when I thought I loved Marine, I was just in love with the intrigue, the forbidden, the adoration, and, of course, the sex.

When I first met Sadie, I expected it to be more or less the same thing.

I was ready for it.

Yes, she was different, but more than that, she made me feel different. But I didn't know what it meant, what it could mean. I always thought in the back of my mind that no matter how passionate our lovemaking was, that's where it would stay. In the bedroom. And when it was her time to go, I would be prepared and ready. That she would fly away, and I would chalk it all up to an American girl I knew once.

But that wasn't the case at all. By the time I invited her up to Paris, I knew I had it bad for her. That I was in deep, like it was a place I couldn't escape, and if I did, I would be on my hands and knees.

That's where I am now.

On my hands and knees.

My heart belonging to her.

I wouldn't have it any other way.

I was so wrong about love, so quick to avoid it, so effortless in passing it off.

But that was never the true me.

Only with Sadie have I finally felt my mask slip away and the shackles falling off my feet, no longer tying me to the person the world needs me to be.

Just the person that I need myself to be.

The person she needs me to be.

I love her, and that has changed my whole world at a time when my whole world has just changed.

It makes me realize the lengths I will go to protect us, to keep her safe.

I don't want to go to the office today. I don't care a bit about the heat or the traffic or even the reporters who are more on my trail these days because of my father's death and the recent announcements in the company. None of that really matters now.

I just don't want to be away from her.

And yet she made me promise to see Seraphine, and I do love my sister. I've felt nothing but guilt at the position I've put her in, knowing I'm lying to her, knowing she doesn't understand. She thinks I've turned on her. She thinks I've become one of *them*.

When I get to the office, narrowly missing a downpour, I'm surprised to see that everything looks exactly the same. I would have thought that when Gautier finally got his bloody hands on it, he would have changed buildings, changed logos, changed staff.

But when I walk inside, all the familiar faces are there: Nadia the receptionist and a bunch of people who work for marketing and sales and the different departments. There are some people who look new, but in a company like this, it's always growing.

I do have to say that the vibe has changed.

Though it may still be a mixture of white and black and glass, all the calm elegance is gone. It seems tainted somehow, like if I looked closely enough, I'd see shit smeared in the grooves.

"I'm here to see my sister," I say to Nadia, watching her carefully. Though they're always overlooked, the receptionists are often the backbone of the company, the skeleton off which everything else hangs.

Nadia's eyes seem to swell with relief when she looks up at me.

That is not a good sign.

I should never be anyone's relief.

"I'm so glad to see you," she says to me quietly, her smile wavering. "When I heard the news . . ."

"The good news, you mean?"

My uncle's voice booms across the office, rich as a barrel of tar.

I meet Nadia's eyes for a second, and there's a flash of pure fear in them. Fear that she'll lose her job for no reason, fear that there's worse.

I try to convey that everything will be all right.

But I can no longer make promises.

I've handed this man the reins.

I turn to face my uncle and offer up the fakest smile I can muster.

"Uncle," I say to him.

My uncle isn't an ugly man. In many ways he resembles my father—not as tall, but still of athletic stature. His chin is more pronounced, enough that I think it bothers him, but his hair is thick and dark, black as night, with only the tiniest wisps of gray at the temples, and I don't think he's ever touched a box of dye.

His widow's peak is commanding, and his brows are even more so: sharp, like they're painted into perfect arches with thick strokes of permanent marker. It's a long face, an odd face, yet beguiling and charming all at once.

If you don't know him, that is.

I know him, and I see right through the charm, and I see right through the cold, fathomless depths of his eyes, and I know this man is

211

everything that's rotten in the world, and it disgusts me that the same blood that's in his veins working its way to his heart like black sludge is the blood that's in mine.

I hate that I'm looking at his face right now.

I should be looking at my father.

It takes everything inside me to keep from breaking down right here.

"Olivier, I didn't expect you to be here," he says, and his tongue is sharp, his words honed like razor blades. He thinks I'm here to fuck shit up, I'm sure.

"I'm just getting Seraphine," I tell him. I don't have to tell him any more. He isn't owed it.

"I see," he says. "She's a wonderful girl, isn't she?"

"Your niece? Yes, and she's going through a lot at the moment."

"Aren't we all?" he asks smoothly, with a hint of a smile that doesn't reach his eyes.

"I am, yes," I say. I make a move to pass him. "Now if you'll excuse me."

But he steps in my way, blocking my exit. I glance up at him, trying to control my breath, my fists curling.

"Are you sure you have a right to be here, Olivier?" he asks, his voice so low now that I don't even think Nadia can hear him. "Perhaps you need to be reminded of your place . . . the place you exited."

My jaw clenches, teeth grinding until they hurt. "I'm aware of my place. But we are still family, aren't we?"

His stare doesn't falter. "We are."

"Then I'm just going to see my sister."

I don't know why the fuck he's so suspicious of my seeing her. He should know that I'm not about to back out of the agreement. He should know.

And maybe that finally lights up in his head, because he nods and steps aside.

"Of course." He gestures for me to continue.

I walk as confidently and quickly as I can down the hall to Seraphine's office, my heart pinching at the sight of my father's still-empty one, and I don't even knock on her door. I barge right in.

She's not alone.

Blaise is there. He's sitting at her desk. She's standing up and looks about ready to throw a cup of water at him.

"Did I come at the wrong time?" I ask, pausing in the doorway. "Or the right time?"

Both of them glare at me in unison.

"Shut the door." Seraphine sneers.

I raise my brows but do what she says. I shouldn't be surprised these two are at it like this; without my father as a mediator, they have no boundaries. And Gautier couldn't care less—in fact, he probably sent his son in here to antagonize her. He wants them to eat each other alive.

"What's going on?" I ask, folding my arms.

"Your sister is fucking crazy," Blaise says. His collected demeanor has dissolved for once, his eyes wild as they dart from her to me.

"I won't argue with that," I say. "Seraphine?"

"He knows," she says, pointing her finger at him. "He knows what happened."

"What happened?" I ask carefully. I feel like I've stepped right into a bullring, and I'm not sure who's winning or what the outcome of the game is supposed to be.

"I don't even want to repeat it," Blaise mutters, shaking his head. But for all the ways he's dismissing her, whatever she said has rattled him. The tops of his hands are sweating, and his hair is slightly disheveled from his hand constantly combing through it, something he does when he's nervous. Aside from when he loses his temper and blasts off like a rocket, obliterating everyone around him with the most vicious insults, he's usually as cool as a cucumber.

"We should probably go for coffee," I tell Seraphine, wanting to get her out of this office. "Or a drink. Several drinks."

"We aren't going anywhere without him," she says.

"Why are we his babysitters?"

"We're not done talking," she says in a deliberate staccato, leaning in close to Blaise.

I run my hand down my face, not understanding any of this and knowing it won't become clear anytime soon.

"This office is probably bugged," she says to me, as if that was something obvious. She kicks the leg of Blaise's chair. "Isn't that right?"

Blaise folds his arms and looks away, not saying anything.

"Okay, well, I'm going to turn around and go," I say, "because, believe me, this office is the last place on earth I want to be. If you want to come meet me for a drink and talk, that's fine, but I'm not standing around here getting tangled in whatever game you guys are always playing."

"Father was murdered," Seraphine says in a low voice.

I almost laugh, but her tone was so stone-cold serious that it made my stomach feel like ice. I turn to face her, and that same severity is in her eyes. She's not joking.

Which makes things more difficult.

"What?" I manage to say. "What are you . . . Come on. Don't go down this road."

"That's what I said," Blaise says quietly.

"Shut the fuck up." She sneers at him. "You're the one behind it all."

His head jerks back, and he stares at her with pure animosity. "Do you honestly believe that? That I murdered your father? My uncle? That I would do that to you?"

Do that to you? That's an interesting way of putting it, as if the two of them are supposed to matter to each other.

I shake my head. The whole thing . . . I can't even entertain the thought.

"Seraphine," I say slowly, stepping toward her with my hands out like I'm about to trap an injured dog, "please, what are you talking about?"

"Why should I even tell you? You're acting like I'm already crazy."

"Because you are fucking crazy," Blaise says.

"Fuck you!" Seraphine yells, and then lunges at him with her fist. He's fast enough that he catches it in his grip and holds it tight.

"Hey, hey, hey!" I yell, coming around the desk and placing myself between them. "Jesus fucking Christ, what the hell is going on here?"

There's a knock at the door, and we all freeze.

The door opens silently, and we all hold our breaths. Only one person barges in here without announcing himself. Well, one person other than me.

It's Gautier, eyeing us all warily. "Is everything all right in here?"

I clear my throat. "Just a sibling quarrel," I say at the same time Seraphine says, "Work stuff."

"Do you know where Pascal is?" Blaise asks tiredly. "He was supposed to be in today."

Gautier gives an ever so imperceptible shrug. "I don't know. Not here."

"Okay, great," Blaise says sarcastically, waving his father away. "We're good, thanks for checking in."

Gautier stares at us all for a moment, and then the door slowly closes.

"What the fuck is going on?" I ask them after a moment. "Tell me what you're nearly fist-fighting over, and I'll be on my way."

"I told you," she snaps. "But now I really don't trust talking about it here." She grabs her purse from the back of her chair. "Come on. Blaise, you're coming with us too. I'm not done with you."

"Why, so you can torture me somewhere?"

To my surprise, Blaise actually gets up and follows Seraphine out the door, with me coming up behind them.

Gautier isn't anywhere to be seen, which I take as a good sign. I'm sure he already thinks Blaise is fraternizing with the enemy, or perhaps he was sent in as a spy.

And then there's this talk about . . . murder?

He wasn't murdered.

He had a heart attack.

I saw it happen right in front of my fucking eyes.

Seraphine only came over after he was already dead.

The image is burned into my memory, and I'm so lost in it I barely hear Seraphine asking me if I'm okay.

I nod, trying to bring my mind back to the here and now, even if it's not much better.

The rain has let up to a soft drizzle as Seraphine leads us outside to her car—a small burgundy Fiat—and then unlocks the doors.

I'm about to sit in the front seat as I usually do when Seraphine says, "You're in the back, Olivier."

Blaise passes by me and opens the door, avoiding my eyes.

Maybe he wasn't too far off with that whole torture thing.

With a sigh I resign myself to the back seat and buckle in, completely confused and wishing I hadn't promised Sadie I'd come here to talk to Seraphine today. My goal was to avoid these offices for as long as I lived. Without my father here, and with Gautier in charge, I'm just making things worse.

"In the future, you're meeting me at a café," I tell Seraphine as she swings the car onto Avenue Charles de Gaulle, heading toward La Défense. "Where are you taking us, anyway?"

She doesn't answer. Her hands just grip the wheel harder.

"Seraphine?" I say. "I don't even think you should be driving right now."

"It's fine," she says quietly, and I meet Blaise's eyes in the rearview mirror. He still looks a little shaken, which makes me wonder exactly what they were talking about before I arrived.

"So does someone want to explain why you were talking about murder?" My face scrunches up as I say that. I can't even fathom it. I feel like we're betraying our father just by saying the word.

"Why don't you ask Blaise?" Seraphine says. "He's the one who knew all about it."

"Oh, shut the fuck up," Blaise says. "Do you even know how insulting that is?"

"Why would Blaise murder our father?"

"I didn't murder anyone."

"I agree," I tell him. "And you need to stop using that word. Look, I know you're upset and looking to blame someone, Seraphine, but this isn't the answer. Father had a heart attack. I saw it happen."

"You saw him die. He was poisoned. Heart attacks don't work like that."

"Actually, I think they do."

"He was in perfect health. He just had his checkup the week before. He's never had high blood pressure or heart disease or cholesterol or anything like that. Why on earth would he just—no, it doesn't make sense. Someone poisoned him that night."

"And you think it was Blaise?" This is getting more and more ridiculous.

"No," she says. "Maybe. Yes. I think Blaise at least knows."

"I'm not even going to talk about this with you," he says, crossing his arms and staring out the window.

"Fine, I'll talk about it with Olivier," she says, eyeing me. "I know this sounds crazy to you, but it's something I feel and believe, right in my heart. Don't you feel that something was so wrong about that ball? About the way the company merged? How easy it all was once father was out of the picture? Everyone benefited."

"Except for Olivier," Blaise says quietly.

"Right," Seraphine says as she eyes me intently, "except for you. And me. And Renaud. But you look at Blaise and Pascal and Gautier, and they all moved up and over and now have complete control. If I wasn't in the picture, they'd have everything."

"You'll stay in the picture if you do your job right," Blaise says, but even as he says it, he looks uncomfortable.

Seraphine takes a left turn just as the light turns red, the Fiat skidding slightly on the wet roads, pulling onto the D1 and racing along the Seine, parks and tennis courts whizzing past us.

"What are you doing?" I ask her. "You just ran a red light."

"I thought I was being followed," she says.

"Followed?"

Oh, now my sister has really lost it. Even Blaise looks over his shoulder at me, brows raised, as if to say we're screwed.

"Yes," she says tersely, paying constant attention to the cars behind her. "It was a black Land Rover with Polish plates. It followed us all the way from the office."

"Which wasn't very far."

"It looked like it waited to pull out only when we did. I noticed the driver. Bald, with glasses. Watching me."

"Honestly, Seraphine," I say to her, leaning forward and putting my hand on her shoulder, "I'm just looking out for you as your brother. But you need to drive yourself home. Blaise and I will find our own way back. First this talk about father being murdered; now you think we're being followed. I hate to—"

"Look out!" Blaise yells, and I whip my head around to see a black SUV come barreling out of a side road by a polo field, heading across the lane of oncoming traffic right toward us.

Seraphine has the reflexes of a cat. She yanks the car into the far lane and steps on the gas at the same time, the car hydroplaning on the wet road before correcting itself.

I fall back into the seat and manage to turn around in time to see the Land Rover right on our ass and getting closer.

"What the fuck!" I yell.

"That's him!" she yells.

"Fucking hell," says Blaise. "Who the fuck is that? What does he want?"

Suddenly, the Land Rover comes at us full speed and smashes into the back of the Fiat. All of us are propelled forward, the car spinning out of control, knives of pain stabbing my neck from the whiplash.

Seraphine is screaming but manages to get control of the car.

"Fuck, drive, drive, drive!" Blaise yells.

Seraphine makes a garbled cry and steps on the gas, briefly veering into the opposite lane and almost smashing into a car head-on before she swerves back. Meanwhile, I'm holding my neck, trying to watch the Land Rover copying our every move and gaining on us.

This guy isn't just following us.

He doesn't want us to pull over either.

He means to kill us.

"Where the fuck are the police?" Blaise yells, his voice ripped by panic as we whir past traffic, trying to get out of the way. "Why isn't anyone doing anything?" He brings out his phone, about to dial when it starts ringing.

It says *Father* on the screen.

Blaise stares at it for a moment, as if he's not sure he should answer, as if he'd rather let it go to voice mail, as if we aren't being fucking chased down the streets of Paris by a maniac.

"Blaise!" I yell at him, but it's like he's in shock.

Actually, he probably is in shock.

"I'm taking this exit," Seraphine says and guns it up the ramp onto the bridge heading over the Seine into Hauts-de-Seine. There's traffic on the bridge, but it doesn't slow Seraphine down. She just maneuvers between the cars and the concrete side of the off-ramp, clipping the mirror on Blaise's side.

But the traffic doesn't slow the driver of the Land Rover down, either, who is hot on our trail, plowing through traffic just the same until we're both racing over the bridge toward the other side.

"Well, are you calling the fucking police or what?" I yell at Blaise, trying to fish out my own phone. Just as I do, the Land Rover speeds up, darting to the left of us into the opposite lane of traffic and then bringing the car right into our side.

Seraphine screams, and I duck as the side of the Land Rover collides with our Fiat, the side windows shattering and sending a spray of glass all over me.

The car spins around, and, somehow, before I can even lift my head, I can feel the car gunning it the opposite way.

I sit up in time to see Seraphine driving as fast as she can, her arms and cheeks dotted with glass and bits of blood, and the Land Rover doing a sharp U-turn and coming around after us.

Relentless.

"Are you okay?" I manage to ask just as Blaise's phone rings again.

Seraphine nods, but her lip is trembling, and it's clear she's surviving on just adrenaline and instinct now, much like I am.

I look over at Blaise, and he's answering his phone.

"Father," he says, his voice slow and methodical, "you have to call the police. There's a man on the road trying to kill us. He's driving a . . ." He pauses. "Yes, I'm with Seraphine and Olivier. I don't know, I came along for the ride, I—" He removes the phone from his ear and stares at it. "He hung up on me. He must be calling the police."

"I don't think they're going to arrive in time," Seraphine says grimly as the Land Rover gets closer again. It's almost as beat-up as this car, and yet it keeps coming, even faster now since I think either the Fiat or Seraphine is losing their energy.

I stare back at the car, trying to absorb the look of the driver, and then notice him answering his phone. In the middle of a high-speed chase, trying to kill us, he answers a call.

And then, just like that, he hangs up.

And he slams on the brakes, turning the SUV around and taking off in the other direction.

Leaving us alone.

Like he had never been there at all.

"What the fuck? He left!" I yell.

"What?" Seraphine yells, frantically looking over her shoulder.

Blaise turns around in his seat, frowning, watching with me as the Land Rover disappears over the hump of the bridge.

"Tell me you got that license plate number," Seraphine says.

"I did, but I bet it doesn't exist."

"And I bet that car will be turned into scrap in about five minutes," Blaise says slowly. "Maybe even sooner."

"We have to go to the nearest station," I tell them. "Then the hospital. Fuck, I'm surprised that we didn't have news vans and helicopters for that . . . chase? What the fuck was that?"

"It stopped as quickly as it started," Blaise says in a strange voice, staring blankly out the window.

I look at him closely. He's way more shaken up than I thought. "Hey, you okay? Are you hurt anywhere?"

He shakes his head no. Then he blinks, as if snapping out of a trance, and looks at Seraphine. "You're bleeding," he says, horror rising in his throat.

"I'm fine," she says. "It's just a bit of glass."

"Pull over, right here," I tell Seraphine, and she pulls off onto a narrow road that curves through a wooded park, stopping on the gravel on the side.

Except there's no relief.

The car feels claustrophobic.

I climb out of the other door, the one that isn't smashed in, and get to my feet. I only manage a few steps before I'm putting my hands on my thighs and trying to breathe.

None of this makes sense.

Who was that man?

Why was he trying to fucking kill us?

Why?

In broad daylight, without a care in the world, as if he could never get caught?

And why did he stop, just like that?

It's like whoever was on the phone told him to quit.

I take a deep breath, trying to put it all together, trying to figure out our course of action.

We have to report this to the police.

We have to go to the hospital.

We have to figure this out before it gets buried.

I walk back to the car and open Blaise's door.

He looks up at me with pained eyes, but whether it's from actual pain, being scared, or something else, I don't know.

"What did your father want? Why was he calling you?"

"I don't know," he says softly. "I told him . . . I told him I was with you, and he sounded so shocked. He hung up . . ."

I don't want to say my next words. "And right after that, the driver behind us got a call. You saw that. And you saw him quit. Just like that."

He swallows uneasily. "What are you saying?"

"He's saying that you weren't supposed to be in the car," Seraphine says quietly as she gets out of the car, taking a few steps and leaning on the hood. "That's what it means."

"Are you saying my father orchestrated that? That he just tried to kill us all?"

I shake my head. "I don't know he was trying to kill us. Maybe just scare us."

"He was trying to get rid of me," Seraphine says. "Perhaps poison was too subtle for him. Perhaps he has experience with it. You know, I never wanted to accuse your father, Blaise. I always assumed it was a

Pascal thing to do, to kill someone, to get rid of them, considering who he knows and hangs out with. But now . . . now maybe your father is just as fucking sick as I feared he was, to murder his own brother. To try to off his niece next."

"You're not making sense," Blaise says, but there's something in his eyes that's telling me it all does make sense to him. It's just he doesn't want to believe it.

"It's quite the coincidence," I tell him, "if that's what you want to believe. But I can tell you know the truth. We have all the reasons, Blaise."

"No," he says. "No, they would never go that far. I mean, they've done some fucked-up shit, believe me. They've done things . . . things to you, Olivier. But not to Seraphine, not to Ludovic. This doesn't fit. They're bad, but they aren't this bad."

"What do you mean they've done things to me?" I ask him.

His eyes dart to Seraphine, and she frowns. He looks back at me. "You know."

And I do know.

So Blaise knew about the blackmailing too.

"Were you always in on it?" I manage to say, feeling anger swirling up through me. "Did you always know? All this time? All these years?"

A ripple of fear goes through his eyes, then shame.

His head hangs just a little lower. "Only recently. I'm always the last to know."

"Know what?" Seraphine asks.

"Why don't you tell her?" Blaise asks. "Why don't you tell your sister what you did. And what it's cost everyone." He pauses, a smug look coming across his face. "You like to pretend that you're so good and noble and loyal, but instead, you're just a fraud. No better than the rest of us. Just a dirty, lying son of a bitch who doesn't even have the guts to admit he's—"

I don't even think.

My arm swings back, and my fist comes forward, and I punch Blaise right in the nose.

His head goes flying and smacks against the doorframe of the car with a metallic thunk. Blood trickles from his nose as he covers it with his hand, yelping in pain.

"Olivier!" Seraphine yells at me.

But I don't care. He's had it coming for a very long time, and it takes all I have to not punch him again. The rage is burning through me at a terrifying rate.

"You're an asshole," he growls at me.

"And you've been an accessory to fucking blackmail." I sneer at him. "Do you know how you've ruined my life? Do you know the pain you helped cause?"

"Olivier, please, what are you talking about? Blaise, what blackmail?"

He shrugs. "Olivier slept with Marine," he says tiredly. Seraphine gasps, and I can't believe it's finally coming out. "Ten years ago. My father found out and made a bargain with Olivier. Actually, several bargains," he says and then glances up at me, wincing through the pain. "One was that you would feel the same as you had made Pascal feel . . . Tell me, if you think that driver was after you, where do you think he might go next?"

I blink at him, breathing hard. "I don't understand."

"Sadie," Seraphine gasps. I meet her eyes. "Your girlfriend. Where is she right now?"

Oh fucking no.

I climb into the back seat and start looking frantically for my phone.

"No, no, no," I repeat under my breath, refusing to think about it, needing her to be okay. I finally find it under the seat; the screen is cracked, but I'm able to dial her number.

"I'm not saying it's what's happening," Blaise says. "I don't know what's happening anymore. But if what you think is correct . . . then there are other ways of coming after you if the job didn't get finished the first time."

I barely hear him. I have the phone to my ear, and it's ringing, ringing, ringing.

No answer.

No answer.

CHAPTER SEVENTEEN

SADIE

"Un billet, s'il vous plaît," I say to the woman behind the booth. Either she doesn't know English or my French is finally good enough to understand, because she answers me in French—rather cheerfully for someone who works at the catacombs.

When Olivier went out to talk to Seraphine, I knew it would do me no good to spend another afternoon moping inside of his apartment. But with rain in the forecast, it was either the museums, which would be absolutely packed, or a visit underground to the Catacombs of Paris.

I'd never been before—Tom was too disturbed by the idea of passageways filled with bones—and I wasn't about to wait for Olivier to play tourist with me.

It was kind of a pain to get the various Métros here, and I got off at several wrong stops, but now that I'm here, I'm glad I came—even though I'm currently descending a very narrow, very twisty staircase, deeper and deeper underneath the streets of Paris. I pull up my phone to check the reception, and, naturally, there is none.

Once I reach the main level, the creepy factor ratchets up several notches. It really is just a lair of bones. Actual human bones. It's a winding labyrinth with stacks and stacks of skulls, all dimly lit, the bones dusty, the air damp. It's cold, too, the kind that clings to you.

But there's something rather beautiful about the way the bones are displayed, artfully and with reverence, an artistic way of paying respects if not just a space saver when it comes to burials. After all, there are six million people buried in these tunnels, which absolutely blows my mind. The fact that the public is allowed to see only a tiny fraction of it is pretty disturbing.

I feel like I've been walking for a while now, passing tourists taking photos and selfies with skulls and femurs. It's confusing, the way the tunnels go, and the damp and darkness really seem to put you in a weird headspace.

It doesn't help that this is a pretty morbid thing that I'm doing, especially after seeing Ludovic die, then the funeral, and hearing Seraphine's theory, not to mention the truth of what happened to Olivier.

A cold breeze washes over my bare arms, and I shiver, wishing I had paid more attention to the online reviews and brought a sweater. It's like even with the rain happening far aboveground, it's gotten even colder down here.

There are not a lot of tourists, either, not as many as I'd thought there'd be. There are some passages of the tunnels where I don't see anyone at all. I just hear hushed voices. And when I turn the corner, there's no one there. Maybe the rain has them all cooped up in the Louvre and the Orsay museums. Maybe they were smart and figured the catacombs were actually the worst place to be on a gloomy summer day.

There are various darkened passageways that lead away from the main tunnel at any given time. They all have NE PAS ENTRER and STOP signs, warning people not to enter. Some have doors that are locked; others are just long, dark cracks that disappear into the limestone.

I shiver when I hear the wet smack of footfalls behind me.

I whirl around, but see only a round column of bones rising from the middle of the slimy floors. No one at all.

It must be the water dripping from the ceiling, I tell myself.

I take a deep breath and keep walking, relieved to turn the corner and see an older couple reading one of the plaques on the walls.

Still, again I hear the sound of footsteps and feel the wash of a cold breeze, goose bumps prickling my arms. I swear I see a shadow move backward, deeper into the other shadows.

"Hello," I call out, but the only response I get is a curious "Hello?" from the couple in front of me.

I give them an awkward wave and then walk past them, wanting now to get the hell out of here.

But there's only one way out of the tunnels, at least for the public, and the exit never seems to come. I keep walking, sometimes through rooms with a few people in them, sometimes through spaces with no one else.

And all this time I have the disturbing feeling that I'm being followed.

And, yeah, of course I'm being followed. There are always tourists coming up behind me, though at my pace I'm passing everyone.

No, this feeling is something else.

It's shadows that won't stop moving.

It's the gleam of eyes before they disappear into the dark.

It's knowing deep in my core that I am being watched.

Hunted.

When I get that feeling for the millionth time, I whirl around, prepared to face my attacker.

I don't see anyone but a lone kid at the very end, touching a skull.

Then I turn around and see it.

This time in front of me, not behind me at all.

A man passing across the tunnel and disappearing into the dark, going to and coming from a place he shouldn't.

I walk forward and peer around the corner.

There are two passageways, both with Do Not Enter signs. One is completely dark. One has a dim light hanging from somewhere farther inside, like it's a large cavern.

I know I should keep going.

I know I should get out of this place.

But now I'm curious, more curious than afraid.

I carefully walk through the narrow passage, ignoring the sign, my fingers brushing along the damp limestone walls.

And then I see it.

A small room carved into the stone.

A stack of busted crates in one corner.

Piles of broken bones.

A single swinging bulb giving off a dull sepia light.

And Pascal, standing right below it.

Waiting for me.

I should have expected to see him, I should have known it was him following me. This place looks like the sort he'd emerge from, somewhere between the real world and hell.

Yet, I'm surprised.

Surprised enough to freeze in place, my breath catching in my throat.

"You're a hard girl to get ahold of," Pascal says in a low voice. He steps forward, the light of the bulb hitting his eyes, making them gleam with intensity.

"And you don't seem to take a hint very well," I tell him, raising my chin and fixing him with my most confident glare, even though inside I want to run, maybe throw up somewhere.

I turn around and start out the way I came, because I may have been stupid enough to come in here, but I'm not stupid enough to stay.

"And you don't seem to take threats very well," he says sharply. There's such an edge to his voice that I have no choice but to stop. "You're a smart girl, Sadie. You know what's going to happen to you, to

Olivier, if you don't start making the right choices. You can walk out of here and pretend you never saw me, but I'll make sure to follow you wherever you go. Wherever your loved ones go. Wherever your loved ones are." He pauses. "I've heard Seattle is lovely this time of year."

My heart booms loudly in my ears, and I slowly turn to face him.

He can't be serious.

Did he just threaten my mother?

But he is serious. He's more serious than I've ever seen him. That mask he sometimes wears is gone, and there is nothing but ice-cold ambition, the kind of look that I'm sure most serial killers have while they're planning their next kill.

"What do you want from me?" I ask quietly.

"I want to show you something," he says, smoothly taking his phone out of his pocket and walking toward me.

I back up until I am pressed against the cold wall and wonder if I scream whether my voice would echo out into the tunnels or be swallowed up by the bones.

"Don't panic," he says to me, coming so close that he's almost pressed up against me, leaving just a few inches that feel like no space at all. I can hardly breathe. His face comes in closer, his lips going into that lopsided smirk, one that enjoys what he's doing far too much. "I'm not going to hurt you. We can discuss things like adults. We can decide what we're going to do next."

I don't say anything, just stare at him, and I know my eyes are showing every ounce of fear rolling through me.

"You have such beautiful eyes," he says. "Like an animal, caught, cornered. Once trusting, now afraid."

I lick my lips, my mouth going so dry it's like a bag of sand was poured in it.

"You don't have to fear me if you listen," he murmurs, his gaze now raking over my mouth. "You have nothing to fear at all if you play this the right way."

"And what way is that?" I whisper.

He raises his brow. "You're curious. Curiosity killed the cat, isn't that what they say where you're from? But you're smarter than that. That's why you're going to listen. That's why you're going to leave."

"I'll gladly leave." I make a move to go, but he flattens himself against me, positioning himself so I'm stuck between him and the wall. I suck in my breath, trying to muster enough energy to scream, when he puts his hand over my mouth.

"Shh, shh, shh," he whispers harshly. "What did I just say? You stay quiet and you listen, and everything will work out. If you scream, if you run, then it will be me on that next plane back to Seattle, not you. Do you understand me? I know my English can be bad sometimes, but I'm trying to convey something very important here. Do you comprehend any of this?"

I don't.

All I know is the fear.

The fear that something terrible is about to happen to me.

But at the same time, how could it?

I could fight, I could escape, I could yell, and people would come running in a second. We're in a room with one way out, and there's a world of tourists just around the corner.

I could do all of those things and escape.

It would only make things worse.

I try to will myself to relax, to play along, but with his hand pressed against my mouth, his hard, strong body pinning me in place, it's impossible.

"Good girl," he says. "You're learning. You're listening. This is good. Hey, let me show you something." He takes his hand away from my mouth, and I gulp for air. He brings his phone right up to my eyes and presses "Play." "Do you recognize this?"

It's a video. The footage is grainy at first; then it focuses in.

It's of a hotel.

A hotel room at the Rouge Royale.

It's of a window. I'm naked and pressed up against the glass. Olivier is screwing me against it. The camera zooms in closer and closer, and though I'm facing away for most of it, occasionally my head turns to the side, either in ecstasy or to look down at the world below, and you can clearly see that it's me.

My cheeks immediately go red, and I close my eyes from the shame.

I knew that it was a mistake to be so brazen. To fuck where anyone could see us. It was part of the thrill. I was so taken with the meeting in the hotel, with everything.

And Pascal saw the whole thing.

He filmed the whole thing from the building across the street, maybe that dark room with the half-closed shutters.

He puts his phone away. "At first I thought you were an incredible performer," Pascal murmurs into my ear, his breath hot. "I thought that there was no way my cousin could be that good. But I guess it's the truth. Though you know, if I had my way with you, Olivier would barely be a memory."

"Dream on," I manage to say, glaring at him.

"I don't have to dream," he says with a smile. "I have this. Do you know how many times I've come watching this? How many times I've imagined it was me with my cock inside you, making you writhe against the glass? I'm getting turned on just talking about it again, being able to feel you like this, to smell you when you're hot and desperate. Do I make you desperate right now?"

I look away from the lewd excitement in his eyes, refusing to answer him, knowing no matter what I say, he'll find some fucking way to twist it around to suit him.

"Bashful suddenly? I see. Well, I suppose it's always a shock to see yourself in such an intimate moment. It will be a bigger shock when the world sees it."

"What the fuck are you talking about?" I snap at him.

He grins. He looks like a fucking maniac. "I have your attention. Very good. Well, see, this is just one of the things that will happen if you stay with Olivier. I'll share this with the press. It will be everywhere. Sure, it's nothing more than a scandal, and I don't think it will hurt Olivier in any way. But it's got to be embarrassing for you. To have everyone back at home see you like this. Your mother . . ."

"Don't you fucking mention her."

He shrugs. "I have to. It's part of the plan."

"Your fucking plan to break us up, to keep Olivier from any happiness, isn't that it? That's what you want?"

He tilts his head, frowning as he studies me. "You make it sound like I hate my cousin."

"You do. And he fucking hates you."

"Oh, I am very aware of that."

"That's why he fucked your wife," I spit out, expecting Pascal to look shocked or insulted or something.

But that crooked, twitching smile returns, and his eyes are practically dancing with joy. "That's not why he fucked my wife," Pascal says. "He fucked my wife because it bothered him how little his own family thought of him. How little I cared for him. He fucked my wife because she was beautiful, and she said she wanted him, and he fell for it."

I frown. "Fell for it?"

"Why, yes. Fell for it. Marine was ambitious but stupid, a terrible combination. A lot like my mother, actually. That's probably why I first asked her to marry me—you know how messed up all these relationships can be. Anyway, when you're stupid but ambitious, you'll do anything and never think of the consequences. Marine never wanted to be with me—she just wanted my money. It happens to all of us. I'm sure with my mother it was the same. It was certainly the same for Seraphine's ex-husband. You can never really be sure of someone's intentions. When you're a Dumont, everyone wants a piece of you, even if it means cutting themselves in the process."

He runs a finger down the side of my cheek, slowly pressing harder and harder. "Marine was an easy target, and she was disposable. I told her the plan. She would seduce Olivier, have an affair with him, lead him on, and let him believe that she loved him. Then we'd wait for them to be discovered."

Oh. My. God.

"After that, the deal was done. Olivier lost everything. My father and I gained everything—we would just have to bide our time. It came a lot sooner than I thought, to be honest with you."

"Marine . . . you made your wife seduce Olivier? You set him up!"

"*We* set him up. It was my father's idea, naturally. He always has the good ideas. I was rather young at the time, I hadn't evolved into it yet. Don't worry about Marine, though, she got what was coming to her. As soon as it was over, I divorced her, and she didn't get a single penny from me. You see, she was cheating on me with my cousin, and there was that infidelity clause in our prenup."

Just when I didn't think this guy could get any more evil . . .

"Oh, I disgust you," he says to me, amused. "I'm all right with that. It's better to get a reaction than no reaction. It's like art, you see."

"How dare you compare murder to art."

"Murder?" Pascal says. "You're being a little dramatic, don't you think?"

"I know you did it. Everyone knows. You murdered Ludovic to take over the company."

Pascal purses his lips for a moment, and I can tell this has caught him off guard, the fact that I know the truth. "He had a heart attack."

"You killed him."

"I can assure you I didn't. I didn't agree with my uncle, but I didn't hate the man either. I would never do such a thing. So messy."

"I saw you. I saw you leaving the study with him and your father, right before Ludovic died. You could have done it in there. Poisoned him."

Pascal frowns, seeming to think something over. Then shakes his head. "You believe what you want. I don't really care at this point. What I do care about is you, leaving now. And by leaving, I mean catching your flight tonight."

"What flight?"

"The flight you're going to take in three hours, back to Seattle."

I balk. "I'm not going anywhere."

"Yes, my dear, you are. You know the consequences if you stay."

"Why do you want me to leave so badly?"

"Because you have no place here, in this. Maybe I'm just looking out for you. Maybe you're right, and I do hate Olivier and want him to know that I have all the power, all the cards here. I can make his beloved leave him. I can make him stay here, alone. You know he'd never follow you. Not with Seraphine here, all alone and exposed. Not with his hotels. He'll mourn you, and it will break his heart, and he will never see you again."

I swallow hard, barely flinching as cold water drips onto my shoulder from above. Pascal is still so close to me, I feel like he's this big black hole that's slowly devouring me, eating away at my resolve.

"I'm not going anywhere."

He closes his eyes briefly and sighs. "I do like you, you know. Very much. I think if you were more open-minded, you might even prefer me to my cousin. But that's neither here nor there. The point is, I don't want to have to hurt you or Olivier or your family. But if you don't do exactly as I say tonight, I will." His eyes focus in on mine with stunning conviction. "And I will make it hurt more than you can imagine," he whispers.

Then he pulls back, and the damp of the underground cavern rushes over me, making me feel ill. He takes out his phone again and pulls up an airline ticket on the screen.

"Your flight," he says. "If I were you, I'd rush back home, pack, and go." He scrolls along until another ticket pops up. "As you can see, I have a ticket too. I'll see you at the airport. Or maybe, if I trust you, I won't. Either way, someone will be flying to Seattle to see your mother. *Comprenez-vous?"*

I nod. "Yes."

"It sounds better when you speak French," he says.

I can barely get the word out. *"Oui."*

"Ah," he says, "okay, perhaps you stick to your English then." He puts his phone away and strides out of the cavern, calling over his shoulder, his words echoing off the walls, "Don't be late, Sadie. You can't afford to be late."

And then I'm alone.

I collapse against the wall, sliding down it, trying to breathe, trying to think.

Trying to figure out the right thing to do.

And if it's the only thing to do.

CHAPTER EIGHTEEN

OLIVIER

"Can you drive a little faster?" I ask my driver, Hugo, even though he's already going twenty over the speed limit as we burn down the Quai d'Orsay toward my apartment in Le Marais.

He raises his brows but still steps on the gas.

I turn around and look back at Blaise and Seraphine. "Well?" I say to Blaise. "You were saying?"

The moment he hinted that Sadie might have been compromised by Pascal in some way, I knew I had no choice but to get to her immediately. The Fiat wouldn't cut it after all the damage it had taken, so we abandoned it in the park, and I called one of my drivers to get me.

I also made sure I wasn't going alone. I need Blaise with me. He is the key to this whole thing, the only person who can make things right.

Which is pretty naive of me to think, because Blaise is still one of them, and I'm not sure I can ever trust him. But, currently, he's all I've got.

Then there's Seraphine, who I can tell is reeling both from nearly getting killed in a car crash and from the truth of what I signed with Gautier.

She's mad at me, I know. If she's not, when the shock wears off, she will be. I can't blame her. Even if she chooses to push me away, cut ties with me, and disown me as her brother, I can't blame her. I've lied to her for a long time, and it's a lie that might cost her personally, a lie based on my own selfishness and stupidity.

But for now, she's picking bits of broken glass out of her hands and doing her best to prod Blaise for answers. I insisted we take her straight to the hospital, even though she said it's not as bad as it looks, so that she can get the ball rolling with the insurance filings and the police reports and everything else, even though I know in my heart that it will be futile. Sure, she'll get some money for her car—not that she needs it—but it's all just lip service at this point. The man behind the wheel might as well have never existed, and even if this does have something to do with my uncle—which I'm trying to get to the bottom of—it won't ever see the light of day.

That's the thing about being that corrupt. When you have the power of the mafia and various crime organizers at your beck and call, when you have all the fucking money in the world, then you control what the police do or don't do.

"I wasn't saying anything," Blaise snipes, still rubbing his nose and groaning when he presses too hard.

"Yes, you were," Seraphine says. "You said Pascal had a screw loose, which, frankly, is a surprise to no one here."

"If he hurts her," I warn him, the anger rising in my throat like bile, "I hurt you. More than I already have. More than you can imagine."

Blaise frowns. "What Pascal does is none of my business."

"So why are you ratting on him then?" Seraphine asks.

He looks at her, his eyes meeting hers and latching on for longer than usual. He swallows, rubbing his lips together for a moment, as if wrestling with some monster inside him. Then he says, "Because I hate him."

Seraphine looks to me, shocked, then back to Blaise. "What?"

Blaise takes in a deep breath. "I thought you would have figured that out."

"Why on earth would I have figured that out? You're always with them."

"Like the third musketeer," I say.

Blaise glares at me and then looks back to Seraphine, like I don't exist. "I'm working with you more than I ever did with them," he says. Then he shrugs. "Whatever. I don't need to explain myself."

"My God, you're a moody little bastard," she says.

He grins at her. "And you wouldn't have me any other way." Then he winces, holding his nose. "Ow."

"I'm sorry," I say, "but we have more pressing issues at hand. Sure, we almost died, and, yeah, it's shocking that you suddenly hate your brother—but Sadie's life is at stake here."

"He's not going to hurt her," Blaise says snidely. "Maybe rough her up a little. You know how he is. Scare her. But he won't hurt her."

"So now you're standing up for him?" Seraphine asks.

"I'm not standing up for anyone. I'm just telling the truth. Pascal is going to threaten her, and he's going to get her to leave."

"Why?" Seraphine asks. "What did she do to him?"

"Nothing," Blaise says. "It's just a game. You should fucking get that by now. It's a game to those two, and it always has been. They have to be on top. They have to be controlling the ride at all times or . . . things get ugly."

"Things are already ugly," I tell him gruffly. "Just fucking look at us."

"So that's why it's happening," he says, like talking about it all is exhausting him. Or boring him. "Sadie is something new in your life, and she doesn't really belong in this world. As far as they're concerned, the more they run you into the ground, the higher they rise. Don't forget . . . they're scared of you."

"Scared of me?"

"You don't send out Polish thugs when you're secure with yourself. They're very aware that they've been blackmailing you to get to the top.

They didn't want to kill you today, they wanted to scare you, to remind you of your place."

"So it was them," Seraphine says. "You admit it."

"I know nothing," he says quickly. "But it makes the most sense. Unlike your murder theory, which doesn't. Sorry, I know you want to blame someone, but I think you should just let it go."

"Our father is dead," Seraphine says coldly. "I can't let that go."

"Then I think you're in for a world of pain if you keep pursuing it," Blaise says, staring at her steadily. "Trust me on this. Please. I don't think my father or brother had anything to do with Ludovic's death. But if you start looking around, if you start acting like they did, if you start to twist things . . . they will retaliate. You're better off forgetting it. Mourn your father and grieve. But don't go looking for something to make it worse."

I have to say, I agree with Blaise on this one. Maybe it's because I don't want to think about it, maybe because I know it will make things worse, but we'd all be better off if we let it go.

For now.

Besides, that's not at the forefront of my mind. I'm not sure I trust Blaise when he says that Pascal won't hurt her, and I hate to think what roughing her up means. All I know is that if Pascal has Sadie, she's going to be terrified and lost and confused. She's going to be hurting in some way, and, knowing her, if Pascal makes her choose, if his whole intent is to make her leave, she will leave.

She'll do it to protect me.

It's part of the reason why I fell for her.

She's one of the few people who would go above and beyond for me, just as I would for her.

God, it seems so long ago, those blissful days in that sun-soaked hotel room, where our only problems were what to order for room service.

I miss that life.

I miss her.

I miss us, that us.

Now everything is fucked right up.

"Hey," Seraphine says gently, touching me on the shoulder. I turn my head to see sympathy in her eyes. "She's going to be okay."

"Yeah. And if she's not?"

"She will be."

"It doesn't mean we'll be okay."

I can tell she understands exactly what I mean.

This has become too much for any couple to weather, let alone a new one.

Thankfully, it's not long before the car is screeching to a halt on the wet street outside my building. I run past the concierge, who does a double and then triple take as Blaise and Seraphine sprint through the lobby behind me. I'm actually amazed that Blaise is still here, but perhaps he's trying to distance himself from Pascal and Gautier.

Or maybe it has something to do with Seraphine.

He does seem protective of her in a strange way. Maybe in a brother-sister way, which would still be quite strange, because they're from different sides, and they've never gotten along. All I know is that if Blaise truly hates Pascal—and it sounds like he's not too fond of his father either—maybe Seraphine isn't alone in this game after all.

Once I get inside my apartment, it's obvious that Sadie is gone.

Her bag is packed for one.

And there's a note.

The note brings me a bit of relief, just to know that she's okay.

Dear Olivier,

I am so sorry, but I have to leave. I have no time to explain, but I'll be catching a flight out of Charles De Gal, or however you spell it, and I'll be heading home. Please know that I'm okay and I'm fine and I'm not hurt, but I have to go home. Please understand that. It has nothing to do with you.

I'll call you when I land. I love you.

I really, really love you.

I'd write it in French, but . . .

I love you.

Sadie

"Is she okay?" Seraphine asks, trying to look over my shoulder to read it.

I fold it up and put it in my pocket, away from her prying eyes. "She's fine, I guess. I don't know. She's going home."

"Home?"

"She caught a flight back to Seattle."

"Which means Pascal bought it for her," Blaise muses as he stares at a painting on my wall, hands clasped behind his back. "I figured as much."

"How do you feel?" Seraphine asks me, rooting through my liquor cabinet for a bottle of something to drink.

"I don't know," I admit.

Because I don't. She's gone.

My love is gone.

And yet I know I won't let her go so easily.

Seraphine selects a bottle of brandy and pulls the cork out with her teeth. "If you don't mind, I feel like helping myself to this."

I watch her absently as she takes several long gulps from the bottle.

"Impressive," Blaise notes, his attention on her now, watching her swallow in a way that I don't think is family friendly.

I frown at that, but my mind pushes on. "Why do you hate your brother?"

Blaise smirks. "Why do you hate him?"

"Because . . . he's fucking dirt. Ruthless, classless dirt."

"Oh, we're all a little ruthless, Olivier," Blaise says. "We all have our ways of climbing to the top. You did. Not with the Dumont brand, but with the hotels. And you did, too, Seraphine, to get to the position you have. If you could, you would be at the top. I see that ambition in you. It runs in our blood. I think my side of the family just fed it more."

He walks over to Seraphine and takes the bottle from her hands, taking a swig himself, not breaking eye contact with her. When he's done, he wipes his mouth and says, "Is this our label, or is it actually something good? It all tastes like fire to me."

"You never answered the question," I remind him.

He shrugs. "What does it matter why I hate him? Just because someone is your brother—family—doesn't mean you have to like them. Let's just say that I have lived a different life from you in a different house. But my aspirations, my goals, they're all the same."

To get to the top, I think. If he can get Pascal out of the picture somehow, then he can take his position. But I don't know if Blaise realizes his father and Pascal are a united front he will never get past. There are favorites in that family.

"So what are you going to do?" Seraphine asks me as Blaise hands me the bottle.

I take it. Why not?

It does taste like fire, but the kind that baptizes you.

The kind that burns away the fog and brings a certain type of clarity to your head.

I know what I have to do as I'm saying it.

"I'm going to Seattle," I say. "Tonight. And I don't know if or when I'm ever coming back."

I expect Seraphine to make a fuss. I expect her to tell me that I'm doing what they want, that they'll win this way, that father would disapprove.

But the truth is, father only ever wanted me to be happy.

And I know what makes me happy.

It's Sadie.

It's Sadie and nothing else.

"Good," Seraphine says, and even though they aren't related by blood and don't look at all the same, I can see my father in her, hear him in her voice. I know he's speaking through her, or she's speaking through him. "I think that's the right thing to do. Maybe it's the only thing to do."

"You don't mind?"

She laughs dryly. "Mind? I'll miss the hell out of you, but if you're worried about leaving me on my own, don't be."

"I'll make sure she's okay," Blaise says.

Seraphine looks at him, eyes wide in surprise. He just holds her gaze, and in that moment I know he's telling the truth. For what it's worth, she'll be okay without me. Maybe she'll even be better. Maybe we'll all become better versions of ourselves once we're left alone to figure out who we really are.

And what we really want.

And what I want is about to board a plane and fly thousands of miles away, across an ocean, to another land.

And I know I'm about to follow her there.

"I think I have a flight to catch," I tell them, heading into my bedroom to grab my passport. When I come back out, Blaise and Seraphine are passing the bottle of brandy back and forth between them. "Can I trust you guys in my apartment?"

"You think we're going to start fist-fighting?" Seraphine asks.

Not particularly.

"Fine. Can I trust you guys to get yourselves to the hospital at least?"

"I'll take her," Blaise says. "You just get the hell out of here."

For a split second, I'm hit with the feeling that I'm doing exactly what they want, that my leaving Paris would only benefit Gautier and Pascal, as well as Blaise.

But that doesn't mean I'm turning my back on any of this.

I'm just moving forward.

There's just one stop I have to make on the way to the airport.

Gautier's house is located just outside of Paris in a peaceful part of the country where rolling hills meet oak forests, a place I know like the back of my hand. All those summers I spent there as I was growing up, my days at that house and running around their property, rotating with all the days my cousins spent at my house.

On the surface, the memories seem pure. Untainted. Maybe that's the way it is for so many people. Your childhood is full of sunshine and the smell of fresh grass, the taste of ice cream, the feel of nostalgia. You remember everything good and bury the bad.

Until recently, I believed that my interactions with my uncle and aunt and cousins were as innocent as they could get.

I'm starting to realize that I was wrong.

That even through the rose-tinted glasses of childhood, things were already set in motion. Gautier and Camille used their children and us against each other like chess pieces, all in an effort to undermine the family bond.

And now, as I'm driving down the wooded road toward Gautier's estate, the memories slam into me. The real memories—the slices of nastiness that cut through all the smiles and the laughter and the games.

I remember seeing my mother crying in the bathroom after an altercation with my uncle. I remember my aunt telling Pascal he wasn't as handsome or as smart as I was, which then made Pascal lash out at me. I remember Blaise pushing me down one day, telling me I wasn't welcome. I remember my uncle continually comparing me to his sons, using me as something to measure up to, even though I was just a boy and hadn't done anything wrong. I remember he used fear to drive them into doing anything he wanted, and when things didn't go his way, he'd turn into a violent beast.

I remember seeing Blaise with a bruise on his cheek.

Pascal crying after his father locked him in the basement during his own birthday party.

Camille trying to get my mother more and more drunk.

My uncle telling me that I come from a line of liars.

Now I remember all those dark moments I had tried so desperately to hide away, and they're creeping through like that dying summer light through the lines of oak trees.

I pull up to his house, and with all the shadows and new memories, the sprawling three-hundred-year-old estate looks especially sinister.

It also looks like no one is home. There is only one car parked outside. I would have thought at least Pascal would be home since he lives here most of the time, but I'll have to do with my uncle.

He's the one controlling Pascal at any rate.

I park and get out of the car, looking up at the top windows of the house. I see my aunt's shadowed figure as she peers down at me and then disappears.

I knock on the door, and there's only silence for a long time. If this were a horror film, there would be big demonic dogs barking from somewhere in the house, but Gautier and Camille have a hatred for most animals.

The memory hits me hard, just a flash of when we picked up a kitten named Felipe from the shelter, thanks to Seraphine's wish for one.

Pascal was so in love with that cat, every time he was over at our estate, he would spend hours with it.

He'd kept asking for one from his parents, but they were adamant that they would never have filthy animals in their house. The most Pascal could do was save up enough for a hamster. He bought the cage and the animal from money he'd saved, and I remember when he brought me up to his room to brag about the fact that he had finally gotten a pet too.

Except the hamster was gone. The cage was empty.

And after we spent a good twenty minutes frantically searching the room for it, his mother appeared and told him she flushed the hamster down the toilet.

Pascal changed after that moment. It's like whatever boyish innocence he possessed at that age was snuffed out, and something cold and impersonal took over. I remember feeling all the shock and horror and disgust at what his mother had so casually done to a living creature, but, most of all, I recall being afraid of Pascal after that, as if the one good side of him was flushed away too.

I take a deep breath, about to knock again, when finally the giant doors open, and Charlotte, the young, petite maid, appears.

"Hello?" she says in her soft voice.

"Charlotte," I say with a nod. "Is Pascal home?"

She shakes her head, looking fearful.

"Is my uncle?"

She swallows, and from her body language I can tell she's getting ready to close the door on me.

Then from behind her, "It's quite all right, Charlotte, let him in."

Gautier's voice.

She opens the door wider and moves out of the way. I stride inside to see Gautier by the entrance to his library, holding a glass of sherry.

"Good to see you, Olivier. Come, join me."

He turns and walks off, disappearing into the room.

Charlotte gives me a worried glance and then scurries off down the hall, disappearing into the dark bowels of the house.

I go into the library, trying to control the anger rushing through me, the impulses that make my fists clench and unclench.

Gautier stands in the middle of the room, dressed in a suit—though I think it's Gucci, not Dumont. The man doesn't even wear his own fucking label.

"To what do I owe this impromptu visit, Olivier?" he says, taking a casual sip of his sherry.

"Where is Pascal?" I ask. I've stopped where I am, just inside the room. I don't want to get close to him. I'm afraid of what I might do.

He shrugs. "I haven't a clue," he says. "I don't keep tabs on my sons."

I smirk, letting out a dry laugh. "Yes, you do. You sent him today. You sent him today to harass Sadie, just as you sent that driver to have us killed."

Gautier raises his brows. He doesn't look surprised. "Sadie? Have you killed? Are you sure you're all right there, Olivier? You haven't been drinking? Because you're not making any sense at all."

"You can pretend all you want," I seethe. "It won't make a difference. I know what you did. I know your plan. I know you wanted us out of the picture today, not to just give us a scare. Well, it worked. It worked on Seraphine and me. It worked on Blaise too."

His eyes narrow. "Don't mention my son."

"Why not? You almost had him killed today, do you know that? How do you think that made him feel?"

He wants to take the bait. He wants to know how Blaise feels. He wants to know if he's okay. But he reels himself back in. "I don't know what you're talking about."

"And Sadie. You had Pascal threaten her, do your dirty work. You thought that if you got rid of her, that would weaken me. That it would lower my resolve and I would flee with my tail between my legs. You were wrong."

"Olivier, please. I don't even know who this Sadie is. Some new whore of yours?"

I don't know how it happens, but I fly across the room and lunge at my uncle, knocking him to the parquet wood floors, the sherry flying through the air.

All logic and restraint have left me, and I'm punching him, a blast to the cheekbone, to the nose, to the jaw. I think I might just beat his head into the floor until it resembles ground beef.

My uncle is yelling for help; he's trying to fight back. He's strong for his age, and through the blood on his face I can see the anger in his eyes and the fear that I might just kill him, or maybe the shock that he's losing. Loss of pride is a dangerous thing in this family, especially for him. It's the thing he fears the most.

And I won't stop delivering it.

Not even when my knuckles are raw.

Not even when Camille and Charlotte are trying to hold me back, and Camille says she's calling the police.

Not even when I'm standing over Gautier's bruised body, panting hard, feeling more animal than man, and I know that I've won this one small round.

"I know what you did, Gautier," I snarl at him, very aware that Camille is trying to get the cops, aware that they're in Gautier's pocket and will do their worst to me. "We all know what you did. You might think for now that you've gotten away with it, but you haven't. When your guard is down, when you think no one is looking, that's when your own world is going to collapse, and you're going to wish that all you got from me was this beating."

Then I strike out with my leg, kicking him in the side. In English, they say don't kick a man when he's down. But they also say karma is a bitch.

With Gautier groaning and swearing at me, I shrug off Charlotte's and Camille's half-hearted grasps, and I leave. I get out of there before the police have a chance to do anything to me.

I get out of there knowing that I've damaged his pride in front of his wife.

I get out of there knowing exactly where I'm going next and who I'm going to see.

CHAPTER NINETEEN

SADIE

I'm not sure if it's because of everything that's happened, or if it's the way the jet stream and the world work, but the flight home from Paris seems to take a million hours longer than the flight I took there.

I spend all eleven hours writhing in my seat, chewing on my nails, and downing glasses of wine until the flight attendant kindly suggests I've had enough, and the person next to me is convinced I'm the world's worst flier.

The only thing I've been able to hide are my tears. Every time I feel my nose growing hot and my eyes burning, I get up from my seat and try to make it to the bathroom. They're all probably thinking I'm throwing up in here, but I'm actually crying my eyes out.

I'm mourning everything I've lost.

I'm mourning Olivier.

The man I love, the man I fear I won't ever see again.

After Pascal antagonized me in the catacombs, I knew I didn't really have much choice in the matter, and there wasn't a lot of time to make any decisions. Yes, I wanted to go to the police and tell them that I was being threatened, that my mother was as well. I wanted to fill them in on what has been happening.

But I knew it wouldn't be easy. I'm a backpacker who has officially been in Europe for too long, overstaying my visa, and the person I would be accusing is one of the richest men in France. I would be laughed at—the idea that Pascal would have any interest in me. In fact, because Olivier had kept me hidden, there was no real evidence that I was even involved with him at all.

And the fact is, my flight was leaving soon. I couldn't risk all that, only to not show up for it, to have Pascal get on the flight instead.

So I did the only thing I could do.

I left.

I went back to Olivier's, and I packed my bags in a flurry. I left a note that, if I had more time, would have been filled with a million sentences of how much I love him, how much he matters to me. How much he's changed my world, my life. I'm not just leaving him behind, I'm leaving the person I never knew I could become.

The only thing I could write was that I loved him, and that I had to do this, and I was sorry I couldn't think of any other way.

"We're landing soon," the flight attendant says to me, motioning to the seatback that I've had reclined as far as it will go—which is pretty far, considering I'm in business class. I don't know what Pascal was thinking; you'd think he would have gone out of his way to be extra cruel and stick me in a middle seat in coach by the bathroom, but instead it's business class with all the perks. Too bad I can't enjoy it one bit.

"Sorry, I must not have heard the announcements," I mumble as I make the seat pop upright.

"That's okay," she says and then gives me a sympathetic smile. "Don't worry—I'm sure you'll be back in Paris before you know it."

She continues her walk down the aisle, checking on everyone else. I guess she knows the face of someone who has to leave before they're ready.

The truth is, I would have never been ready to leave. When I decided to stay with Olivier, I never gave any thought to how long it would be. To what my future would be. Did I think I would live in France forever, illegally? Did I think we could continue our honeymoon period for months, years? Then what? Would I ever go back to school? Would I ever see my mother? Did I expect Olivier to come over to the States and live there?

I mean, Pascal was right. I hate to admit it, but Olivier's life is rooted in France. It was always a one-way street with us. Even though we loved each other, things were always on his turf, in his life.

Maybe this is for the best. Maybe Pascal is doing us both a favor.

I shake my head, having a hard time accepting that. Pascal is pure evil, that's what he is. Or at least partially evil. Even though all signs point to his having something to do with Ludovic's death, I have a strange feeling that he had nothing to do with it. Or, rather, that maybe Seraphine's theory was just that: a theory. Perhaps it really was a heart attack. It happens all the time, even to healthy people, and it was no secret that his father was under a lot of stress at the time. It's the whole reason Olivier was helping out to begin with.

Oh, it doesn't matter what the truth is anymore. The only truth that really matters is that I'm on a plane about to land at Sea-Tac Airport without the man I love. His absence feels more real now than ever.

But even with my heavy heart, I go through the motions of coming back home. I get off the plane, get my bags, marvel at the sounds and sights of something as simple as the airport, the transition from the easy but chaotic European rhythm to the brusque and efficient way things are in the States. I get myself in a cab and am immediately reminded of how much the cabbies here love to talk, and now I can understand every word.

In a way I wish I could still sit in silence, remain anonymous, at least until I sort myself out and become something human again.

But I survive the inane chitchat, and soon we're pulling up in front of the apartment I shared with my mother.

No, share, I remind myself sharply. *Present tense. Things are going back to the way they were.*

I sigh, stepping out of the cab and tipping the driver with the last of the cash I have. Good timing to officially be broke.

But the moment I knock on the door and my mother opens it, a rush of relief comes flooding through me.

"Sadie?" she exclaims.

"Mom," I cry out, bursting into tears and falling into her arms.

She clutches me—well, mostly my backpack—and we stay like that for a few moments while I cry and cry and cry.

Then she leads me over to the couch and tells me she's going to make me tea, and I look up and around. For the first time in a while, I feel safe. I always felt safe when I was with Olivier, but never when I wasn't. Here, I am safe, I am home, just sitting in my living room and looking at the crappy pictures I drew when I was young that my mother insisted on framing, and the photo albums with my father's face cut out of them, and the cat lounging on the bookshelf, and . . .

Wait. Where the hell did that cat come from?

"Mom, did you get a cat?" I ask. "Or are you aware there's a cat in here?"

The cat has been watching me this whole time, and now that I've noticed it, its tail starts twitching. It's completely black except for one white paw.

"That's Kismet," she says to me, bringing the teapot into the room and placing it on the worn coffee table. "We're best friends."

I raise my brows and look at her. "I thought you—"

"Didn't like cats?" she says with a chuckle. "Well, that's what I thought. But while you were gone, I was getting lonely, and after a while I realized it might be good to take care of something else. I thought I was finally well enough to do it. So I went to the shelter and saw him, and when the volunteer mentioned that black cats rarely get adopted, I knew I had to take him home."

I can't help but beam at her. "I'm proud of you." I never really thought that my mother would be in a place where she could not only keep a job and make friends, but adopt a pet—but here she is.

And here I am.

She gives me a wan smile. "I'm just taking it a day at a time. That's the only thing that's really keeping me going. If I mess up, well, that was today. There's always tomorrow, and tomorrow is never the end." She pours me a cup of green tea and hands it to me. "I'm sorry that you're here."

I take the cup, blinking at her. "You are?"

"I mean, I'm glad you're here. It was the greatest surprise I could ever get. But I know that if you're here, that means things didn't quite work out. And I so wanted them to for you, darling."

I exhale loudly, suddenly exhausted at even the thought of trying to tell her everything that's happened. "I wanted them to work too" is all I can manage to say.

"Well, we don't have to talk about it right now. You've had a long flight. You must be so tired. Let's just have some tea, and if you're hungry, we can order in pizza. I bet you haven't had real pizza in a long time."

I don't bother telling her that there was a lot of real pizza when I was in Italy. Instead, I say, "Pizza would be awesome."

But even before she can place a call to Domino's, I'm lying back on the couch, closing my eyes, and slipping into a deep sleep.

◆　◆　◆

The next morning, I wake up at nine o'clock, having slept more than twelve hours. Jet lag doesn't even know what to do with me anymore.

Somehow I ended up in my old bed, and I assume my mother put me there, even though I have no memory of anything after falling asleep on the couch. The house is quiet, and when I walk into the kitchen to make coffee, the cat darts between my legs, making me yelp.

The cat also yelps and then runs across the room, scampering for safety in the heights of the bookshelf.

"Sorry," I mumble, my hand at my chest, trying to bring my heart rate down. I'm jumpy as fuck, and I guess I can't really blame myself, considering I was pretty much forced on a plane back home in order to save the ones I love. That whole thing.

That's one thing I'll leave out of the conversation with my mother. The less I say about Pascal or Gautier or any of them, the better. It's just about Olivier and me, which is what it should have been about all along. It's like the minute we went to Paris, whatever precious thing Olivier and I had between us was torn in a million different directions, whether by work or his family duties or his perverted and conniving cousin. I'm starting to wonder if Olivier and I really ever had a chance to become more than what we were. It was like the sex we were having every night was the only thing holding us together.

And yet I know that if we had been given a chance to make it, just the two of us, somewhere else in some other life, we could have been something amazing.

I pour myself a cup of coffee from the pot and spy a note from my mother, saying she's gone to work and is doing a double shift, and she'll see if she can get off early. Also, there's pizza in the fridge.

I open the fridge and pull out a slice of pepperoni and start munching away on it, trying to figure out the next course of action.

The first thing I did after the plane landed was open up my phone to see if there was anything from Olivier. Then I sent a few texts and emails, wanting to talk to him on the phone, to make sure he's okay, to explain what happened to me. The last thing I wanted was for him to think I actually left because I wanted to.

But the texts weren't delivered, and the emails were never responded to.

I can't tell if he's mad at me—I wouldn't blame him if he didn't know the whole story—or if he's okay. I wish I had Seraphine's phone number so I could check in on him that way.

I know I should start making real plans. Figuring out if I can still go to school, albeit a week late. If not, if I can pick it up next semester. Or maybe—maybe even transfer schools. I don't want to set foot in Europe for a while—in fact, I don't even think I'm allowed to go back anytime soon. But maybe somewhere in the US. I don't want to leave my mom again, and yet as I stand here in the kitchen, sipping the lukewarm coffee, this doesn't feel like home either. I feel like I won't be the person I need to be until I'm somewhere else, whether it's a place that's near or far.

And yet, even with that realization giving me some purpose and some strength, I know that no matter where I am, my heart won't be with me.

I left it behind in Paris.

Back in that apartment.

With the person it belongs to.

The person who deserves it.

The person who needs it.

The heartache comes at me so fast, I barely have enough time to react.

One minute I'm holding the cup of coffee.

The next minute I'm buckling, the cup falling to the floor and smashing to pieces.

Of course, that reminds me of Olivier too.

That very first morning.

After he saved me.

He saved me in so many different ways.

And now it is my turn to save him.

257

I let out a garbled cry, the kind of violent sadness that overtakes your whole body, makes your heart and your guts and your lungs feel like they're being ripped in half. I cry, and I sob, and I'm on my knees now, hands covered in spilled coffee, tears falling from my eyes and onto the sticky tiles.

This wasn't what it was like with Tom.

That was just a scratch.

This is a full-on gash, created by the sharpest blade, slicing me from head to toe until I wonder if I was ever whole at some point.

I don't know if I'll be whole again.

I don't know if you ever get your heart back into one whole piece after you've given it to someone else.

I stay on that floor for a long time, long enough that the cat is curious enough to come and investigate me. Kismet nuzzles my head, then starts to lap up the coffee before he saunters off, looking disgusted.

It brings me back to life a little, just focusing on the cat, and on the fact I'm lying on the kitchen floor, the same floor that's been here since I was a young girl, when my mother and I moved from Wenatchee, abandoned by my father to fend for ourselves. In a way, it's almost full circle, only I'm the one who left.

At first I don't hear the knock at the door. My brain kind of processes it as background noise along with the loud whir of the fridge.

But then I hear it again. Loud and commanding.

I slowly ease up to a sitting position, listening.

One by one, the hairs on my arms stand up.

My nerves are razed.

Adrenaline is buzzing somewhere back in my primal brain.

Don't get ahead of yourself, I think to myself. *Relax. It could be the postman, a neighbor, a Jehovah's Witness. Anyone.*

I get up, wishing I wasn't shaking. I slowly and carefully make my way out of the kitchen, careful not to step on the broken ceramic; then I think better of it and grab a knife from the drawer.

Holding it at my side, I sneak past the cat, who watches me with wide eyes.

If it really is no one, just a normal person, I'm going to look like a crazy woman, with my bedhead and tears and red eyes and coffee-stained pants, wielding a knife.

God, please let it be a normal person.

The knock happens again, the door almost shaking, and my heart ricochets into my throat, making it hard to breathe.

I peer through the peephole, but it's always been so rusted and marred with scratches, all I can see is the tall silhouette of a man.

Oh my God.

I'm afraid what might happen if I don't answer the door. I think maybe I should put down the knife and get out my phone and get 911 on the ready.

I'm about to do that when I hear a booming voice. "Sadie?"

I can't hear it clearly, and even though it's familiar, I don't think Pascal or Gautier would announce themselves before they murdered me.

Still, I grip the knife harder and open the door.

I almost drop the knife.

A worn-out, disheveled, and desperate-looking Olivier is on the other side. His shirt is dirty, his hair is a mess, his eyes are haunted.

But when they look at me, really look at me like I'm looking at him, they come to life again.

"Mon lapin," he whispers hoarsely. "It's you."

"Olivier," I cry out, my breath returning to me, my body reeling from shock. "What are you doing here?" I drop the knife and instinctively throw my arms around him, and he holds me tight, so tight that I can't breathe.

But I don't need my breath now that I'm with him.

"I was so worried about you," Olivier says into my neck, his voice breaking. "You have no idea, the things I thought."

"I'm so sorry I had to leave like that," I tell him. "I didn't have a choice . . . Pascal . . ."

"I know," he says, pulling away, his eyes full of fire as he cups my face. "Blaise told me everything."

"Blaise? And you trusted him?"

"Let's just say that Blaise is no more a fan of his father or his brother than we are. I don't trust him at all, but I do trust what he told me. That Pascal threatened you . . . and I knew you would have done anything to protect your mother. And me."

"I didn't know what else to do," I explain, holding the door open for him to come in. "I couldn't risk it."

"I know," he says, stepping inside and looking around. "Is it odd that I pictured it this way?"

"I don't know what that says about me," I say. "How on earth did you even find me here?"

"You aren't so hard to find."

"Oh, really? Because I recall you once saying that you knew nothing about me, that I was practically untraceable online."

"That may have been my way of making you talk," he says with a smirk. "It sort of worked."

"Don't tell me you have access to French spy networks."

"I might," he says. "I also might have access to a little something called Google."

I laugh. I laugh because he's here, and it's so amazing and impossible that he's here.

He's here.

"How did you even get here?"

"An airplane," he says, pulling me toward him. "The same kind you took."

"Oh, was yours bought by Pascal too?"

His grip on my arms tightens, and Olivier's eyes grow hard. "I need you to tell me everything that happened. Did he hurt you? Did he"—his voice breaks in anger—"do anything to you?"

I shake my head. "No. I mean, he's an asshole and a creep and a fucking pervert."

"Pervert?" he asks sharply.

"Are you surprised?"

"What did he do to you?" he grinds out. He looks like he's ready to throw the armchair across the room.

"Calm down," I tell him. "He didn't do anything. He just . . . he's lewd. And he may possess a video of us having sex, and he may have jacked off to it more than a few times."

Olivier's eyes narrow into green slits. "What?" he hisses.

"I saw the video. It's, um, hot—us against the glass at your hotel. But it's nothing you should worry about . . . or perhaps maybe the next time you see him at the office, you can confiscate his phone." As if there isn't a chance it exists on some online drop box. I try not to think about it.

"What a sick fuck," he swears. I can see veins throbbing in his temples. Jeez, I probably shouldn't have told him that.

"Yeah, but on the plus side, we did look pretty hot," I manage to say, but he doesn't return the humor. "So I guess he's going to deserve a punch or two in the face when you get back?"

"I'm not going back."

I stare at him blankly. "What?"

"I said I'm not going back."

I look him up and down. "You don't even have any luggage."

"The moment Blaise told me, the moment I saw the note you left, I had to come. I went right to the airport and got the first flight out. I told Seraphine there was a chance I wouldn't come back for a while."

"How long is a while?" I ask, both hopeful and afraid to hear the answer.

He chews on his lip for a moment as he gazes at me, perhaps feeling the same way I am. "As long as it takes. Maybe years."

"Years?" I practically spit out.

He shrugs. "No pressure. But I figured now was as good a chance as any to finally get that hotel in Napa Valley going. At Renaud's vineyard."

"You're kidding me?" This feels all so precious and fragile, I'm afraid to question it in case it breaks, but . . . "You're not going back home?"

He shakes his head. "Things are fucking crazy back there. I don't want any part of it."

"But Seraphine! She's your sister."

His face falls at that, and I immediately feel bad for the guilt trip.

"She is my sister, but she's a big girl. She wanted me to come after you. She wanted me to go."

"But the company . . . they'll eat her alive."

"She can fight back. She will fight back."

"But . . ."

"I know," he says with a sigh, running his hand down his face, "but it is what it is. And I don't think she's as alone there as you think."

"But this way they win. You could take over, protect your family name."

"Like it or not, the family name is Dumont. If Gautier wants to ruin it or make it rise into the next century by adapting to the times, that's on him. It's not on me. Look, I am not cut out for it. Maybe I was at some point, but I'm damn good at what I do now, and I like it. And I think cutting my ties with Paris for the time being might be the best idea I've ever had. Didn't you feel the same way when you left here?"

I nod slowly. I guess Olivier's only worked and worked and worked. Maybe this is his time to be someone else.

"I didn't like the person I was in Paris, and it wouldn't have gotten any better, only worse," he says. "You know it. We had the odds against us the moment we stepped foot in the city; we were never able to capture what we had at the beginning."

"Don't all relationships go that way?"

"Maybe if you accept it and give up on them. But I'm not going to give up on us. I'm not going to give up on you. We deserve better than that, *mon lapin*."

I'm smiling and crying all at once, floored by happiness, my body shaking from the transition from pure heartbreak to fear to suddenly having everything I ever wanted.

"And," Olivier goes on, "I hope you'll come with me. To California. Maybe you could finish your studies in San Francisco. Or do whatever you choose to do. I just want you with me for every single step of this new life."

"Of course I'll go with you," I whisper to him, my voice choked, standing on my toes to give him a soft kiss. "And I'm honored to be part of any life you choose, but . . . aren't you still worried about the life you're leaving behind?"

He nods. "I am. There was a lot that happened before I left, more than you know."

"So what happened with Seraphine? Did you hear what she had to say about her theory?"

"Oui," he says slowly. "I did."

"And?"

"And I don't know. I really don't."

"Yeah, well, I talked to Pascal about it."

He cocks a brow. "You talked?"

"A lot of things were said. But honestly, as horrible as he is, I'm not sure he did it."

"I don't think so either. Which leaves my uncle . . . and I know to never put anything past him."

"So what are you going to do? You can't investigate when you're over here."

"I can't investigate anything. I'm not the police. And, well, let's just say I'm not sure the police are on our side. I think they're on *their* side."

"What makes you say that?"

"Nothing for you to worry about," he says smoothly, which of course makes me suspicious. I'm sure whatever it is, *is* something for me to worry about. But I know that I'll take baby steps with Olivier now. After all, we have all the time in the world.

But still . . .

"So when you said that Blaise told you everything, what exactly did he say?" I ask.

"Just that Pascal might have interfered with you. Oh, and that I was set up."

"By Marine and Pascal?"

His jaw clenches and he looks away. "Yeah. What bothers me the most about all of that is I should have seen it coming. I should have known this was all set up from the start. I was just so young. Just a young, stupid fuck."

"And you were in love. Don't be so hard on yourself."

"No," he says, his hands trailing through my hair, gripping me by the neck. Possessive. The way I've needed him. "No, I wasn't in love. I know what love is now, Sadie, and it lives in you. It's why I'm here. Because you're here. Because you're mine as much as I'm yours."

I can't help but grin. "Look at you, being all romantic."

"I'm always romantic," he says, kissing my neck. "Because it's impossible to be anything but a lovestruck slave around you." He rests his forehead against mine, breathing in deep. "Tell me I did the right thing in coming here. Tell me you want this. That you want me."

Oh God. Doesn't he know by now?

"I only left because I had to," I tell him. "Maybe Pascal is full of empty threats, but maybe he's not. I don't know. There was no time to decide."

"I know. You had to protect what you love. And that's why I followed. Because I love you. And I will always follow you."

"And I will follow you. To Cannes. To Paris. To California. Every step of the way. I love you."

We kiss. Long, deep, sweet, brimming with all the emotions of the past few days, spilling out with lust, with love, with longing.

We kiss and kiss until I feel the cat twining around our legs.

"Whose cat is that?" Olivier asks when he breaks away, watching as Kismet winds around us, purring contently.

"My mother's. Who I guess you're going to meet later today."

"I can't wait."

"She's working a double shift and will be home late, but, boy, is she going to be surprised to see you."

"What did you tell her about me?"

"Well, I only said nice things, of course."

"Even though you came back early?"

"Yes, well, I know she wanted things to work out between us. I think moms have an instinct for young love, or at least they like to give you advice and pretend they do," I say with a chuckle. "In the meantime . . . pizza?"

"Pizza? For breakfast?" He shrugs. "I guess I am in America."

I hit him across the chest. "Hey! It's leftovers, and I'm going to assume you're on Paris time, and you look like you haven't eaten a thing. So, pizza?"

"Lead the way."

I take him over to the kitchen, and he eyes the broken coffee cup on the floor.

"Were you practicing your Hitchcock this morning?"

"Something like that," I tell him, opening the fridge and pulling out the pizza, then heading straight for my bedroom.

"Where are you going?" he asks, following me. "Don't you want to heat that up?"

"Cold pizza is the American way," I tell him, and once we're both inside, I close the door and gesture for him to get on the bed. "Take off your shoes, get on the bed."

"This is very bizarre," he says as he slips off his shoes. "Is this how you all eat breakfast?"

"No," I tell him, climbing on the bed with him. "I just knew I'd ravage you after I had a few bites, so I figured I'd kill two birds with one stone."

He grins at me. So damn beautiful. "Ravage me?" he asks, brows raised. He takes the pizza box out of my hands and tosses it across the room. "The food can fucking wait."

Olivier pounces on me like an animal, and I let out a loud yelp and dissolve into giggles as he proceeds to attack me from head to toe with kisses, his hands trailing all over my body.

I feel nothing but relief with him on top of me.

I feel nothing but butterflies in my chest and love in my heart.

I let myself be ravaged by my Frenchman—mind, body, and soul.

EPILOGUE

Olivier

Six months later

"Bon matin," I hear Sadie whisper in my ear.

I push the fragments of my dreams aside and slowly open my eyes to see soft sunlight spilling in through the windows. The light here in California is so similar to the light in the South of France, especially in winter. It's pale, and it glows, just enough to give you warmth, enough to keep your spirits lifted.

But the light isn't the only thing that keeps me up.

It's Sadie.

My dear, beautiful Sadie, lying on her side in bed with me, positively angelic in this light, in every light.

When I decided to come to America and start over with her, in what she would call a ballsy move, I knew it would be a risk. I knew it would be a challenge. But I didn't for a moment think it would be a regret.

It hasn't been. It was worth it ten times, no, a million times over to take that leap with her and focus on creating a life together.

At the moment, our life is just starting to settle down, find its footing, put down roots.

We're actually living in a guest cottage on Renaud's vineyard.

His house is on the other side of the thousands of rolling acres of merlot and cabernet sauvignon. And in between us, nestled near the Dumont Napa Winery and production facilities, is the foundation for the Dumont Hotel.

People work fast in the US. We broke ground a month ago, and in a few more months, just in time for summer, the hotel just might be up and running.

I've never been so excited about a project in all my life.

Especially now that I have two projects.

The first is the hotel, set to be not only my first real boutique hotel with only twenty rooms, but also my first one in America.

The second is that I plan on making Sadie my wife.

I know on the surface we've known each other for only seven months, but the truth is, I've discovered more about myself in those seven months than I have in my whole life. And more than that, I've learned what it is to know my heart. To know what it is to love.

To know what it is to be loved.

With Sadie, I've found all that. I've found myself in her—the true Olivier who isn't bound by contracts and deadlines and guilt. A place where I can finally be free.

But, of course, it all comes at a price.

The company is still in the hands of Gautier, Pascal, and Blaise.

My sister is still working there . . . working for them.

It pains me to even think that, to know that what we worked so hard for, all my father's morals and accomplishments, has been washed away. Sure, his legacy will always survive, but Gautier is running the company completely differently now. The online store is up and running. He's collaborating with artists such as Jean-Michel Basquiat in limited-edition runs, which is producing a flurry in stores. Even the branding has changed, becoming something flashy and cheap.

Sales are up. I guess I never assumed his plans and ambitions for the company wouldn't work—rather, that they were never needed. Sales are up because this is a novelty, but I have doubts they will stay up in the long run.

And Seraphine is there, trying to deal with it all, knowing that my father is most likely rolling in his grave.

But she won't give up. I talk with her at least once a week, trying to convince her to leave, or at least to come here and visit.

She won't. She's too loyal for that. Too determined and stubborn. She wants to do this for our father. She wants to stay on board to have her say, even if no one listens to her. She wants to be there just in case, to keep our enemies closer.

She says it's the only thing she knows how to do, the only thing she wants to do.

I worry about her. Not just about her safety, I worry most about her sanity. What it's like to work in that building alongside Blaise all day. She insists he drives her crazy, and I believe that. I also worry that she may start putting trust in him when she shouldn't. She says that Blaise has been distancing himself from his brother and uncle and that his confessions to us are still holding true. But I don't know. She can be too trusting about the wrong things, and I wish I were there to keep an eye on things myself.

But I don't want to leave Sadie, even though she's used to having my brother, Renaud, around, and I often fly her mother down to visit. I don't want to leave construction either, not at this crucial time.

I know that going back to Paris will have to happen sooner or later. I'm able to conduct my business here without having to be in Europe, especially with a board of managers and directors underneath me doing the work, but even so, I need to check in on Seraphine.

I need to check in on my uncle.

I need, in some way, to let him know that I haven't run away, I'm just biding my time. Neither he nor Pascal have contacted me. I guess there's no need. I'm out of the picture. I lost. My father is dead. I have no control over the company. They set me up, and they won.

Still, I have a feeling my uncle isn't going to let me forget what I did to him. He doesn't take humiliation lightly. I can only hope that he's too wrapped up in the company to come after us, even though I'll be watching my back for the rest of my life.

But I don't mind.

Because I have the love of my life by my side.

I have a new life here, one that transcends the one I had before, one that feels more truthful and real than I could have ever imagined.

That's what love does to you.

It wakes you up. It makes you real.

Even so, I have a hard time believing that Sadie is lying here beside me, as she does every morning. That I could be so lucky to have found her, that I didn't let her go, and that she didn't let me go.

"What is going on in this brain of yours?" she asks, reaching over and running her finger between my brows. "You're not normally so frowny first thing in the morning."

I give her a wry look. "I think you have me confused with someone else." Ever since moving here to our quaint little cottage in the vineyard, I've discovered the joys of sleeping in and taking things slowly.

"Okay, well, you don't normally think so much when you get up," she says. "What's on your mind?"

"Only you," I tell her. I lean over, brushing her messy hair off her forehead and kissing her gently. "You're always on my mind."

"Even when I'm right in front of you?"

"Even when you're right in front of me." I reach out and try to pull her closer to me, but she laughs and rolls out of bed, looking adorably sexy in her lacy underwear and tiny T-shirt with a unicorn on it.

"Oh no you don't," she says. "I've got places to go and people to see."

"You know that we have to go to the same places and see the same people, right?" I tell her as she walks off to the kitchen.

"And I know what you're like in the morning," she calls out, and I can hear her filling the Nespresso machine with water. "You like to take your time, and we don't have time this morning."

She's right. We're driving down to San Francisco today, first to pick up her mother, who is coming to visit for a few days, from the airport, and then to check out the University of California, Berkeley, together. Sadie had been thinking about transferring her studies over to that school so she can continue her communications degree in the fall, but lately she's been thinking about other options.

As much as I want her to get an education, I don't like the idea of her moving to the Bay Area for so long, even though of course I'll move with her. I just like the little life we've built for ourselves at the winery. Luckily, one of the options that Sadie wants to explore is becoming a sommelier. Being here and being around Renaud and seeing his passion for wine is rubbing off on her.

Frankly, I think she'd be great at whatever she sets out to do, as long as she's happy. But in the end I feel like today's visit to the university is just to appease her mother. Even though her mother loves me and approves of this new life we have, I think she still worries for her future.

Hopefully, when I propose and Sadie becomes my wife, she'll worry a little less.

With that on my mind, I go into the kitchen and stand in the doorway, watching her push the buttons on the machine and getting discouraged when nothing happens. I don't know what it is about it, but she's always struggling with the damn thing.

"Why can't we have a normal American coffee maker?" she whines, hitting the side of it and then opening it, peering in where you put the cartridges. "I could even deal with a French press. I mean, that's French, you should approve."

"Tell you what," I say. "How about we ask for an old-fashioned coffee maker as a wedding gift? I'm sure someone will give us one."

She stops her frantic fiddling with the machine, tensing up.

I really wasn't planning on doing it this way, but I figure now is as good a time as any.

"Wedding gift?" she asks, her voice high and squeaky as she slowly turns around to look at me.

I grin, and I hope it looks steady, because I'm starting to shake inside.

Maybe I should have thought this through better.

I was going to do it in the vineyard under the stars.

I was going to do it on a sailboat under the Golden Gate Bridge.

I was going to do it in a million romantic moments.

I'm French, damn it. I shouldn't be proposing in the kitchen first thing in the morning when the two of us are barely dressed.

But here I am.

Walking over to her, grabbing hold of her hand—the very hand that was grappling with the coffee machine—and I'm dropping to my knees.

Asking my love to be my wife.

"Sadie, *mon lapin*. Will you marry me?"

She's speechless.

She didn't see this coming. I didn't see this coming.

But the best things in life are like that.

"Are you serious?" she asks, her other hand going to her chest in shock.

I nod, feeling the tears, the heat prickling in my nose, my throat. "Never been more serious before in my life. Even if I don't look it right now."

"Yes. Yes, *mon Dieu*," she says, and I laugh. I laugh so hard because I'm so excited, and I'm so scared because she just agreed to marry me. "I'll marry you, Olivier. Of course I'll marry you."

I grin at her. My heart is exploding from joy. I'm not sure I'll survive it. "You're not just saying this because of the coffee machine, are you?"

She's laughing now, smiling from ear to ear, and I get to my feet, pulling her to me, kissing her hard. "I'm saying yes because I love you," she says, and then she glances down at her hand in mine. "Don't you need a ring?"

"Be right back," I tell her and run into the bedroom, quickly fetching the ring that I've kept hidden in my sock drawer. It's been there for a few months now, a sapphire-and-diamond ring that matches her eyes. The moment I stepped inside the antique store, I knew it was the one.

Just as I knew she was the one from the moment I first saw her. First saved her. From the moment I first realized that she was the one who saved me.

I go back in the kitchen, get down on my knees again, and then propose with the ring.

She accepts.

The ring fits.

She fits.

Into my heart, into this life, into the next life too.

"I love you, Sadie," I whisper to her as I wrap my arms around her and hold her tight. I'll hold her forever. "Thank you for getting off that train."

I feel her smile against me as she realizes what I'm talking about. "Best decision I ever made," she says.

"And deciding right now to become my wife?"

"Easiest decision I ever made," she says. "I was yours from the start."

"Now you're mine forever."

"*Bien sûr,*" she says and then pulls back to look at me, frowning through her happy tears. "I said that right, didn't I?"

I laugh. "You'll get there, *mon lapin*. You'll get there."

We'll at least get there together.

ACKNOWLEDGMENTS

I've written close to fifty acknowledgments at this point in my life, and I imagined this would be one of the hardest, simply because this book was the hardest I've ever had to write.

But since the hard part is over, I've decided to make this as short and sweet as possible (though something tells me it's wishful thinking).

First, a little about why this book was so damn hard.

I have to say, it really has nothing to do with the book itself. It's not the characters or the plot or the subject matter. When the idea for the Dumonts first hit me, I sat down at my computer, and for the first time ever, I was able to crank out more than ten thousand words in one day. Now, that's not unusual for me: I write fast, and when I'm on deadline, I'm often writing that much. What made it unusual was the fact that I wrote that within a day of getting the idea. Usually, I have to let an idea and characters and plot soak in for a few days to a few months before I can start writing.

But it just came to me, and I was so damn excited about it all. The intrigue, the sex, the money, the French—my God, I do love the French (especially my French readers—*bonjour!*). We travel so often to France that it feels like a second home, and I knew that this series had to be set there (I also knew that I had to incorporate my Chanel obsession in there, too, hehe). I was all about the Dumonts.

Then . . . I took a break from writing (I actually went to France to do a bit more research), and that's when everything sort of fell apart.

November came along, and so did my usual bout of SAD (seasonal affective disorder). Usually we're down south as soon as the days grow dark and gloomy, as this disorder actually interferes with my ability to work, but this time we weren't going until December. And we live on an island that not only has no lights—you need a headlamp to cross the street to get the mail—but sits under a dark cloud for months with almost no sunlight and very short days.

Then I got sick with a nasty, never-ending flu, and that, combined with my SAD and the fact that I was also dealing with other big health problems for the first time, meant everything went downhill.

And I mean everything. I fell into a very deep depression from which there didn't seem a way out. And though I'm no stranger to depression, especially that time of year, this time it was directly affecting my writing. I couldn't conjure up the will to care about anything, let alone my characters or the book. The spark was gone. There was no joy to be found. And it wasn't this book . . . it was everything. It didn't matter if I wrote something else or nothing at all; I just couldn't conjure up the mental energy or the will to do it. Every time I tried, a brick wall came down in my mind, and I had no strength to fight my way over it. I stopped caring, and I needed so deeply to care.

Yet, somehow, I kept going. Kept trying to climb over that wall or dig under it or pick my way through it. It must have worked, because, eventually, the book got finished. Deadlines got pushed back. The first ten days of vacation were spent writing from morning to night, fighting this story every step of the way, fighting for it to be told, fighting my depression. But somehow I got it done.

Looking back, I'm not even sure how. Mentally, it was the hardest thing I've ever had to do, and I know to many of you reading this, it won't seem like that big of a deal, but, believe me, it was. Losing any hope and joy in something that once brought you those things is so devastating, and it's scary when you start to believe you'll never feel normal again.

All I knew is that if I could just get Olivier and Sadie's story out there, then that meant depression wouldn't have won. It meant that I hadn't given up. It meant that I prevailed when it felt like I never would.

So while this book conjures up some painful memories for me, the number one thing I feel is triumph. This is the book in which I overcame. Depression did not fuel this book. Depression fuels nothing but darkness and despair. But this book became the fuel to beat my depression.

Of course, I could not have done this alone, and I really, really mean that. I needed help from all directions of my life, and I am so grateful and lucky that I got it.

I have to thank my most wonderful editor, Maria. Thank you so much for always believing in me and wanting this to happen. You've been so understanding, and it was a doozy of a first book with you, but—yay!—we did it, and I am so looking forward to more. Onward and upward!

Holly, you are a soldier and a champion (and, well, a genius). You put up with all my crap (and writing that I'm still not sure made any sense), and you turned it into something I can be proud of. I am in awe of you and your patience and skillz (with a z), and I can't thank you enough.

Taylor, you are the bestest agent that ever agented. Thank you for never giving up on me and for always listening to my long rants and rambles and turning them into something to get excited about!

Sandra, Nina, Kathleen, Kelly, Ali, Chanpreet, you guys rallied around me when I felt like giving up, you listened when I just needed to talk, and you made me feel like I wasn't alone when all I felt was lost. Thank you for believing in me and being there.

Also, big thanks to my Anti-Heroes. Another outstanding group of readers and friends who always show up and make me feel like I'm better than I really am. And my IG family, your messages of strength and support and solidarity (and, above all, compassion and understanding) meant the world to me.

Hmm, I guess the Kauai Beach Resort gets a shout-out, too, even though when we drive past you now, we just shake our fists and yell, *"Discretion!"* You didn't have any room service, and the weather was borderline hurricane, but without you I wouldn't have spent those last four days by myself writing up a storm while an actual one was going on outside, so, hey. *Mahalo.*

My biggest thanks, as it always is, is to my husband, Scott. I'm going to start crying as I type this if I say anything too mushy, but the fact is, I would be nothing and nowhere without you. You are such a good, good soul, and I'm so happy our souls are together. You're so talented and kind and beautiful and lovely, and I love you more than anything in this world.

Honorable mention: Bruce. You weren't here when I wrote this, but I could feel your four-legged support from across an ocean.

Extra honorable mention: My mother. For watching Bruce. Oh, and for that always-believing-in-me part. Let's add my dad in there, too, for good measure.

I know I said I would make this short and sweet, but at least I got that sweet part done.

Merci!

ABOUT THE AUTHOR

Karina Halle, a former travel writer and music journalist, is the *New York Times*, *Wall Street Journal*, and *USA Today* bestselling author of *The Pact*, *A Nordic King*, and *Sins & Needles*, as well as fifty other wild and romantic reads. She, her husband, and their adopted pit bull live in a rain forest on an island off British Columbia, where they operate a B&B that's perfect for writers' retreats. In the winter, you can often find them in California or on their beloved island of Kauai, soaking up as much sun (and getting as much inspiration) as possible. For more information, visit www.authorkarinahalle.com/books.